The Andromeda Effect

The Andromeda Effect

CORBIN DECKARD

 Third Season Press

Printed in the United States of America

First Printing, 2018

ISBN 978-1-7325877-0-0

www.thirdseasonpress.com

To the nevers. You made it all possible.

1. The First Machine, 1945

"There," he said while pointing from the back seat of the Kŭbelwagen to the plaza ahead. "Pull in over there." He then hunched his shoulders to get a better look through the cracked windshield. It was a welcome change from the bombed out and burnt up areas of the Zitadelle sector. The plaza, incomplete as a result of the outbreak of war, was to be the centerpiece of the airport of Germania, Tempelhof. The half-finished circular drive led up to the main Luft Hansa terminal, their last commercial flight leaving just days before.

"Jawohl Herr General," the driver replied, pulling up through the zig-zagging barricades of sand bags and barbed wire into a square that led to the entrance of the largest building in the world. He stopped, reached over to the control panel in the middle of the dashboard and with a flick of his wrist turned the key shutting off the motor. The two men sat silently in the shadow of Ernst Sagebiel's accomplishment, wondering its fate not long from now. The rumble of Opal Blitz troop transports pulling up nearby regained the two men's attention. The driver quickly jumped out of the automobile to open the general's door.

"Seven hundred men," the general lamented as he looked back at the roughly one-hundred remaining. He reached to his side pulling the latch to open the stamped steel door himself, the driver catching the corner as it swung open. The general preferred the simplicity of the Kűbelwagen. It was easy to produce, easy to maintain, and more importantly, it worked well in the field. He was fighting a war after all, not driving to a dinner party.

The general stood, took another look at the building before him, stepped down and straightened his tunic. With his right arm in the air, making a circular motion, he signaled the Opal drivers to head to the flying field on the opposite side of the terminal. There they would set up a temporary camp, a defensive zone, holding off the Soviets long enough to accomplish their mission. The Blitz's roared to life, spewing black smoke from their straight six engines, then drove out of sight. "Seven hundred men." The general was standing at the base of the steps of the main entrance to the terminal when he was met by another German officer.

"General Krukenberg?" The officer, a lieutenant, stepped to attention, his arm extended before him in salute as he waited for the general's reply. "Heil Hitler!"

"Yes. Yes. I am General Gustav Krukenberg." He returned the salute, walked up the stairs, then reached out to shake the lieutenants hand.

"Lieutenant Haas sir."

"Lieutenant. I was expecting Oberstleutnant Böttger, will you take me to him?"

"I am afraid that is not possible Herr General."

"No? Why not? Is he not here?" the general inquired, his tone now more authoritative. "I was given orders to contact him at Tempelhof. Did he not receive word of my coming?"

The lieutenant, nervous, remained at attention. "No sir. He did not."

"Why not? I have orders to contact him here. I demand to speak with the communications officer immediately."

"Herr General, I am the communications officer." A bead of sweat formed on the lieutenant's temple. "I assure you, I gave the Oberstleutnant the orders myself."

"Then what do you have to say for his failure to meet with me Lieutenant?"

The lieutenant's eyes slipped from attention as he answered, "Böttger is dead." He immediately straitened up as he met Krukenberg's eyes.

Krukenberg took a step back not believing what he just heard. "Dead?" *How could Böttger be dead? American airstrike, or maybe Soviet artillery fire.* "How?"

"He shot himself this morning, after receiving orders to prepare to destroy the airport. He considered Tempelhof a treasure, he couldn't destroy it, so he committed suicide rather than disobey orders."

"He shot himself?" Krukenberg took another step back. It wasn't the first time he heard of a senior officer committing suicide. It was more frequent now, especially how things were going in the east. Not wishing to delay his actions any longer, and anxious to get things moving, he asked, "Who is his replacement?"

"His replacement sir?"

"Yes. His replacement. Who is now in charge? I presume Böttger wasn't running this entire facility by himself. Who is the next highest-ranking officer?"

"Sir, I am sir," the lieutenant said confidently.

"Well then, I have accomplished one of my orders. I was to make contact with the field commander, Tempelhof. Now that we have that out of the way, I will require your assistance. Please, stand at ease." The lieutenant relaxed his shoulders, finding it hard to believe he would be entrusted to command such a vast and important complex as Tempelhof. "I have further orders, from General Wielding, Vistula. Are you familiar with the General, Lieutenant?"

"Yes sir, very. He has used the facility on more than one occasion. He was also responsible for Böttger's orders."

"Good. By his order I am to evaluate the progress of the destruction of this facility. Now that Böttger is dead, I will presume nothing has been done in that regard."

"That is correct sir. We have been waiting for new orders from Vistula since this morning, no word."

"I would have expected so. The Soviets are a stone's throw from the Spree river, and Montgomery continues to sweep through France almost unchallenged," Krukenberg said now beginning to pace. "Vistula has their hands full. So, you will see that it gets done."

"Me? Sir, with all due respect, I would be better suited to lead a company of men to the Spree than to- "

"You are the commander of this installation, Lieutenant." The statement, and order, snapped the lieutenant to attention once again.

"Yes sir."

"Stand at ease." Krukenberg ordered once again, now looking through the entrance of the terminal to the interior and beyond. "You can have one of my men to take over as communications officer. As of now I need someone who is familiar with this facility to lead efforts to keep it from the enemy's hands. Understood?"

"Jawohl, Herr General."

"Lieutenant. I realize how unexpected this may seem," Krukenberg's tone softened, "but we all must do what we can given the circumstances."

"Yes, Herr General."

"Good." Krukenberg turned and walked toward the lieutenant. "I also have orders to meet with a Dr. Henke. I presume you are familiar with his whereabouts?"

"Henke, General? Yes, he and his team are almost always in their lab in the bunker, I can take you to him."

"Bunker? I thought Tempelhof was merely an airport. There is a bunker here as well?"

"Yes sir. It's out of sight, under the Luft Hansa terminal. The two structures were built at the same time, Böttger had once told me, to hide from prying eyes. I can take you to see Doctor Henke now." Haas reached for one of the doors of the entrance and held it open, inviting Krukenberg to head into the facility. Stepping inside, his footsteps echoed against the high stone walls and the vast space beneath. In awe of the great structure before him, Krukenberg slowed to a stop to take it all in.

Haas was about ten meters ahead when he realized he was alone. He looked back, calling out, "Herr General?"

"Hmmm? Oh, yes." Krukenberg snapped out of it and began to follow, the sound of his leather soled boots echoing against the walls once again.

"It's only used on special occasions," Haas added. "When someone or something needs to get to Command quickly, it comes through here. Any other time it's simply a monument." He kept walking through the terminal building, heading for another set of doors opposite the entrance. When Luft Hansa was operating, passengers would arrive through the same doors the two men were approaching, but that's where the similarities stopped. There were no more boarding agents, no lounges, and more importantly, no Junkers JU-52 trimotors waiting to take passengers to parts unknown. It was all empty, a shell of its former self.

"A monument," Krukenberg whispered. An appropriate description for something that represented this Reich, and he was going to see to it that it was destroyed leaving nothing for the Soviets.

"Through here, we can get there faster if we go outside. There are doors leading to the bunker from the interior, but they are at the opposite end of the terminal."

"Why would Henke still have his lab here and not toward the rear lines? Do you know what he's working on?" Krukenberg asked while Haas held open another set of doors leading to the flight line. Krukenberg stopped once again, this time standing under an immense umbrella that made up the ceiling of the hangars. It was a canopy that stretched out like an eagle's wings for over a kilometer from end to end. This is where the airliners, JU 52's, would wait, and passengers board. "A monument," he agreed.

"Not entirely sir. Böttger at first suspected it was part of the Wunderwaffe."

"Wunderwaffe? Such as the V-1 and V2?"

"Yes, he even hosted Von Braun and his team for a short while which lead us to suspect it was a secret development site. We quickly came to the conclusion it was not."

"How?" News of Von Braun's visit had peeked Krukenberg's curiosity and would have explained the situation; he wanted to know as much as Böttger and Haas knew.

"To put it simply, Doctor Henke."

"Henke?"

"He is, to say the least, not capable of such feats of engineering as V-weapons. It wasn't until we were ordered to assign a security detail in his lab that we confirmed it was not. It is, in my opinion General, a gross waste of resources. Henke refuses to discuss it."

"What do you mean Lieutenant?"

"Henke will not discuss the project with anyone who is not directly involved. I've been in the bunker though, and whatever it is, it's not a V-weapon. Maybe Wunderwaffe, maybe not."

This left Krukenberg confused, trying to understand what was so important that he and his men had to get to Tempelhof. He knew there were many projects in Wunderwaffe, from the V-1 and V-2 weapons to a German version of the British Sten gun. *If it is truly a waste of resources as Haas says it is, then why am I here instead of fighting on the front lines?* "I wasn't given any details to his project... only that I-" he stopped. Without warning, the conversation was cut by an explosion at the far end of the flying field. Soon after, the unmistakable screams of Elektror L1 air raid sirens filled the air.

"Quickly, we cannot make it to the bunker from here. We must find shelter." Haas started to make his way toward one of the barricades just outside the reach of the hangar canopy above. Krukenberg stood still, trying to determine what had been hit. Before he knew it, an Ilyushin Il-2 Sturmovik attack aircraft strafed the field with gunfire in front of him and screamed out of sight over the hangar. He could hear the Flakvierling 38 anti-aircraft guns in the distance, trying to chase the airplane away. "Herr General! There may be more!"

"They fly in pairs. Always. If he is alone," Krukenberg turned for a moment to get a better angle to listen, "his partner was shot down. He won't be back." He was still trying to make out what was hit when he glanced down to see Haas peering up from a bomb crater left from an earlier attack. Stepping closer, he asked, "What's over there?"

"Fuel depot," Haas answered as he started to climb out of the hole. "It was a waste of a bomb. There hasn't been fuel in the depot for weeks. If he was alone, he probably had no chance at getting back behind his lines. It was a suicide run."

"That would be my assumption. Why hasn't the main terminal been bombed?" Krukenberg was curious. The terminal, and surrounding building's that made up Tempelhof looked relatively untouched. With such a large facility, that seemed unusual.

"It's not that they haven't tried," Haas replied, brushing dirt from his sleeve. "It's of little military importance, at least now. Weser Flugzeugbau made dive bombers and attack aircraft here up until last year," he said while pointing to the broken up remains of Junkers Ju 88 Stutka and Focke Wolf Fw 190 airplanes littering the field. "Tempelhof has never officially been used by the Luftwaffe as a base, so the enemy has chosen targets they see as more strategic."

"And are they?" Krukenberg asked.

"To the enemy maybe, but they don't have the whole picture." Haas turned and started to walk toward a rather conspicuous set of steel doors. They were set in the corner of one of the hangars, a short walk from the exit a passenger would have made when walking to and from awaiting aircraft. They were unseen from the sky above, and out of place from the two men's vantage. "This way. Henke and his team should be inside. They rarely come out, less so when there are sirens."

Krukenberg turned again to look out to the fuel depot and to what little smoke could be seen. The sirens were now moaning quietly and eventually could no longer be heard.

"Anyone on the grounds has access through here." Haas twisted a heavy metal lever to unlock the doors from the outside. He swung one of the heavy doors open and walked in.

"Anyone?" Krukenberg asked.

"Yes. There's a shelter on the other side. Beyond that is another set of doors, heavily guarded. They lead to a set of stairs, then to the bunker and Henke." He kept walking, through the open space of the shelter, with its painted murals and poems on the walls, until he made it to the far end. Krukenberg could hear his boots clicking on the ground again, the way they did when they were in the terminal. He followed, stopping to get a better look at something on the wall.

"What is this?" Krukenberg pointed. It was a painting of a traditional looking country farmer, pulling a cart behind himself.

"The painting? There are many like it. It's to help calm children of families who happen to be caught here during an air raid. Some have poems written with them too," Haas answered, now standing next to Krukenberg. "Shall we?"

"Yes, yes, let's find Henke." Krukenberg started to walk toward the doors when he could hear the unmistakable sound of steel grinding on steel. He could see the handles of the doors move by themselves, slowly until they could move no more. The guard on the other side recognized the lieutenants voice and started to open the doors from the inside.

"They knew we were coming. I delivered the orders from Vistula this morning, before Böttger...", Haas stopped, "before he was gone." The door swung open, and two guards with MP-40's came out to meet the lieutenant, taking the opportunity to present themselves before the general.

"Herr General," the two guards said simultaneously while snapping to attention. It would have been the general's nature to review the soldiers, but he didn't have time. Not today, he needed to get moving and free up the lieutenant who now had work to do. "Heil Hitler!" the guards added. The general waived his arm in response, then walked past the two men and into the bunker.

"This way sir." The lieutenant didn't say anything to the guards. He stepped past the post on the other side of the steel doors where another soldier began to log their arrival in the books. The two officers proceeded down a flight of steel stairs dimly illuminated by two of the three working phosphorous lights hanging overhead.

Krukenberg stopped and looked over his shoulder to see if he could see the guards post. "Just out of sight," he said, turning to follow Haas to one more set of doors.

"Here. His lab and office are behind these doors, along with his team. Before I introduce you, may I ask you a question, Herr General?"

"Lieutenant." Krukenberg said, straightening up.

"Am I really to destroy Tempelhof? Are those really our orders? Such a magnificent structure. Surely there is a mistake."

"Those are the orders Lieutenant. It's magnificent, but Tempelhof will not be a prize of the Soviets. Do you understand?"

"Jawohl, Herr General." The lieutenant turned and opened the steel doors. "This way." They headed only a short distance inside when Krukenberg stopped, unable to understand what was now before him.

"What the devil is that?" he asked.

"No devil, Herr General," a mousy voice said from the corner of the lab. Krukenberg and Haas walked right by not even noticing him. "It's my life's work, and by virtue of your comment, that would make me the devil."

"Herr General," Haas said, motioning to the direction of the voice with a vexed look on his face, "Doctor Henke." Standing in the corner of the lab was a man of about one hundred sixty centimeters. He could easily have disappeared should he have stood behind any one of the control panels.

"Herr Doctor," Krukenberg turned and looked at the machine towering in front of him, "what is this?" A moment passed before he caught himself. "Ah, you must forgive me. Pleasure to meet you." He turned back and extended his hand. "What is all of this?"

"This, Herr General, will turn the tide of the war." Henke returned the greeting, then started to walk toward the machine.

"But what is this? What does it do?"

"We call it... M31," Henke answered, taking a moment to look over his creation. "More than that Herr General, I am afraid I cannot tell you under strict orders from the Führer himself." Henke turned and walked quickly to his desk. "I wasn't at all shocked to hear about Böttger."

Krukenberg's attention was diverted for a moment to the sound of Henke's footsteps, a fast paced but light walk. He squinted at the Doctor, as if to try and get a better feel for the man as he found his statement odd and somewhat cold.

"Tempelhof is astounding. It was the showcase of Berlin to every passenger that walked through her doors." Henke reached behind his desk and pulled out a long tube, sealed at both ends. "Böttger could not destroy her any more than Breker could of one of his sculptures. Are you familiar with Breker, General?"

"Somewhat. In my position, I am afraid I don't have much time for the arts. But, this is truly a masterpiece of the Reich. I can understand your views."

"Yes, Herr General, yes indeed. I believe this is what you came for." Henke handed a long storage tube to Krukenberg. "It has been sealed, and it is my understanding that it will go directly to General Wielding."

"Those are my orders. I plan to leave this afternoon." Krukenberg turned once again to look at the machine in front of him, placing the tube under his arm.

"Ah. I almost forgot." Henke turned and headed back to his desk where he picked up a small attaché. "It contains further instructions for M31 should something happen to my team. It's been Enigma coded, you will not be able to read it."

Krukenberg briefly looked over the case, noticing that printed on the outside flap was simply 'M31'. "He will know what all of this is?"

"Most definitely. We have been working on this project for months, and all communication is done by code and delivered personally. Wielding is expecting it."

"That must take some time Doctor."

"Yes, but it is the only way. It is too dangerous otherwise. We cannot take any chance that this will end up in the wrong hands."

"Tell me Doctor, how do you plan to get it out of here?" The general motioned with his left hand over to the M31, the centerpiece of the lab. "We have orders to destroy this facility. I have no orders to transport-"

"Ahem," the lieutenant, standing near the doorway, cleared his throat. Krukenberg looked over to him, then dropped his shoulders. He understood now. Böttger, now Haas, was tasked with destroying the facility, and that included the machine. What the general was about to carry on to Wielding are its blueprints, and presumably coded instructions.

"It was a pleasure to meet you Herr General. Will you and the Lieutenant be joining us for our test today?"

"I am afraid I must go Doctor. I need to contact headquarters and await further orders. My field operations will be directed from the terminal above. I will, as it seems, be right outside the bunker should you need me." Krukenberg turned to make his way out of the bunker with Haas staying behind.

"Herr General, one more thing."

Krukenberg stopped just outside of the steel doors. He turned and said, "Doctor?"

"Your company patch, it's not like any I have seen. Charlemagne, and those colors. Who exactly do you command?"

"That should be obvious Doctor." Krukenberg resumed his exit, starting to climb up the stairs. "The French."

2. Class of 2018

The future's nuclear science,
Power for the masses,
Made in the shade,
Wearing sunglasses.

Close enough, Williams thought. Nuclear science isn't any more the future today than it was back when his world wasn't so complicated. In fact, he didn't know much more about nuclear energy than he had to teach, and that wasn't much. "Dang," he mumbled, thinking about that line while he pushed up his sunglasses with his forefinger. It was already warm out and his perspiration had caused the pads to slide down the ridge of his nose.

He was listening to a tape he made of Atomic Day, his old high school garage band. It was one of his rituals, something he did every morning while walking to class. As a matter of fact, he listened to it almost every day since it was recorded, before everyone went their separate ways. It reminded him of a different time. "Close enough," he whispered.

Things aren't so bad,
And the future's looking better,

That line always struck home with him. Was it really? Was it really looking better? Sure, working at the college gave him some sort of freedom, way more than the outside commercial world ever did, but was it better? He stopped to think it over, taking a look around at the students walking by, then started again. "At least I can write what I want, I guess."

His classroom was only a few minutes from Bohr Hall, just enough to get him through the first track. He used the time to guess how many students would show up. It was a game he played, it was never a full class. Sometimes he would get it right, then walk around with this feeling of accomplishment; he knew he wasn't going to get it any other way. But most of the time he was wrong, it didn't bother him.

Life is going pretty good,
Just a little fade,

He tried his hand in the real world for a while, but soon realized the real world wasn't anywhere near exciting. Neither was teaching at a small New York college, but here he didn't have a nine-to-five schedule, and he could write and research pretty much anything in relation to physics he wanted. To him, it was the next best thing, it was the closest to a particle accelerator he was going to get, and it didn't bother him. Eventually, he thought, some of the old relics who refuse to retire would move on and he would naturally take over some of the more interesting subjects like advanced thermodynamics or nanophysics. At least that's what Dean Tarkarov would tell him during their semiannual one-on-one meetings. But for now, it was basic Physics, entry level gen ed type stuff and that was okay.

There was nothing really special about his lab room. It was your basic auditorium seating with florescent lights overhead, half didn't even work. He had a lab desk that was center stage, perfect for his needs, and a chalkboard. An honest to god chalkboard. Nothing special. The aforementioned relics, the ones who have been there since the dawn of time, they had dibs on the labs with real technology; simulation software, PC-based oscilloscopes, data loggers. None of them knew how to use any of it, but the labs were closer to Bohr, which meant less walk. Williams didn't care, it was a job, no one bothered him, good enough.

I'm taking it in stride,
Guess I got it made!

This is where Williams sang along. "I got it made!"
"Right on Dr. Williams." It was Travis Washington, walking up from behind Williams. He was always good for providing his two cents on any subject, even when not asked. He shot by the Professor and headed up to where he normally sat, near the back of the class away from most everyone else. Williams was five minutes late today. By his standards, and those of the rest of the class, early.

Out of the ten or so songs Atomic Day managed to put together, he liked this one the most. It basically summed up his life now. He pretty much attended college, graduated, then took the first job offer that came around. It was a middle grade technology firm, R&D type work. He quickly realized he was just being paid to provide 'research results' so companies could say they did due diligence in the event they were sued. It opened the door to a part-time community college position teaching night classes, then here. He liked this better, the campus was small but, big enough. It was a suitcase school, most of the kids packed up for home on the weekends, so he had some sort of life off campus. And when he didn't, there was beer. *Made in the shade.*

"Crap...full house," he mumbled as he stepped through the doors. He kept listening to his Walkman until he opened his briefcase at the end of the lab desk. He tapped the stop button, pulled the headphones off, and dropped them both inside. Most of the kids thought it was cool, eccentric maybe, that he used the Walkman instead of an mp3 or smart phone. Williams just never bothered to join the next century. He waited long enough, it was now vintage.

"Okay....sorry I'm late but the Dean wanted to chat before class." He listened. He was sure he used that excuse for the third or fourth time this month, and he knew the students were going to catch on sooner or later. He watched carefully for signs they were on to him. Nothing. They either weren't listening or didn't care. *Damn, my sunglasses.* He quickly grabbed them off his face and tossed them next to his Walkman and headphones.

"Okay...as promised, let's talk about paradox. Try holding your excitement." He tried to toss in a joke here and there, just to see if the class had a pulse. Again, nothing. "Specifically, paradox that relates to physics, so yeah, it should be a lot of fun." The class laughed a bit. Williams knew most of the kids in the class were here because they had to be. Sure, there were some aspiring physicists in the room, but they were grossly outnumbered. Williams tried, but didn't always succeed, to keep everyone interested. "Everybody knows a paradox is a statement, or action, that contradicts itself." *No, no one knows that, except maybe Bosch. But you all know it now.* "There are literally tons of paradox in the world of physics, but since we only have an hour and twenty minutes" Williams looked at the clock hung over the doorway remembering he was late, again "make that an hour, we are only going to talk about a few. Some of my favorites."

"Professor?" one of the aspiring physicists interrupted. "May I suggest the Fermi Paradox?" It was John Bosch, Physics major, major pain in the ass. He was one of those students who couldn't just hang out and enjoy the show, he had to be part of it. Williams always has one in his class. They usually try to show that they are light years ahead of the material being covering in class, as if that would get them somewhere. It never did. They were always there right after class wanting Williams to clarify a point, or brown nose, or both. Usually both. That was one thing Williams didn't care about, not at that level. You could basically show up, take the tests, fail miserably, and that was good enough. Most of the kids would never use any of this again anyway, at least not realize it. Treating students like they were going to put a man on the moon next week didn't make much sense, and one or two of them acting like they were made even less of it.

"That's a good one Josh, but I'm going to keep with a theme. I have a few others in mind. We're going to talk about paradox as they relate to time. Grandfather paradox, Bootstrap, and some dude named Polchinski, his paradox."

"What about the Sony paradox?"

"Don't think I've heard of that one Travis."

"You know, listening to music about the future on an old Sony Walkman." The class was aware of Williams's eclectic song catalog and his method of listening, they laughed.

"That's more irony, I think, and that I am cheap, but I like it." Williams still enjoyed interacting, even if his students didn't want to be there; it made the time go by. "Let's start with the grandfather paradox. Anybody ever hear about this one?" He paused, looked around, no one said anything. "This one is similar to the Hitler paradox, but before anyone gets bent out of shape I'm not saying your grandfathers were Hitler or anything." In this day and age, he needed to make sure he didn't offend anyone, and didn't want to chance it. "But it's important to understand the paradox in these terms. So here it is, I'll start by asking you a question. Would you travel back in time to kill your grandfather? Let's say he did something heinous before he married your grandmother; before they had one of your parents. I don't know what he did, but you have it in for him."

"What does heinous mean?" one of the students asked. It was the type of questions that always had Williams wishing he said it in other terms, the word itself taking away from the point being made. But at least he knew they were listening.

"Well, you know, he did something terrible." He began to pace back and forth trying to think of an example. "For instance, maybe he invented a weapon of some sort that was used to kill thousands of people. Something like that."

"I'd go back," a voice said from somewhere in the upper rows of class. He was surprised by how fast he heard someone respond, with a small rumble of agreement from the class.

"Okay, someone here would go back and kill their Grandfather, given the circumstance. But," Williams paused for a moment, no longer pacing, "what if I said you wouldn't?"

"Why not?" another student asked. "If it would save thousands."

"Well, consider this. Although whatever the reason, if you went back in time and killed him, again, before one of your parents were born, then you wouldn't have been born." He again paused for effect but heard nothing. "If you weren't born, then you couldn't have gone back in time. You see?" Again, no response. "Let's move on from the Grandfather example. Consider the same paradox, but your target is now Adolf Hitler. Would you do it?"

"Hell yeah!" said a student again from the back row, the rest of the class in full agreement.

"You wouldn't go back in time to kill Hitler either. Let's say you decide to go back and eliminate him as a teenager. Doing that though, means he would never grow up to do all the things he did. You wouldn't have a reason to go back in the first place. And in the grandfather example, killing your grandfather would effectively eliminate you, therefore there would be no you that would go back and kill him, understand?"

"That's messed up." said Travis, adding his two cents. Williams liked Travis, he never shied away from dropping his opinion and that kept the class interesting and moving. "Hitler I can understand, but why anyone want to off their grandpa, psst." Travis could also miss the point entirely.

"Yes, yes, it's messed up, but you can see the dilemma. Now let's shift to another type of paradox. I don't want to talk too much about whacking people from the past. Here's another one, the Bootstrap Paradox."

"The booty what?" The class erupted from the quip.

"Thanks Travis." Williams said, giving Travis the look. The one that said he was pushing it, time to get back to discussion. Travis complied. "This particular paradox has to do with creation. It's easiest described using this example. Say you won the Nobel prize in literature for a novel that took you ten years to write. Okay?" Williams paused and started to pace again, anticipating an irrelevant question about the book. He looked up, and to his surprise the entire class was looking directly at him. "Well, now you go back in time, hand your past self a first edition of your book, whatever you wrote, and call it a day. Sounds awesome, right?" He waited for any sort of response.

"If I was writing a book, yeah," one of the girls answered from the middle row of the lab.

"Right. And you just saved yourself ten years' worth of time and trouble by giving your past self what she would have achieved in ten years. What's the paradox?" He paused, waiting to see if anyone would answer. "The paradox is in the fact that if you just handed yourself the novel, you never would have taken the ten years to create it in the first place, so how could you give yourself something that has no origin?"

"That's messed up," Travis's said, his mind was definitely blown.

"Are you starting to get the idea?" Williams took a glance at the clock. "Looks like we have time for one more. I mentioned this Polchinski guy when I started class. Doctor Joseph Polchinski Jr to be exact, and a little more respectful. His contribution to string theory and co-founding of D-branes are well known. But it's his paradox we are interested in; he took the grandfather example a bit farther. Around 1990 he wrote to a colleague discussing, guess what? Yep, paradoxes in time travel via a wormhole."

"Wait, you mean like Star Trek?" a student asked.

"Yeah... pretty close," Williams replied, not wanting to lose time explaining the differences. "But in his example, it's not a person that's travelling time through the wormhole, but an object, a billiard ball to be specific."

"How is that even possible?" the same student in the middle row asked.

"It's theory, but here's how it would work. Now I know you guys don't hang out at the billiard parlor, but I have been wrong before." There was a slight rumble from the class. "Let's say you cue up the eight ball and hit it into the corner pocket. That pocket is a hole in time."

"Is that the wormhole?" Travis asked.

"Yep, the beginning of it anyway. You shoot the eight ball into that pocket, but it comes out the opposite sides corner pocket. Pretty awesome party trick I know." Williams heard a slight rustle, he still had their attention. "But let's say that wormhole makes it so that any ball that enters the first corner pocket will come out the other corner pocket a few seconds earlier than when it went in. Everyone with me?"

"Yes Professor," Bosch answered.

"Good. So, if that were the case, when you initially hit the eight ball, it would actually get knocked out of the way by itself emerging from the other pocket. If that happened, it never entered the first pocket to begin with, which means it couldn't come out to hit itself. Think about it." The class was stone silent once again. Lost, or maybe not.

"Okay. Those are just three examples from many paradoxes that exist in the physics world. I would invite you to Google paradox in physics and see what else is out there. Maybe even take a look at John's suggestion of the Fermi paradox. Who knows, it might make its way to the test we are having Thursday." A collective sigh could be heard throughout the lab. "You don't need to go to extremes or anything. Tip from the future....it will be multiple choice...and maybe even open notes. Also, check out Doctor Polchinski, extra credit if you can tell me about string theory. Alright, speaking of time, class is out early, get out of here."

One thing Williams would see in each class he taught, no matter what, was that students would go the extra mile if he didn't keep them for the whole hour period. And when he let them go early, they moved.

"Later Dr. Williams," Travis said, holding up his hand while racing out the door. That's when Williams noticed the man again, sitting in the corner of the room, in the upper rows opposite of where Travis sat. He thought he'd seen that same man somewhere before, a month ago. He didn't look like a student, like everyone else, he wasn't wearing the uniform; jeans, t-shirt. He wore a dark blue suit, no tie, clean brown leather shoes, and carried an ivory colored fedora and brown leather briefcase. Williams brushed him off as some old guy just sitting in on a lecture. It happened from time to time, someone wandering the halls and decides to sit in on a class. For the most part they were harmless. It wasn't like they were taking tests or answering questions, they just wanted something to do, so he didn't care. But here he was again, a month later, a different class.

Williams started to pack up the few things he had out from his briefcase when Bosch stepped down to ask him about today's lecture. It would be an abnormality if it didn't happen with at least one student after each class. Williams used to stay there until Bosch, or any other student for that matter, got in all their questions. That all changed when he had to catch a flight to Cincinnati one fall. He just packed up and started answering their questions as he walked out the door, they followed, and it's been that was ever since. Bosch must have had something else to do, he only had one question today.

"Dr. Williams? I was wondering, since I have a pretty good knowledge of paradox, you know, like Fermi and others, do I need to take the exam? Maybe I can help administer?"

"Well, Josh, yes. Yes, you will still have to take the test. Of course, you should ace it with flying colors." Williams didn't care much for brown nosing. "But I'll tell you what. Write a short explanation of the Fermi paradox on the back of the exam, I'll give you extra credit, fair?" Williams knew Bosch didn't need extra credit, and he wasn't planning on reading what Bosch was going to write anyway, but it made him feel more special than the rest of the class, and that's all Bosch was really looking for.

"Cool, okay, okay cool. I'll do that, thanks Dr. Williams." And with that, Bosch started to head out. By that time all the other students had gone, and curiously, Williams glanced to the back of the auditorium. Just like that, the visitor was gone too. *Until next time,* Williams thought. Reaching into his briefcase, he took out his headphones and put them around his neck, slipping the Walkman into his pocket. He then put on his sunglasses like he has always done after class. Closing the case, he slid it off the lab desk, turned, and started to make his way to the door.

He didn't get more than a few paces when he stopped and looked back to where the man was once sitting. He again thought about how well he was dressed. *I swear I've seen him before, but where was it? Another one of my classes maybe? Walking around campus?* Without an answer, he turned and continued on his way out of the lab. As he left he slid his left hand down the wall to hit the light switches, the buzz of the fluorescents coming to a stop.

It was already late morning, early to the Professor. He decided to stop at the Union Coffee Yards for some caffeine and maybe a piece of carrot cake. Since he was running late in the morning he didn't have a chance to stop like he normally does, and that was also why he let class out early. He was feeling the withdrawal and needed to get his fix. He refused to drink the coffee at Bohr, it made him sick more than anything else. The coffee shop wasn't far anyway. It was in an old brick ticket booth built in the nineteen twenties with a green glazed French tile roof at the center of campus. Some of the relics told him that's where they had to buy tickets back in the day for any event on campus before everything was computerized.

"We want to be recognized!" blasted from someone holding a megaphone. It came from the middle of the Union area, where a group of what looked like students where gathered, protesting. Williams had seen them every day but had yet to understand what they wanted to be recognized for. He was also sure none of them actually went to the school. This was the place though, where one could stand on the corner and scream anything they wanted, and sometimes even change things.

The green shutters that covered the two arched openings of the coffee shop were swung to the sides during the summer, with seating outside. In the winter months, you waited in the cold and ordered through a small window on the opposite side, much like visiting a teller at a bank. It was nice out today, and Williams planned to take in some people watching with his coffee. Being in the middle of campus it was the perfect place, and since there were protestors, he wanted to get a good seat.

Williams remembered his Walkman just as he was rounding the corner into the plaza. *Man, must be withdrawal, I knew I was missing something.* He usually listened to it because he liked to walk with music, but also because it had big headphones. That meant people would notice and leave him alone. *Would have been 'Life is Hard' too, maybe I'll dedicate that to the megaphone dude another time.*

Once he rounded the corner he could see the Yards, so he didn't bother pulling the Walkman out now. He could just make out the seating surrounding the brick building. *Cool, only two people.* As he got closer, he noticed something odd, one of the people sitting outside, glancing over his shoulder toward Williams, had an ivory colored fedora sitting on the seat next to him. *I've seen that hat before. Wait, a month ago, and today. That's the guy who was in my class.* He could see the man turn away just as Williams got within view. Williams stopped, curious about the man, and what he wanted with him. He decided he was going to get a closer look. "Coffee first."

As the Professor got closer he could see the stranger was having an espresso by the size of the small cup on his table.

"Can I help you?" the barrister asked through the part in his blue hair that hung purposely in front of half his face.

"Hey. Yeah. Espresso, please."

"Huh...second one in ten minutes," the barrister said, thumbing over to the direction of the stranger, "except that guy called it a silver parfait."

"Silver parfait?" Williams at first thought he heard it wrong.

"Yeah, silver, or something, sounded like silver parfait, I don't know. He started to speak French; I don't know what he was talking about."

"I'll have a piece of that cake too." Williams pointed to the glass case, then glanced over again to the man with the hat. He decided he was going to introduce himself once he had his coffee and cake. The blue haired barrister disappeared behind the mountain of coffee making machinery, presumably to fill Williams's order.

"We want to be recognized!" blared once again. This time the protestors were headed in the direction of the coffee shop. Williams began to think he was in for a less than peaceful spot of coffee. But just as they neared the booth, the protest stopped. Williams looked back to see the leader let his megaphone drop to his side while he and the other handful of protestors got in line waiting to place an order.

"Coffee break," Williams whispered. After some commotion, and a hiss or two from the espresso machine, he was handed a small cup on a small saucer, a piece of carrot cake taking up space on its side.

"Espresso," the barrister called out, even though he could clearly see Williams standing there.

"Thanks." Williams took the saucer, balancing it in one hand, holding his briefcase in another. He took a few steps, paused for a moment to get a look at the stranger, then made his way over to his table. *Something in French. Maybe he's from a French university.*

"Bonjour." Although the barrister was probably not the most reputable source on the origins of the stranger, Williams thought French wasn't a bad way to break the ice. It wasn't new to him as his mother would speak it all the time when he was a child; his grandparents immigrating from near Chaumont. The man, delighted, quickly turned to face Williams.

"Bonjour Monsieur. Comment allez vous?" After a brief pause, the man smiled, pleasantly surprised by the French greeting.

"Tres bien," the professor answered, then pointed to the empty chair at the table. "May I? I am afraid my French doesn't get much use anymore, I hope I said that right."

"Please, be my guest Doctor Williams, and yes, it was said quite well. I sometimes forget I am not in France at the moment. I asked for a coffee, Un café, un café, s'il vous plait, is what I said to the young man. He said they don't serve silver parfait. Would you happen to know what that could be? Some American concoction perhaps?"

"Never heard of it," the Professor said while he smiled and laughed inside. "I see you were able to get a coffee at least."

"Oui. I used my finger, the universal language." The man pointed at Williams coffee cup with his index finger. "I am pleasantly surprised; the coffee here is not bad."

"You must have only had the espresso." This time it was Williams who paused. "I apologize if I sound a bit up front, but have I met you before? I get the feeling you might know me, but I don't recall meeting you."

"Pardonne-moi Monsieur. Forgive me. Doctor Legard, Paris France." Legard stood, extending his hand to Williams who was caught off guard by the gesture.

"Pleasure to meet you Doctor." Williams, now standing, had forgotten to let go of his case when he sat. Awkwardly, he dropped it by the foot of his chair and shook Legard's hand. "Was that you in my class an hour ago, and perhaps a month ago?"

Legard smiled slightly. "Oui Monsieur. I thought perhaps you didn't notice. I was looking for a more opportune time for us to meet, and, I wanted to get a sense of whom I would be talking."

"Well then...here we are. I hope I don't disappoint. What brings you to New York?" Williams didn't want to prolong the surreptitiousness any more than he had to.

"To the point, I have heard that about you Professor." Legard motioned once again for Williams to sit, then took a seat himself. "I am with the Ministré l'Interieur, France, partnering with the Université Pierre et Marie Curie, Paris."

Aha! Williams shouted with confidence inside. He was right, Legard was an observer from another university. *Why didn't Dean Tarkarov mention it? Legard's been here for at least a month and no heads up from him, odd.* Usually that sort of thing is set up through the head of the department. He couldn't remember the last time someone from another university just showed up, let alone from Europe, and for a month.

"Well, I hope you enjoyed the class today. It was a little shorter than usual, but productive. I was doing some.... research, late last night, couldn't get to class on time." He wasn't, and sort of felt bad for lying to Legard. He didn't know why, he just met the man a few minutes ago, but there was something about him.

"Indeed Professor. And the others."

Others? I've only seen you one other time.

"Paradox. It intrigues me. It's a subject I almost always have interest... when I have time of course. The Fermi paradox." Legard stopped, looked up at the sky for a moment, then went on. "Fermi was nothing less than genius. But he has me looking out into space and waiving my hand every now and then, au cao ou." Legard waived at Williams slightly. "Where are the visitors from outer space? I would be interested to hear your student's views."

"Me too, that's why I told them about the test. But, it's almost the end of the semester, most of them have checked out." Williams could see Legard struggle to understand. "It means they already have their minds on other things, like the summer. They really aren't going to spend any time studying, but I would like to think they will. The test is just so they will at least attempt to look like they are trying."

"Ah...of course. I can relate. I felt the same way when I made plans to come to see you. I have obligations you see, in Paris. But, they will be there when I get back."

"I always wonder what they think, new eyes on new concepts, a fresh perspective and things like that. Maybe from someone other than Bosch, he was the student who brought it up. I get a run down the moment class lets out, always." Williams paused once again, he wanted to see if Legard would add to the story of why he was here. If for anything Williams didn't want to seem rude for asking so many questions, but there seemed to be just that, so many questions. "So, uh, Université...."

"Université Pierre et Marie Curie, Paris," Legard finished.

"Right. I confess, Dean Tarakov didn't mention you would be observing my classes. Those types of arrangements are usually cleared through the department. I would have ended my research night early if I would have known."

Legard took a sip of his espresso, then cleared his throat. "Doctor...if I may clarify. I work with the Ministré l'Interieur, a liaison for special projects. It is mostly a l'iabri, and with resources from the Université, and others. I do not teach as you do, and I am not here to observe, quite frankly."

Alright, I'm confused. Why are you here then? "Professor....I..." Legard struggled to find the right way to say what he wanted, "we, need your help."

"You need my help? What exactly would you need it for? I have to tell you this seems a little strange. I've seen you in a few of my classes, but you are not a student or visiting Professor. You are from France, a university in France, but you don't teach there, and you work for the Interior did you say, that's Government right?"

"That is exactly the truth Professor." Legard didn't hesitate to answer.

"And you're here to ask for my help." Williams tried to be easy, but he felt like he was being spied on. Now that the cover has been blown, the agent has been found, he is asking for help.

"Exactement, Doctor." Legard sat upright, confirming exactly what Williams said, which was the opposite reaction he thought he would get.

"Okay...shoot."

"Shoot?" Legard asked, with a confused look on his face again.

"Yes, I have about an hour, what can I help you with? I am all ears."

Legard, not used to American slang, laughed. "I am afraid Professor, what I, that is we need from you, cannot be asked in one hour. We wouldn't even begin to scratch the surface. And indeed, cannot be displayed here. Let me explain." Legard folded his hands together, leaning on the table before him. His eyes were looking down into his cup of espresso. "Monsieur Williams, what if I told you we, that is my team and I have made a discovery that will fundamentally change the world as we know it?"

"Change the world as we know it? I'd ask you if that was such a good idea."

Legard smiled at Williams response. "Let me put it this way. Have you ever dreamed of standing in front of a doorway in Paris, only to walk though and be in New York?"

"What do you mean?" Williams heard him but was thrown off by the shift in conversation. When Legard asked for his help, the first thing that went through his mind was help with lesson plans, teaching style, something mundane, but this wasn't like that.

"You know what I mean, don't you Professor?" Legard just sat there with a slight grin, now looking directly at Williams, waiting for his response.

"Matter pathways. The ends of the earth in a short distance, that sort of thing? Yeah I've dreamt of that." Legard just sat there silent, wearing that grin. "Wait. Are you saying you created a matter transporter? You have a teleporter?" Legard didn't answer, his grin only getting larger. "Is that how you got here? Is that how you've been travelling?" Williams had a new question before he could get out the last.

"Doctor, we have created something unlike anyone has ever seen. It will fundamentally change our world."

"My god man, how does it work? What are the energy requirements? How long have you been running?" Williams had a million questions, but Legard had a few things to say first.

"All in good time Professor. But first, no."

"No?"

"Exactement. No, I have not used it to travel. I am afraid I still have to fly the friendly skies as they say. In fact, at this point, what we have does not work."

"What doesn't work? Did you create a teleporter?" Williams realized Legard never answered that question directly.

"Professor, at this time I must exercise some discretion, but what I can say, is that all attempts to make our project function have failed. We are in an impasse." Legard looked down at the table again.

"Impasse? How long have you been working on this? How big is the team working on it? If it's what I think it is, you have some of the best people working for you, right?"

"Professor, I am embarrassed to say.... I must be cautious with what I am telling you from this point on." Legard reached into his briefcase, pulled out a small envelope, and laid it on the table. "My team indeed is of the brightest talent, that which didn't scoff at the very idea of a project such as this."

"What's this?" Williams thought at first Legard was going to hand him some more detailed information revealing what the project actually was. After handling the envelope, he realized it was way too small for anything like that.

"Your travel arrangements. You will find information on your flight, facility badge, and directions to where you will be staying in Paris. You leave in two weeks."

"I leave for Paris? In two weeks? Wait a sec. I have a ton of questions."

"I am sorry Professor, this is all the information I can give you here. If you want to know more, you will have to come to Paris." Legard stood up and shook Williams's hand. "It was good coffee," he said, pointing to his empty espresso cup, then started to make his way toward a waiting car.

"Wait...why me?" Although Williams was fascinated by the idea, he couldn't understand why the French government would want him, and for what.

"It's quite simple Professor," Legard said, stopping to face Williams, "you were selected."

"Selected?"

"Based on your research, unconventional I would say, not entirely suited for mainstream publication. But, for our needs, entirely practical. You scored the highest probability of success."

"I did?"

"To put it another way," he said, starting for the car again, "there are only four people in the world capable of solving our problem."

"Well then, why don't you ask one of the others?"

"That's impossible, Monsieur Williams."

"Why? Why is it impossible?"

"Three already work for me. You are the only one left."

"I don't..." Williams was uneasy, he took a step back from the table. He *was* being spied on and he didn't know how to react. "Hold on," he said, hoping Legard would stop again, thinking that he wasn't interested.

"Au revoir Monsieur," Legard added. Williams watched as another man stepped out, walked around to the passenger side of the car, and opened the door. Legard turned and held up his hat.

"What makes you think I'd go?" Williams asked.

"Your curiosity Professor."

3. A Walk in the Park

It was the first time Williams flew business class, so far, he was impressed. He was early so he decided to check out Air France's passenger lounge while he waited for his flight's boarding call. The lounge seemed like it had just been renovated, it even smelled new. It was a very clean and modern lounge with as much natural lighting as could be had. Williams stepped in, not wanting to seem like he was new to all this, which he was, and quickly began to scan for an available seat. He headed for a corner spot, completely void of anyone, and near a window overlooking a complex system of roadways that lead into JFK. It would be perfect for looking over the things Legard gave him.

He took another look around, making sure he was alone, then poured out the contents of his attaché on the table in front of him. He's looked it over more than once in the few weeks the two men spoke, but he couldn't help going over them again. "ID badge. With, my picture from my passport. I'll have to ask him how he got a hold of that." A woman a few seats over peered over at Williams talking to himself. "A spy maybe?" he joked quietly. "NICHOLAS G. WILLIAMS, at least they spelled it right. And then there's these." Williams picked up two cards, each with a different name of a place and address. "Le Emporeur, I guess that's where I'll be staying." He placed the card and ID on the corner of the table. "But what does the museum have to do with anything?" Williams was now holding the second card, on it printed the name of the army museum, Musée de l'Armée, and an address.

"Nous souhaiterions la bienvenue à nos passagers de classe affaires.... We would like to welcome our business class passengers..." It was time to board. Williams heard his flight number and started to gather his things. He quickly slid the remaining items with his hand into the open attaché he had positioned at the end of the table, the two cards and ID falling inside. He stood, took a few steps, then glanced back at the table he was using, making sure he didn't leave anything behind.

"Guess I'm committed now." He took a deep breath. "What the hell am I doing?" He was one of a few passengers called to board and quickly made his way to the attendant, handing her his boarding pass. She glanced at the pass, then at him and smiled. With a brush of the paper document over the scanner, the bar code registering into the computer beeping in acknowledgement, she handed the pass back to Williams.

"Merci. Bon voyage," she said smiling, then waived him on.

He walked down the jetway when he realized, after catching a glimpse through one of the windows, that he would be flying in a Boeing 777. He secretly hoped it would have been one of the new Airbus A380's, or even one of the older Boeing 747's. It didn't matter he thought, it would still be a good ride.

He was greeted by yet another friendly member of the flight crew when he reached the doorway. With a quick glance at his seat assignment, she escorted him to the business class section. "This will do," he whispered after seeing his spacious and private reclining seat near a window, to his approval.

It was late in New York, but Williams thought there was no way he would be able to sleep on the plane. He kept imagining what the teleporter was like, if indeed that's what it was. "Enter Paris, get out in New York, that's what he said. It has to be. Damn my curiosity." He envisioned some machine straight out of a science fiction movie. Some large round doorway, lights flickering on and off, a bank of computers manned by top scientists monitoring every piece of data emanating from its ports. But once he was in the air and the night set in, there was only so much he could do before exhaustion started to take hold. For the remainder of the flight he would drift in and out of sleep. When he was awake he would think about what he would see when he arrived in Paris, when he was asleep he would dream about it.

"What time is it? Crap, is it still New York time or did it change?" Williams was holding his phone out in front of him, not sure if he had the auto change function set. "It had to have been at least five hours, it's getting light outside. Might as well look over them again." He reached for his attaché he had tucked in a drawer that was built into his business class seat and pulled out one of the cards. "Rue Grenelle. Army Museum. Why is that significant?" He took advantage of the on-board Wi-Fi and searched every detail of the museum only to nod off when sleep took hold again, the card falling to his lap.

"Bonjour!" a voice said over the intercom. "On behalf of Air France, the crew and I would like to say thank you for flying with us, and we hope you have enjoyed your trip. We will be arriving in Paris in one half hour, where the local time is ten A.M. Bonne journée!" A slight French accent woke Williams from a light sleep, in a half hour he would be one step closer to seeing the reason that brought him here. He was in and out of sleep throughout the night, using the moments he was awake to put together his questions. Sleep had just taken hold again when it was time to land, and the announcement started to get his mind going. "Rue Grenelle." He kept what Legard gave him in a separate attaché so he could take the items to the museum after he dropped off his things at the hotel. Legard left instructions to meet soon after landing, and he didn't want to waste any time.

De Gaulle looked different than Williams remembered it. From the air he could see the old circular terminal building where he walked through as a child. This flight de-boarded on the other side of the airport, in the newer terminal 2 that was completed in the 1980's and 90's.

He stepped out of the jetway and immediately stepped to the side so he could stop and get his bearings. This was new to him, and he had places to be. He thought the best option was to follow some of the other passengers, at least until he started seeing signs for the baggage claim. But before he knew it, he was lost in the architecture of the terminal hall and stopped once again. It was a modern cathedral, a cylindrical ceiling as far as the eye could see, travelers were its congregation. "Pretty cool," he said.

"Dernier appel d'embarquement..." the announcement snapped Williams out of his trance. "Final boarding call..." he soon heard. The open spaces of Charles De Gaulle airport were flooded with the sound of departure announcements, arrival announcements, flight information, in so many different languages they all seemed to melt into one another.

"Better get going." Williams started again. "Bags, then taxi," he whispered. Starting again down the long hall, keeping to the side as he walked, he eventually found the sign he was looking for. "Bagages, that's it."

It was a long walk down to the claim, the information Legard gave him would soon start to occupy his mind again. *What are they working on? What is it that is causing problems? How am I going to be able to help?* He kept walking, constantly running the same questions in his mind over and over, always coming up with nothing. Williams stopped, realizing he could not remember anything he just had walked past, being completely drawn into the idea of what he would soon get to see firsthand. *Crap. Did I miss the claim, did I walk right by it?* He started again after seeing another blue baggage claim sign with an arrow pointing in the direction he needed to go.

Williams didn't pack much, after all, he really didn't know how long he was going to be staying. He figured if he really needed something, he could buy it, no sense lugging it half way across the world since it might just be a short trip. So, he made quick work of the baggage claim and soon found himself outside. Not far from the exit, he could see the sign he was looking for and hurried over to queue up in the taxi rank.

"Do you want a ride?" a raspy voice asked just outside of the door. Williams stopped, not sure he heard the question. "Do you want a ride? Mine's cheaper, and I get you there fast." The raspy voice belonged to a short man, round, with dark skin.

Williams knew right away he was a gypsy, or illegal migrant, someone who didn't have a license to do what he was doing. Sure, they had their advantages, they were usually cheaper, but they had their risks too. Williams was too tired to take a chance, and instead refused, politely, and headed to the taxi queue.

"Frog," the raspy voice whispered. Williams laughed quietly as he walked away toward the queue. He knew what 'frog' meant and that he made the right choice not taking the ride. The man would have to find another mark.

A few short steps later and Williams was queued up. Almost immediately, a car pulled up with that unmistakable sign on the roof, 'TAXI PARISIAN.' "That's more like it," he said as he looked back to see that the raspy voiced man was gone.

"Septième arrondissement," he said through the open window to the driver. After tossing his bag in the open trunk, next to what looked like the driver's lunch, he hopped in. "Rue Chevert, Hotel L'Empereur." The hotel was only a short walk to Rue Grenelle and was his first stop.

"Oui Monsieur, right away." The driver spoke perfect French, and English too. He wasn't from France though, the small flag hanging from the rearview mirror gave that away.

"Ireland?" Williams asked. The driver just looked at Williams through the mirror. "The flag, is that the Irish flag?"

"Cote de Ivory. Same colors, but reversed." The flag of the former French colony, the Ivory Coast, was green, white and orange, opposite of Ireland. That explained the look.

"Ah, I do that with the flags of Luxembourg and France, Germany and Belgium too, they look similar, sorry."

"It's a big world. Sooner or later, you run out of colors," the driver added jokingly. "It's no problem, as long as the other country is as cool as yours."

"I would have to agree."

The trip from De Gaulle to the hotel was as direct as it could be. Old Paris streets coupled with the city's dense population made it a lengthy drive. Williams again couldn't help but think of what Legard told him. It wasn't much, but enough to peek his curiosity. *What does it look like?* Paris was going by the cab window but Williams was not interested. He decided to take out his pencil and pad from his breast pocket to jot down the questions that kept running in and out of his mind. They were overwhelming, and after a while he put it all away, leaned back against the seat and started to look out the window of the taxi. He wasn't taking in the sights but imagining what was so important about the museum.

"Hotel de L'Empereur, Monsieur." Williams had no idea how long the taxi was stopped, he was too engrossed in his thoughts, just like at the airport. The driver was tapping on his rear-view mirror to get Williams's attention, but then spun around in his seat. "Monsieur, Rue Chevert, L'Empereur."

"Ah...pardon, sorry," Williams said as he reached for his stash of euro's. He knew taxi drivers didn't want to see plastic, they would have to report it then. That meant the cab company would take a cut, the government would get their tax, and there would be a record of his tip. It didn't matter what city, or nation for that matter, cash made things better. The driver saw the cash and hopped out of the taxi, opened the curb side door, then hurried to the trunk to retrieve Williams's luggage. Cash made things better.

Hotel de L'Empereur was a quant hotel a few blocks from Eiffel. More importantly, it was across the street from the Army Museum. Le Empereur was a six-story building on the corner of Rue Chevert and Boulevard de la Tour-Maubourg, Rue Grenelle to its north. Its name was in gold letters just below the second floor, with a small sign protruding from the corner. A small white number two in a blue square hung above the entrance.

The exterior was sandstone and shone brightly in the near noon sun. Williams entered under the arched doorway, directly under the number two. It was a small hotel, but from what Williams could see, it was going to be perfect. It wasn't where all the tourists went, and it was quiet which meant he could get work done. That was assuming he wasn't going to spend all his time with Legard, wherever that might be. Williams turned just before entering and looked across the street. *What do they have hiding over there?*

"Bonjour Monsieur, comment allez vous?" The receptionist smiled at Williams as he made his way to the front desk. There was no one else in the lobby, and it appeared she had been waiting for him to arrive.

"Bonjour. I have a reservation, it's under...." *What was it under?* Legard took care of everything, except some of the basics, like what his reservation was under. He had one, he was sure of that, but he only had the small card in his attaché to show for it.

"Monsieur Willam?"

That was close enough. "Yes, that's me."

"Monsieur Legard confirmed your arrival early today, he said you would be arriving around this time."

Yep, he took care of everything.

"The gentleman will take your bags and show you to your room. You will be in room 237, facing the Musée de l'Armée." The receptionist held out a small envelope with an electronic key card, handing it to Williams.

"Merci, thanks." Williams took the key card, holding it up to get a better look. He turned to see the porter stepping into the elevator. Taking his attaché, he quickly rushed in behind and was then off to the second floor.

The porter walked out and to the left the moment the elevator door opened. Williams followed holding his card key in front of him anticipating its use for the room. The porter stopped and spun around, quickly snatching the key from Williams, then holding it up to the keypad until it beeped and unlocked the door. Williams just stood, his hand in front of him as if he were still holding the key, not registering what was happening. The porter simply slid the key back into Williams's fingers and walked into the room with the bag.

The room was spacious and pleasantly updated. From the outside Le Empereur was a typical French design, old Paris looked like that everywhere. But it was on the inside that made everything different. *Cool.* Williams saw a set of double doors that opened to a small balcony. *Real coffee. Outside. That is Paris.* For a second Williams lost himself. Before he knew it, the porter was gone, closing the door behind. Williams looked at the five euro note he had in his hand that he planned to give the man for helping him with the bags. "I forget sometimes." He tucked the euro in his pocket and went to open the double doors to let in some air.

Williams forgot about Legard, the machine, everything, and saw what everyone saw when they came to Paris, a beautiful city around every corner. It wasn't long before the view from his balcony led him to Mansart's gold Dôme des Invalides. All his questions and curiosity came flooding back, and he was reminded why he was there. He quickly slammed the double doors shut, spinning around to the table where he placed his attaché when he walked in. He couldn't remember if he shut his room door before he was already on the first floor and into the street.

Williams was quick to make his way to Musée de l'Armée. The army museum was housed in the Hôtel national des Invalides, what was once a retirement home and hospital for military veterans, now, a museum. Williams walked quickly; it was just east of the hotel, the dome clearly visible in the noon day sun. As he walked, he tried to understand the connection between the museum and the project, but could see none. *It's a museum. Legard talked about a doorway, Paris to New York. Why didn't he tell me anything else? Why are we meeting there?* "I have no idea," he said to himself. He tried to think of anything, anything at all that could be of significance. By the time he reached the entrance he was no closer to an answer.

Williams wanted to enter as inconspicuously as possible, which meant as a tourist. He was to enter from the main entrance, with no further instructions left by Legard. "There it is." He walked up to the baroque entrance, stopping for a moment to take in the stone guards standing watch on either side. "I'm never going to find him here. This was a mistake." Williams was having second thoughts. He came all this way, not even knowing what for, and here he was standing alone in front of an entrance to a military museum. But his curiosity was pulling him in, and he had to see what this was all about. Just then, a familiar voice.

"Monsieur Williams?" A man waived his hat from a distance, Williams had trouble seeing him over the tourists, and even more trouble hearing him over the echoes and reverberations from the stone and marble structure. At first, Williams thought it was just another person calling for someone else, but as he edged closer, through the mass of people taking pictures and queueing up to enter, he realized who it was.

Standing off to the side, hat in hand, and looking directly at Williams, was François Legard. They never had a planned time to meet, just some time after he arrived. There was no telling how long Legard had been waiting. But if Legard knew him as well as Williams thought he did, it wasn't long. Legard probably counted on Williams wanting to get to it as soon as he checked in.

"Well, that's him. Here goes nothing," he said under his breath. He started to walk toward Legard.

"Monsieur Williams, s'il vous plaît." Legard called out again, this time extending his arm in the direction of a set of brass doors, very highly polished. Williams could see a small sign in dark green with white letters framed in the center of one of the doors. 'PAS D'ENTRÉE!' Williams stopped, then looked at Legard. Here he was, in Paris, on the invitation of someone he spoke to once. He was staying at a hotel where he had a room he didn't reserve. And now he was being asked to go through a door that without a doubt says no entry. He was once again starting to question his wisdom, and why he was there. Legard, without answer from Williams, reached into the breast pocket of his jacket and started to walk toward him.

Damn. What have I gotten myself into?

Legard pulled out a small ID badge, identical to the one in Williams's attaché. "I knew I could count on your curiosity. It's a trait with everyone on the team. Insatiable. Shall we?"

"Hello....er, bonjour." *Okay, it was just a badge, nothing else. Let's try to get that pulse rate down.*

"If you would display your ID, you will need it on all levels once we go through the doors." Legard started to walk toward the brass doors, Williams reached into his attaché and pulled out his ID, attached to a lanyard he had from the university, and lifted it over his head and around his neck.

"I gotta be honest with you...I was a little worried about this. I had a few thoughts as to what you were going to pull out of that pocket," he said, trying to break the ice.

"Ah monsieur. I am, but a scientist. Besides, there are weapons everywhere here." Legard pointed toward a cabinet of early eighteenth century rifles near the entrance, then pointed toward a small dark glass panel just below the ceiling. Williams could only imagine what was behind the glass, designed so one could look out, but not in.

"Venez par ici, s'il vous plait." Legard lead the way through the brass doors, Williams followed. They entered into a small room, not more than three meters by three meters, with another door at the far end. This one appeared to be very heavy, and from Williams's perspective, it looked like something out of a bank vault. In the middle was a key pad and ID scanner. He could make out more small glass panels near the ceiling.

Cameras, cameras, and more cameras.

"Monsieur, please insert your badge, I would like to see that it is working." Legard inserted and removed his card, then one of the two small red lights on the key pad flickered and turned green. Williams did the same. The other light turned green and the two men could hear a small mechanical noise from inside the door as it unlocked. If you are alone, there will be one red light, the two of us, two red lights, three, three red lights, and so on." Legard walked over to one side of the room and pointed to a small bulbous feature which undoubtedly was hiding another camera. "Facial recognition software identifies anyone who walks through that door." Legard used his thumb to point to the brass doors behind them. "Everyone in the room must have a badge or the door will not open. If matching ID's are not inserted within fifteen seconds, this room will fail secure."

"Fail secure? What does that mean?" Williams was pretty sure he knew what that meant, but he has never been in something as secure as this, so he wanted to make sure.

"It will lock you inside this room until security decides to release you, and to whom." Just as Legard was finishing what he was saying, the brass doors locked behind them. Williams thought something was wrong with his ID until he heard a quiet hiss from the steel door as it slowly started to open. "Those will lock behind you," once again Legard thumbed over his shoulder to the brass doors, "so as to not allow any unexpected visitors, you see. Once locked, this door will unlock and open automatically. These two doors can never be unlocked at the same time."

"Okay, seems secure," Williams said. *Why would a museum need this much security? Motion detectors, alarms, cameras, I can understand all that. But facial recognition software, doors that fail secure, why is there this much security in a museum with a bunch of crusty artifacts?* Then Williams caught a piece of the puzzle that would start making the picture clearer. 'MINISTRE L'INTERIOR.' A polished plaque hung just on the other side of the steel door, which by now had swung open completely.

"The machine.... it's here, isn't it?" Williams felt the flood of questions entering his mind again.

"Monsieur, it would be best to not discuss such things here." Legard, nodded slightly to a security guard stationed just on the other side of the second set of doors where the two men entered. It looked like the guard wasn't paying attention to them, but Williams could tell behind the dark glasses, he had checked them out thoroughly. The guard wore a dark blue uniform with black boots, a radio on his belt with a transmitter clipped just above his left breast pocket, and a pistol.

Williams could see a rifle, a FAMAS F1, held in front at the ready. "Right," he said. *Is that a bayonet?* He could see what looked like a dark steel protrusion from the front of the rifle but didn't want to stare and turned to look at Legard. "Understood. I can wait." He couldn't wait. There were so many questions, he didn't know where to start. He did however understand it wasn't yet the place.

"Very good," Legard added. The security guard was part of the Interior Ministry, but that didn't mean he had clearance. With what Williams had seen so far, he was sure all information was handled as need to know. If you didn't need to know, you didn't know. Legard continued to walk down the corridor to what looked like an elevator. He pressed the button on the wall and waited.

"No badge needed here?" Williams asked.

"No. Once you are past the recognition phase," Legard pointed to the heavy door they just came through, "you are cleared until you get to the labs."

"Got it." *Okay...so where is that? Up or down? My guess, down. No way they would have this kind of security and have anything on an upper floor.* Without a buzzer or bell noise, the elevator doors opened.

"Voilà." Legard used his hand to point into the elevator, asking Williams to go first. There were no floor buttons, up, or down, and nothing that looked like it could be activated. The walls were the same opaque glass as what Williams saw on the walls in the hall and through the secure doors. He could only imagine what was watching on the other side. Legard stood with his hands crossed politely in front of him, waiting patiently. The doors closed and the elevator began to move, but Williams couldn't tell which direction. With no visual clues, he only felt motion without a clear idea of direction.

"SOUS-NIVEAU UN," an automated female voice said quietly over the speakers in the elevator. "SOUS-NIVEAU DEUX, SOUS-NIVEAU TROIS."

Okay. We're going down. It's below the museum. That explains a lot, hiding in plain sight...magnificent. "Security is serious business here, but one wouldn't know if from the other side of those doors." Williams was trying to get Legard to say something, anything, if just to keep himself from blurting out all his questions.

"Oui Monsieur. We find the best security is not letting anyone know we are here. And in case they do, well, you saw our friend up there. There are many more like him, all over the facility."

"SOUS-NIVEAU DIX." The elevator stopped. Ten levels below ground.

"I guess we're here." *Wow. Ten floors below the museum. I guess that would be enough to guard against any type of prying from the outside, or...some problem from the inside. No one on the surface would even have a clue.* The doors opened, Legard stepped out and Williams followed. Another armed guard, almost identical to the one topside stood in one corner.

"Bonjoir François, " a receptionist said, standing to greet the two men. She looked at Legard for several seconds with a subtle smile. He reached out for her hand. They knew each other, intimately.

"Bonjoir Adriane."

"And bonjoir Monsieur Williams." The receptionist seemed to have been told of his arrival. She slowly released Legard's hand and held hers out to Williams.

"Hello...eh, bonjoir." He was nervous, and despite all queues, he forgot he was in Paris.

"This way monsieur." Legard led the way down a dimly lit hall. Williams could barely see them but could tell there was surveillance everywhere. He started to think every inch of the facility was being watched or recorded. That would usually make him nervous, but this time he welcomed it.

"So, the lab is ten floors down. Impressive." They stopped in front of another door wired with another badge scanner.

"You can enter individually from here." Legard swiped his badge and then entered a keycode unlocking the door and stepping inside.

The two men walked in to what looked like a control room. It housed three work stations arranged in a way where a center console faced a large open lab area. The other two consoles were on each side, slightly turned toward the center. Each looked to be manned by a member of Legard's team. The floor was divided into tiers down to the base, giving a full view of the open area on the other side of the work stations.

The lab area itself was at least twice as large as the control room. 'Laboratoire Un' was printed on a large sign that was hung on the very top edge of the room. In the lab were no work stations or consoles, and no personnel were stationed there. From Williams point of view, it looked like it was framed in lighting, camera, and sensor equipment, everything one needs to record and analyze data. They looked like they covered every angle, at least from above. From the wires protruding the walls and leading down to the floor, Williams guessed the lower angles were covered too, with more sensory equipment and cameras. Everything looked to be directed at what was in the middle of the room. Williams wanted to get a closer look but could tell something was about to happen.

"Voilà. Just in time," Legard said quietly.

"In time for what?"

"Another test. I was afraid we were not going to make it."

"Test? Where?" Williams started to look around the control room.

Legard smiled slightly, then slowly pointed to the lab room. "Right down there."

4. Closed Doors

"I want ALL cameras functioning this time," Lemaire stated while she looked over her center console to the mass of wires and cables ahead. Her statement wasn't directed to just one person in the lab. During the last test, although the cameras and monitoring equipment were fully functional and rolling, no footage was taken. She thought maybe Engels forgot to trigger the recording equipment and didn't want to take that chance again.

"There all on, again," Engels answered. He sat at the console to her right and was responsible for the functions in the lab that were not directly part of the door test itself. Lighting, power supply, recording equipment, they were all under his control. He insisted the cameras were on after the last test, but the only footage recovered was of the door after they powered everything down.

"I want you to double check. We need to see what's happening on the other side both here and in lab two." Lemaire wasn't going to take his word for it; this test was too important. And although she ordered him to double check, she was busy pulling up the recording equipment diagnostics herself. "What is the ETA for field generation?"

"ETA in five minutes twenty seconds. Everything looks nominal." Vogel made up the third member of the team and occupied a console to Lemaire's left. He would stand periodically to get a visual of the door, then look back to his console for a field generation status. From their consoles they could bring up anything about the test and control room that was needed. The recording equipment, temperature, field stabilization status, power consumption, anything critical to the test they had available.

"Okay. I need a callout when we are at one." Lemaire wanted to be sure she could focus on her tasks when they were ready to initialize the doorway, so in the test plan she had Vogel call out the status at certain intervals. "How are those camera's Robert?"

Engels looked at her with a scowl. He resented being treated like a graduate student. Not wanting to be subject to her anger should something go wrong, he double checked the recording equipment. "There all on, again." He wasn't going to make it any easier.

Williams and Legard remained toward the back of the control room. Since Williams wasn't directly involved in the tests, yet, Legard wanted him out of the way. Williams was uneasy just sitting back. He found himself creeping closer a few inches whenever something would happen in the control room. "Ahem." Legard would remind him not to venture to close.

"Sorry. I'm a little excited." This was the reason he came so far, he was about to see what Legard meant by traveling from Paris to New York. His unsettled curiosity was driving him. He wanted to get his hands on it, he wanted to get involved. No sooner did his excitement take hold, he would realize he didn't even know what he was looking for. All he was able to see, at least from the back of the control room, were what looked like miles of wires and cables. Under all of it was a small fortune worth of what looked like thermal imaging optics, passive IR, ultrasonic, and microwave motion detection devices, light-emitting diodes, pressure sensors, all focused on the open space in the middle of the lab. He would have to wait.

In between what looked like actual events planned in their testing, he took the opportunity to look over the group of scientists working diligently in the lab. Marie Lemaire was French, a Physicist, but definitely didn't look the part, not wearing a lab coat like the others. She was the leader of the group, Williams could tell the moment he walked in. Robert Engels, younger than the rest in his late twenties, was American and looked it. And although he was barely a kid, Legard assured Williams it took a lot to get him from MIT straight to the French Interior. Then there was Gunter Vogel, an older member of the team, a German Physicist from Munich who had been on the project from the start, according to Legard. What Legard wasn't saying, is when that was.

"You are at one minute," Vogel called out, it was the one-minute mark as ordered by Lemaire.

"The cameras are all on, again," Engels added. He took the opportunity to answer before Lemaire could ask. She briefly smirked. Engels looked over to Vogel who smiled.

"I am running the initiation sequence. Are we sure we've got the right sequence this time?"

"It's all best guess," Vogel answered, and also reminded her that they were working with an unknown.

This caught Williams's attention. "Best guess," he whispered. "What does he mean?" Williams asked.

Legard briefly looked at him, then pointed back to the lab. "Un moment, s'il vous plait." The questions were starting to add up, but Legard's answer told Williams it would have to wait for another time.

"Thirty seconds," Vogel called out.

"Initiation sequencing near completion. Robert. System status?"

"Just a sec. Running system check. Yeah, all looks good on my end."

"What about your side Gunter? Your status?"

"I am green on my side, let's try this again. Initialization in fifteen seconds."

Lemaire's hand was resting on the console, her finger hovering over the mouse button ready to go. Lemaire pulled a few strands of hair from her face over her ear, then looked over to Vogel.

"We are at zero," he answered.

"I'm hitting it, keep an eye on your systems. Here we go." Lemaire clicked on the mouse and things started to come to life. All at once, a bright light illuminated the area under all the equipment. The team squinted slightly, except for Engels, who was now wearing his sun glasses.

The control room lights, Williams thought, must have been programmed for this moment, and were off as soon as the door came to life. *Maybe so it doesn't distort any visual records?* He watched patiently for something to happen but couldn't see much from his point of view. He moved up slightly again, to see what he could see. He felt the floor start to vibrate, and the light started to take on a blue hue. Engels took off his sunglasses.

"The fields are holding. Both doors, one and two, everything looks nominal," Vogel said, calling out a status.

Williams came to a realization. *Of course, there's another door, there would have to be. Must be someplace else. Someplace here?*

"Robert. Ready?"

"Yep, ready when you are. Just say the word."

"Wait!" Vogel called out. "I am reading fluctuations in the field. Power spikes. We are all over the place, 1500 Kw to 2000. I don't like the looks of it." Vogel peered out into the lab and could see the blue light emanating from the doorway flicker. "It's unstable. I think it's going to collapse. Scheiße!"

1500Kw, that's enough to power a house for a month. I wonder what it looks like topside? Williams could only imagine the lights in the museum coming on and off. Alarms designed to protect artifacts falsely tripping as a result.

"Should I let it go while it's still up?" Engels asked, holding his hand near the release.

"I don't think we will get an accurate reading if we do. The power is all over the place. Hold on, the power is over max, it's drawing too much. I don't think we want to put anything in the field until it comes down."

"Will it?" Lemaire asked. The blue light flickering wildly in front of them. She pulled up the power readings on her console.

"My guess is the breakers will go any minute." Vogel hoped for the best but knew what they were up against.

"Let it go," Lemaire said, making a decision for Engels to hit the switch. Anticipating the go ahead, he had already pulled up the test menu on his console. He would just need to click the 'GO' option that would release a small red ball down a ramp and into the middle of the door's field. "Let it go before the field collapses."

"Going in five, four, three....", just then a loud hum was heard, followed by what sounded like static over a radio, "...two, one," then a very high-pitched whine. Suddenly, the humming and the static stopped, there was only the whine and the blue light. "Dropping!" Engels shouted. He stood and pointed to the ball rolling down the ramp. But just before the ball could enter the field, everything suddenly powered down. The audible whine stopped, the blue light began to fade, and with a small pop, it was over. The team all looked on as the ball jumped from the ramp, entered the empty space under all the monitoring equipment, then simply rolled to the other side of the lab, beyond the door. It never made it to lab two.

"Gunter, how's the field?" Lemaire asked, looking over her shoulder at Vogel.

"It's down, gone. No readings," he said, not taking his eyes off his console. "It's not drawing any power now. The breakers must have kicked in before we released."

"Same as last time," Lemaire quietly said to herself. She glanced over to Engels to get a report on the second door. She wanted a visual. "What do you see in lab two?"

"Nothing. I don't see anything."

"What? What do you mean?" She was now looking directly at Engels.

"Another blackout. We have nothing," Engels reported.

"Damn it. What is going on?" Lemaire looked back at her console.

"Looks like it went out the second the ball dropped. The spike in power must interfere with all the feeds. We've captured both doors just before the ball dropped, then, gone."

"It does not surprise me, the power the field generates, unlike anything we've ever seen. There must be something causing the spike. The field just cannot stay stable with the fluctuations," Vogel added.

Williams was hanging on to each word, they were all clues. Yet, he and Legard stood quietly in the back of the lab.

"Lab one video went out at the exact same time. Doesn't look like we captured any data from any of the sensors either, except for IR," Engels confirmed. "See if you can see anything."

The rest of the team tried to pull up the captured data feeds on their consoles. "NO OUTPUT DEVICE

INSTALLED", I don't see anything," Vogel reported, shrugging his shoulders.

"Same on my console." Lemaire sat with her arms crossed. "Gunter, can you confirm both doors are powered off?"

"I can see it, it's confirmed, there's no power going to them at all. We won't be able to start them up without full power reset, to get the breakers back into position."

"Are you sure?" She didn't want to take chances.

"Ja, es ist.... yes, it is closed."

"Totally awesome," Engels said, slumped behind his console. "I think we succeeded in frying the cameras. Sending kids toys from one room to another, not so much."

"I don't know. Damn it. What are we missing? This is the same failure over and over?" Lemaire said, clearly frustrated.

"Gunter, did you remember to plug it in?"

Vogel, ignoring Engels joke, made his way into the lab area to retrieve the red ball, now resting where it rolled, in the back corner of the lab.

"Aha! Here you are. Thought you could hide, did you?" He picked up the ball, then tossed it with a smile to Engels who caught it one handed.

"Well, at least we know it didn't work, as if we needed proof."

"I want full data dumps. We need to figure out why we keep having those power spikes, and why that ancient equipment keeps cutting out." Lemaire said, pointing to all the cameras and sensors surrounding lab one. "I don't want to have to replace them with eight-millimeter cameras, that would be taking two more steps back. But, I will if it means we actually record something."

"I'll take a selfie with it during the next test," Engels mumbled.

"Data dumps now Robert. We need to figure out what happened."

"Okay, okay. I'm running the backups. I'll do a status check on the monitoring equipment this afternoon. I don't know what I can do without some sort of shielding."

"Do what you can. We'll figure something out." Lemaire briefly looked up at Legard and Williams. "We're going to have to do something about this equipment François. Most of it, ordures."

"Bonjour Marie," Legard said, making no mention of the equipment. Lemaire did not answer his greeting.

"Bonjour François! Did you enjoy today's exercise?" Vogel was now sitting at his console and spun around in his chair, "It's still in one piece, not bad for a mornings work as we German's say."

"Bonjour Gunter. And humanity thanks you for your efforts. May I introduce Doctor Nicholas Williams. Monsieur Williams, Doctor Gunter Vogel." Vogel reached out his hand.

"And I trust you enjoyed that as well?"

"Nick. And yes, I did.... although I am not exactly sure what *that* was. Pleased to meet you."

"Ich auch nicht," Vogel added, in German, shrugging his shoulders. "Me neither."

"And Monsieur Engels, he's American, too."

"Yo. Hope you like cheese and," Engels motioned to the lab, "not much else happening. There's a lot of that here."

"In moderation," Williams answered. He thought Engels comment was funny, but he could see Lemaire thought otherwise. She turned and looked to the lab. It was clear she was not happy with today's test, so Williams didn't want to push it.

"And may I introduce you to our team leader, the person responsible for getting us where we are today with the project, Doctor Marie Lemaire." Lemaire turned to face Legard and Williams. She at first didn't look directly at them, still working out the issues in her mind.

"Monsieur Williams."

Okay...that was cold. Williams tried to pass it off as frustration and adrenaline at what she just went through.

"You're the one who is going to take over my work." The room went quiet. Vogel and Engels both stopped what they were doing and looked over at Legard, waiting for his response.

"Mademoiselle....mademoiselle, non, monsieur Williams is an extension to the team, your team, as we discussed." Legard could read her attitude, she wasn't happy. "His purpose is to aid you, as a consultant, to try to get us over these..." he looked over to the mass of cables and wires, "issues."

Lemaire turned around, not shaking Williams hand and looked again to the door. "If that were true, you would have let me chose who I wanted. No offense monsieur Williams, but I know physicists at almost every university in France, all would have dropped everything to be here." Lemaire was speaking to Legard, but made sure Williams understood her frustration. "It will not change, no matter how I try." She turned again and looked in Williams's direction, starting to slowly make her way to where he was standing. "A pleasure to meet you Doctor Williams."

Well, that was better. I guess I can stay... for now.

"I hope you enjoyed our rather expensive show." She then walked back to her console briskly, grabbed her laptop and a few papers and made for the exit of the control room. "I'll be in my office."

"Mademoiselle I was hoping we could...." Legard's efforts were for nothing, the door closed behind her and she was gone.

"You will have to excuse her. She has a lot invested in this project. It was the same with me. I thought she was going to kill me on more than one occasion. I thought it was at first that I am German, you know, old wounds. But then I realized it was that I was an outsider, not one of her people, coming here asking her to tell me everything. I probably would have acted the same way." Vogel made complete sense, although Williams expected more of a welcome attitude, especially with what they were trying to accomplish.

"She still treats me like a twelve-year old. Totally lame. Still doesn't call me Bob, but I will take what I can get I guess," Engels added.

"But she still wants to stab you," Vogel joked, "I can tell."

"Gentleman, I am afraid I will need to bid you adieu. I have to prepare a brief on the status of the project, and for that I must talk with Madame Lemaire. In order to do that I must have a glass du vin. Nick, I will leave you in the capable hands of these two gentlemen. Gunter and Bob, I trust you will aid our new member of the team to get situated?"

"He will be taken care of François. We'll see to it." Legard was half way out of the control room when Vogel started to head towards Williams.

"Good, merci. I will be back later to discuss today's test."

"So, she's a tough nut to crack then?" Williams asked.

"Yes, but not impossible," Vogel said, trying to be as diplomatic as possible. "With her it takes time, that's all."

"This is truly amazing. Can you show it to me, up close?"

"Herr Williams. It will be truly amazing when we can get it to work." Vogel turned and started to walk toward the lab. "I am glad you are hear." Williams and Engels followed. "I've read your work. I am glad you are here."

"Me too, I think." Williams stopped in his tracks just outside of the control room. What he saw he couldn't see from his vantage point during the test. Behind all the wires, behind all the cables, behind all the lights and photographic devices, sensors and monitors, was the door, the teleporter. It was situated in the middle of the lab. It spanned about fifteen meters across and just over six meters high and appeared to be a meter wide. The material was unlike anything Williams had seen before; a highly polished material that he assumed was aluminum.

"It's rhodium. Cost a fortune. It's off now. Feel free to look around," Vogel said, giving his okay to Williams to explore.

"Just watch the mess of cables outside of the marked zone," Engels added. "I have to spend all afternoon checking the connections, and it's easier if they are exactly where I left them." He pointed to a zone around the metal doorway that was marked with yellow and red stripped tape. The tape went all around the doorway, leaving about a three-meter zone between the monitoring equipment and the door itself.

"What's that?" Williams wondered aloud.

"It's an exclusion zone," Vogel answered. "We put that in place so we can get confident readings from the equipment when we power on. Nothing is allowed in the exclusion zone when we run a test. I also wouldn't want to be anywhere close to this thing when it is on."

"Doesn't seem to help the cameras," Engels said,

busy checking the video lines. "So, Williams, the old man and I have something we want to ask you."

Williams was inspecting the door closely, and said, "Shoot."

"We've read your papers, like he said, glad you are here. But what's with that college back in the states?"

"I don't follow." Williams now looked at Engels, who was asking his questions while lying on the floor holding two cables he just detached.

"That college you work at. You kill a bunch of people or something, flip out after going corporate?"

Williams thought he was referring to the 'easy' tenured life of a college professor. He started back at the door again and said, "Something like that."

Engels glanced at Vogel.

"Can't say that I've killed anyone though. I just got to a point where I needed to take a break. Step back. Look at the world in front of me." Williams then did just that, took a step back to the edge of the exclusion zone and looked up at the door. "Let's just say I've been looking for something new."

"Good enough. Here." Engels pulled the red ball from his lab coat and tossed it to Williams. "A memento of today's experience."

Williams noticed the ball had the word HABA imprinted on it. "Something new," he said once again. "Or maybe it was looking for me."

5. Need to Know

A few weeks went by, and the team kept making modifications to the doorway and were running more tests. The results were always the same: they would open the door, generate the field, but before they could drop the ball the power would fluctuate and the field would destabilize. Williams's involvement was limited, entirely by Lemaire's influence. He watched from a distance, getting bits and pieces from Vogel and Engels, mostly during alcohol induced nights out. He happily took control of the ball dropping mechanism and sequence, if for anything to get closer to the machine.

"I'm set here," Williams called out. He turned and walked away from the aluminum ramp after setting the red ball atop in front of a release lever. The C-channel structure sat just outside of the exclusion zone, pointing so the trajectory of the ball, when dropped, would put it precisely in the center of the open space of the door. Day after day, test after test, he did the same thing.

They were no further than they were when Williams arrived. He was hopeful they would make progress soon, but with Lemaire keeping him out, he started to question what he was doing there. For the first time since coming to Paris Williams was making plans to leave. He wasn't her idea, and she was letting everyone know it. Williams couldn't blame her. But something had to give or he was going to leave, back to that boring college in New York where nothing exciting happened. At least he was part of that nothing, whatever that meant.

"I want all equipment shut down," Lemaire ordered, her frustration evident. "The only thing I want to see powered are our consoles and the doorways." They tried everything they could think of. They added insulation to all the electronic equipment surrounding the doors, disconnected every non-essential part, camera, sensor, indicator, everything they didn't absolutely need to run the doors. It was a last-ditch effort, one that Williams suggested during one of their nights out, one that he knew would find its way back to Lemaire.

She knew that if they didn't make progress soon, they would have to start from square one. What she, and the rest of the team didn't know, was if they would even be given that chance. Legard was becoming more and more absent from testing cycles and was asking for fewer status updates. It was even rumored the budget office was going to request an oversight committee to do a full review of Interior Ministré expenditures. On covert projects like this, that usually meant complete black out.

"Yeah, totally off," Engels answered. "I even disconnected the mains. Nothing's going to run outside of the exclusion zone." He was relieved, the equipment didn't provide anything useful anyway, and it was one less thing Lemaire could get angry about.

"Check it again," she replied. Spending the last five years on the project, Lemaire had to see some progress. It would be almost impossible for her to transfer to another top-secret project within the Ministré, and even more impossible to explain what she had been doing with all that time out in the public domain. "Let me know when we are at one minute, Gunter." There was no answer from Vogel. "I said let me know when we are at one-"

"Field initialization in two minutes," Vogel said, cutting her off before she could finish repeating herself. It was starting to wear on Vogel and Engels too. Vogel was ready to retire and wanted to go out with something big under his belt. It didn't look like he was going to get his chance. Engels on the other hand, had his whole career ahead of him. He didn't want to waste any more of it on something that was fruitless.

"It's all shut down. I unplugged all the feeds, power, wiring, nothing is connected anymore but direct controls," Engels reiterated, not letting Lemaire ask him a second time. "It should show on you monitor," he added, hinting he knew Lemaire was checking anyway.

"One-minute mark." It was almost time for another test. Williams was standing near Engel's console, getting a better look at the machine, waiting for whatever was going to happen, to happen. Legard, as before, was not there to witness, further worrying the team. "We are at zero," Vogel finished, making a circular motion with his finger, as if saying 'Well, here we go again'.

"Initiating start sequence now." Almost immediately, there was the predictable flash of bright light. The machine hummed to life, the control room dimming in response after Lemaire initiated the start process. It was followed by the blue haze of the field; the doorway was open. "What does it look like Gunter?"

Vogel took a moment before answering, busy pulling up the diagnostics on his console. "Checking," he said, surprised by what he was seeing and deciding to double check before calling out to Lemaire. "The field, it looks like it's activated. Power appears.... the power appears to be stable. 1400Kw, holding!" Vogel didn't mask his excitement. Engels straightened in his chair, he knew Lemaire was going to give the order to drop the ball right away.

"I hope I fixed that ball okay," Williams whispered to Engels, second guessing himself.

"Me too. Wouldn't want to know what would happen if you didn't," Engels answered quietly.

"I'm running a diagnostic. I want to be sure." Lemaire started to pull up a stream of menu options on her console.

"What for? The field is open, the power level stable, let it go!" Vogel no longer bit his tongue; the opportunity was there and he wanted to take it.

"Okay, okay." She looked up at the blue haze. "Robert, let it go."

"Five, four, three," the field was holding, the blue hue not so much as a flicker. There was just a very faint hum from what power the doorways were drawing. "Two, one.... on its way." Engels stood, hoping to get a better look. The lever holding the ball dropped, and the red ball rolled smoothly down the ramp and under its own inertia launched directly in the middle of the doorway. The field held, with only a slight variation of color once the ball entered.

"Gunter," Lemaire stood to try and get a look through the door, "what's the field doing?" The blue haze obscured everything on the other side.

"I only have power consumption. A slight decrease after the ball entered, but now back to a full 1400Kw, and holding. Do we run the shutdown sequence?" Vogel asked, unsure of the next steps. They have never been able to get the field to stay stable, the power always spiked triggering the breakers before they could run any test. But today was different. So far, as it seemed, they solved the problem. Interference from all the monitoring equipment was destabilizing the field, causing it to draw more power to compensate. Inevitably, the destabilization broke down the field until eventually the power consumption was too great and it shut down.

Until today, they have never actually had to run the shutdown sequence.

"Did it work?" Williams asked Engels, who didn't hear him, or just didn't know. Williams took a few steps closer to the machine, standing just outside of the exclusion zone. He wanted to be ready to check if the ball made it through the minute the doorways were closed. His view to the other side also obscured by the energy field.

"Uh, I don't know. I don't know. Merde." Lemaire looked at the door, the blue hue glistening, temporarily overcome by the fact the field didn't disintegrate and the ball was released. "Do we have any reason wait?" It was a first for Vogel and Engels, and they looked at each other briefly. Usually she would do what she thought was the next step. Now she was asking them if it was okay.

"I don't think we should press our luck. Run the sequence and we can tell François we did something!" Vogel answered, now standing, his hands out in front of him in fists, not knowing what to do with them in his excitement.

"I'm running it now." Lemaire sat quickly. "Pulling it up. Come on! Dammit this console is slow." The old Lemaire was back. She worked diligently to enter the codes needed to start the shutdown, following the procedure to the letter. "Sequence started, power should drop off momentarily."

"The Power is dropping. It's at 1000Kw and reducing at 100Kw per second. The field is starting to close." Vogel quickly sat back in his chair, monitoring the power levels, one of the few diagnostics they left intact. "It's at 100Kw." And just like that, the blue light vanished, the hum of the power from the doorway stopped. There was no flickering, no high-pitched whine, just a very slow and purposeful closure. A small pop, and the door was closed. "It's closed. The shutdown sequence worked. It's closed successfully."

"On purpose this time," Engels added, taking a few steps closer, standing next to Williams. He was anxious to see if the ball was gone, which meant it could have made it to the other room. "I don't see it! I don't see it. It must have made it!"

Vogel ran as fast as he could, Williams behind him. "I'll go check lab two!" The two reached the second lab, an almost mirror image of the first, just on the other side of the wall from lab one and began their search. "Where is it? It must be here! Did you see it? It went right through."

"I, I don't see anything. Check under the wiring over there." Williams and Vogel were on their knees now, looking under every conceivable space the ball could have gone. "Nothing." The two stood, disappointed. "Well. If it didn't make it to lab two, where the hell did it go?" They stood for a moment, then headed back to lab one. "You don't suppose it's been vaporized, do you?"

"Ich Weiss es nicht," was Vogel's reply, not even trying to say anything in English, his excitement completely gone. He simply went back to his console in the control room and sat. "It's not there Marie. It's just not there."

Lemaire rolled her head back in disappointment, just as Williams walked in to lab one. "Are you sure? Where could it have gone then?" she asked.

"Wait," Williams said. Something he saw from the corner of his eye. "Well, there's our friend." He walked over to one of the corners of the lab and pulled the small red ball from under some wiring. The ball made it through the door, it just didn't leave lab one. "Still not bad for a test I would say. The field stabilization is fixed. Progress."

"Still doesn't work though," Engels added.

"Progress nonetheless."

"Damn it. What are we missing? We've gone through everything, hundreds of times over. I just don't see it." Lemaire was at her wits end. She straightened up at her console, then stood.

"I don't know. Maybe we don't yet have the power requirements right. Maybe we need to go over the plans again," Williams said, while looking at the ball in his hand.

"So that's it? After all this time, that's what you have to add? I thought you were supposed to have all the answers." There was no mistake, she was looking right at Williams, arms crossed, looking for a way to vent her frustration. For his part, Williams just tossed the ball up and down a few times, then put it in his pocket.

"I wish I did." He turned and walked through the doorway back into the control room. He had a slight smile, knowing this was going to come eventually, and he had a few things he wanted to get out in the open. "But, I don't. I can only add to subjects where I have some sort of background knowledge. I've been here two months, seen dozens of tests, but I don't have any clue to how any of it works. Everything I know about it is from what I have seen from these tests, and maybe a night out with the boys."

"I'm going out tonight if anyone is interested. Just thought I would through that out there," Engels added.

"I haven't seen any design specs, hell I don't even know if you developed this, but I am guessing.... no." Lemaire looked away, caught off guard at Williams's direct remarks.

"Monsieur," she said, wishing she could take back what she said a moment ago.

"So, I am left standing here asking, how did you do all of this? If you didn't develop the specs, create this...doorway, who did?" Williams was a few steps closer to Lemaire's console now. "Look, all I know is we are in the basement of a museum in the heart of Paris. You're now looking for answers from me but I can't give you anything, because you-"

"Because we haven't shared anything with him," Legard interrupted. It caught the team off guard and produced a slight smile from Vogel, and a nod over to Engels, who was now hanging on to every word. He wanted to make sure he wasn't going to miss a thing. "Until now, Monsieur Williams has been here to observe. You," Legard pointed to Lemaire. "and the door. He has seen what we have all seen. Oui?"

"C'est important?" Lemaire faced Legard, arms crossed. "We've been working on this for years now. If anyone can figure it out the three of us can." Vogel again looked at Engels. It was the first time they were acknowledged as valuable members of her team.

"No doubt Mademoiselle. I have no doubt indeed. We do not however, have an unlimited budget. We also do not have unlimited time, 'years' as you have just now mentioned. It is time we give Monsieur Williams full disclosure."

"Bull shit! You mean hand the project over to him. Just come out and say it. You've been trying to sideline me ever since you went to," Lemaire gave a thumb gesture over in Williams's direction, "wherever the hell he's from."

"Frau Lemaire! Das ist est! You know as well as we do no one knows this machine better than you." Vogel wanted to de-escalate, but at the same time couldn't hold back. He didn't care who was the boss, as long as they were able to get the doorway to work, and so far, it didn't look promising. "We can no longer function like this. We need something to change, jetzt!" Lemaire laughed slightly. She wasn't used to people pushing back. She gave in. If the doorway was not going to work, it wasn't going to work because of Williams, not her.

"Fine. Fine. I give up. But understand I'm voicing my objection. I report directly to you, not him, understood?"

"Merci and noted. I will remind everyone here, you are still managing this project, nothing has changed, or will change, in that regard, I assure you." Legard was anxious to get things moving, and also take the opportunity to calm Lemaire's nerves.

"Does this mean you're going to start answering me? And I mean all my questions."

"Oui Monsieur. Anything."

"Okay, let's try this one." It was Williams's turn. As far as he was concerned he had the go ahead to get all his questions on the table, and it was just in time. He had nothing to lose. Lemaire laughed slightly again. "Where did all this come from?" Lemaire laid her hand out in front of her, palm up, pointing to Legard.

"The idea, of course, of a doorway to another city thousands of miles away has been around for most of the last century. This particular device, the one you have witnessed for the last several months, does not have its origins with the French Ministré. In fact, all you see here is from what we had obtained from the Soviet Union." Legard took a second, anticipating what he just said to catch Williams a certain way.

"Obtained? What was obtained from the Soviet Union? What, did you steal it from Russia?"

"Soviet Union," Vogel clarified. "They were not obtained by illegal means, at least not by the French Ministré."

"So where did Russ...the Soviet Union get them?" Williams waited for the answer 'we don't know', or 'they stole them', something like that.

"We obtained the plans you see here," Legard motioned Vogel to pull up a photo scan of the original documents on a large monitor at the rear of the control room, "as part of a larger purchase of data when the Soviet Union collapsed." It took a moment, but the monitor flashed to life, and Vogel pulled up the tattered, worn, and faded plans for the group to see. The color photo image showed ragged documents, yellowed with age.

"There, the plans," Vogel said, sitting back and allowing Legard to continue.

"When the government of the Soviet Union collapsed, well, in the mid 1990's, it was broken up into fifteen independent countries. Many, if not all, found themselves unable to function using the same Soviet scheme of government. In the interim, while these countries formed governments and restructured, they still had to, how do you say, keep the lights on."

Williams stood anxiously awaiting Legard's point. "Okay, I follow," he said.

"Some of those new countries found themselves in possession of material and information that, to them at least, were relics of a cold war past. Now that the Soviet Union was gone, and the new Russia didn't have the means to support or influence these new countries, they began to sell."

"Sell? What do you mean?"

"Sell. Everything and anything with value. Arms, resources, anything. To some of these nations, it was information. Information from the Soviet era that had value. The United States, Britain, France, Germany, Belgium, they would all pay a top dollar for classified information from the former Soviet republic."

"Also paid top dollar for nukes too," Williams went in for a closer look at the document on the monitor, "keeping them out of the wrong hands."

"That would also be true. But what you see in front of you, is a result of one of those purchases." Legard stopped, waiting to see if Williams had any questions.

"I don't see a lot here. How do you know this wasn't some design bureau pipe dream?"

"Pipe dream monsieur?" Legard asked. Lemaire laughed slightly at the idea that half a decade's work was based off a fantasy.

"Well, I mean, the Soviet design bureau's thought up some pretty crazy stuff from what I understand. If they were lucky they came out with something like the MIG, or Soyuz, but those were one in a thousand. How do you know this wasn't just another dud?"

"Because it didn't originate from the Soviets," Lemaire answered. Legard looked at Vogel, asking him to zoom in to a corner of the cover document on the monitor. In bold letters it read 'PROJEKT M31'.

"Project M31 monsieur, that is what the German's called it." After Legard's statement, something caught Williams's eye. He stepped in for an even closer look.

"Wait, what is that? Is that what I think it is?"

"Oui monsieur."

"That's a swastika, and a Nazi eagle? I don't get it." Williams turned away from the plans and looked at the team, puzzled.

"History of Germany Nick, Berlin especially," Vogel added.

"You must forgive us for the history lesson Monsieur Williams. It is quite simple really, the Soviets got to Berlin first."

"You mean, during WW2?" Williams asked, trying to put it all together.

"Oui. They reached the city limits in May of 1945, they surrounded the city. And when the intense fighting stopped, they took whatever weapons research they could back to Moscow never to be seen by the allies."

"That's where all this came from," Lemaire added, wanting to get to the point.

"Wait, Nazi weapons research?"

"Germany had an extensive program for research and development. As far as we know it lasted the full length of the war. Toward the end however, they became desperate. Much of what was coming out of..." Legard looked to Vogel.

"Wunderwaffe."

"Ah, oui, Wunderwaffe. Much of what was coming out of the Wunderwaffe were completely impractical, or not at all cost effective. It is our belief, the plans to the door came out of the Nazi special weapons program toward the end of the war."

"Okay." Williams paused for a second and looked at Lemaire, who just sort of cocked her head as if to say 'what?' He was now even more confused than ever. "This is a weapon? I thought this was some sort of doorway, or teleporter. I didn't sign on for weapons research." Williams started to head for the door. "With all due respect, I'm out. Good luck."

"Monsieur, please. Let me explain." Legard was begging Williams to stay. "Not a weapon. The doorway is not a weapon. May I go on?" Williams stopped, near the exit, then turned to face Legard.

"I'm not working on a weapon. I'm out if that's what this is. I don't want to be part of it."

"It's not. Believe me," Engels said. "I asked the same thing. I think I even told Gunter to F off when he told me about weapons research, remember Gunter?"

Vogel smiled slightly, then nodded.

"At the end of the war Nazi Germany was running out of oil. Without oil they had no fuel, without fuel they had no means to continue their quest for European reunification under Nazi rule. The door was designed as a mechanism to move supplies, troops and weapons, to fronts all over the world in an instant. What limited oil they had could then be reserved for the war machine. With two doorways, tanks, guns, troops, could be moved in seconds."

Williams sat down, realizing the implications of what Legard just said. "Oh man. Wow. That would have changed everything, wouldn't it have?"

"Oui."

"I'm going to ask another question, but I'm not sure I want to know the answer, how close were they?"

"There is some evidence a single test was successful in Berlin in late April of 1945, just days before advancing forces broke through."

"The Soviets however," Vogel taking over now, "did not know this. A single transmission was intercepted from the Wolfs Lair to Field Marshal Wilhelm Keitel. Here is a translated copy of the message." In anticipation, Vogel pulled up a digital file and displayed it on the screen.

FUHRER, ADOLF HITLER

FIELD MARSHAL KEITEL, OKW 28/04/1945

PROJECT M31
KEITEL - SITUATION CRITICAL IN BERLIN.
DEVELOPMENT OF NEW TRANSPORT TESTED
SUCCESSFULLY.
BREAK - TWO OFFICERS AND MEN OF NORDELUND AND
CHARLEMEGNE WILL REGROUP WITH YOUR LINES IN
THE WEST. M31 PROJECT PLANS WILL ACCOMPANY.
YOUR ORDERS ARE TO BUILD TWO M31. THE WAR WILL
BE WON SOON AFTER. STAFF TO OPERATE WILL MEET
IN APPROX. ONE MONTH. END.

"Based on this single message, and what information we put together from the former Soviet archives, we believe a test was successful. As a precaution, Hitler ordered copies of the plans to leave Berlin in case it fell to the Soviets. As it turns out, the doorway couldn't have been used in Berlin anyway."

"Why is that?" Williams asked.

"Soon after this message was intercepted, the doorway was destroyed by Soviet artillery fire. The Soviets believed they destroyed reconnaissance film, nitrocellulose, stored where we think was the actual location of the first doorway."

"What's this 'BREAK'?" Williams now looking closely at the order on the screen.

"During the Berlin assault, Hitler gave the order for any troops in the city to make escape, I believe they called it the break-up."

"Break-out," Vogel corrected.

"Ah, oui. Break-out. Remaining German troops were ordered to leave Berlin and form up with other lines to aid in Germany's defense. It is our belief Hitler ordered as much information as possible to be smuggled out of Berlin in an effort to try and get them to commanders in the field. It was a desperate attempt to provide what was left of the army something they could use to turn the tide of the war back into Germany's favor. It was a noble, albeit hopeless endeavor with the state of Germany at that time."

"Soviet interrogation disclosed there were two sets of plans. This matched the order here," Vogel said, pointing to the screen.

"Interrogation?" Williams needed to know more.

"One set we believe was given to Joachim Ziegler, a Brigadefuhrer with the Wehrmacht. He commanded a foreign contingent of troops, Nordelund, a Nordic contingent defending Berlin and was part of the break-out. He was wounded in Berlin shortly after, the whereabouts of his set of plans unknown."

"Ha. Come on Vogel. I bet he burned them up so the reds wouldn't get them," Engel poked, diligently typing at his console, taking a moment to add his thoughts. "Took himself out too, I bet."

"It is most probable he destroyed the documents before he succumbed to his injuries," Legard clarified, with a bit more grace.

Williams took a look to the lab, not able to see the machine from his point of view anymore but beginning to fill in the blanks. "And what you built was based on the second set, that the Soviets got their hands on."

"Oui. The other set was found on Gustav Krukenberg, Brigadeführer, Wehrmacht. He too was in charge of a foreign contingent of troops defending Berlin." Legard glanced over to Vogel, who then slightly looked away toward the lab. This puzzled Williams.

"Where were they from?" Williams inquired.

"Monsieur?" Legard asked, trying to buy time.

"The foreign troops. Where were they from, a former African colony or something?"

"France," Lemaire answered, then turned around and headed to her console. "They were from France." Legard had hoped he could get past this bit of information, but Lemaire wasn't going to let him off. "They were Vichy, who thought more of the Nazi's than they did of their own countrymen."

"As Madame Lemaire has so eloquently explained, the troops were primarily French. The...hmm."

"Charlemagne," Vogel finished.

"Ah oui, Charlemagne. They were known as unit Charlemagne. What was left of the unit in May of 1945 was under the command of Krukenberg. They too, like Zeigler, made an effort to leave Berlin but to the South. Along with them, the second set of plans, held with Krukenberg himself. He was found hiding out in a bombed-out apartment building in Dahlem. This is all we know."

"That's it?" Williams snapped, but no one picked up on his sarcasm.

"We didn't get all of it," Lemaire added. "Or I should say the Soviets didn't get all of it. They didn't get to Krukenberg before he tried to destroy his set."

"There is some evidence Krukenberg tried to dispose of his documents and was successful in part. Our set is incomplete. We do not have it all," Vogel answered before Williams had a chance to ask.

"This is why the Soviets did nothing. They didn't know what they had. It meant nothing to them. But we had this order. We had something that said it was successful. When we had the opportunity to get our hands on the actual plans, voilà."

"Why now then? If you had this since, what the mid 1990's?"

"Monsieur, now is the only material work we have done on the project. The only time we actually constructed anything. I can assure you research was ongoing since the moment we obtained the plans. The extent however, had not been disclosed to the team here, ah, for security reasons."

Williams glanced over to Lemaire and wondered how she felt about that. He envisioned her first few months here, an outsider, someone who wasn't being let in, much like he was now.

"There was also the facility. One doesn't build such a thing overnight, and without anyone knowing. We spent years putting this facility together. There are very few who know of its existence."

"I can believe that. I can believe almost anything at this point." Williams got up and started to walk toward the lab.

"I know you will want to get a detailed look at the specifications Monsieur Williams. Gunter will show you were to find everything." Legard's phone alarm chimed. "I am afraid I have an appointment shortly and must bid you adieu. I will make time for us to review any of your remaining concerns shortly." And with that Legard stood and made his way out of the lab. Just before reaching the outside hall, he paused and said, "Revoir Mademoiselle."

Lemaire didn't say a word.

"You ready Gunter? My buzz is wearing off," Engels said, stopping mid stride on his way out. "You want to go for a drink Nick?"

"I better not, I need to wrap up a few things here first."

"It's your turn to buy anyway Robert," Vogel answered. The two men made for the exit, leaving Lemaire and Williams alone in the control room.

"And then there were two," Williams whispered. This was his opportunity. They were the only two in the lab, and that scared Williams a little. He could feel the tension in the air. He walked back to the plans, still up on the monitor in the back of the lab. He was standing in front of them but wasn't really looking them over. He was thinking about the best way to approach.

He turned, then began to walk toward Lemaire, who was still diligently working at her console. He could feel it getting warmer, and his mouth was dry. *For crying out loud, it's not like you are asking her out on a date.* Lemaire turned suddenly, stopping Williams as if he were caught doing something he shouldn't have been.

"Monsieur Williams," she said, looking at him frozen in the middle of the isle. "Now you have what you want. Now you can fix what has taken us five years to accomplish."

"I really doubt that's possible. But, I *am* an outsider. I am a fresh pair of eyes, with maybe a few ideas. Please, call me Nick."

"Allons prendre un café, Nick?" Lemaire stood up and started to walk to the door. Williams wasn't expecting the invitation. "Don't worry," she paused, "it's not a date."

6. Breaking the Ice

It wasn't a date, he knew that. It must have been years since he last spent time out with anyone, let alone someone like Lemaire. But for a brief moment, he caught himself thinking about her. Was she married? Did she have someone? What was her favorite wine? Did she even drink for that matter? What did she like to do outside of the lab? He hadn't felt that energy in a long time. There was something about her. Maybe it was her looks, maybe it was her confidence. But, as far as he could tell, their relationship was icy; he didn't want to make it any worse, so he put it out of his mind.

The two departed from the rear of the museum toward the Esplanade des Invalides. She kept to the side, avoiding the rough brick pavement walkway in favor of the cement sidewalk. He still wasn't familiar with the streets of Paris and kept close by her side. He had seen this view of the museum only once before when he first came to meet Legard; the crowds considerably less dense than before. Most of the time he preferred to use the entrance near Napoleon's tomb, if for any reason to admire the gold dome overhead.

Ah, a clear view of Eiffel. Doesn't look that far from the hotel. She turned on Avenue de la Morte-Picquet and headed in that general direction, toward Champ de Mars, the park, or literally 'Field of Mars' on the east side of the tower. She didn't tell him where they were going, he just had to trust her. *If only she would trust me.*

It wasn't really Williams habit to stare at someone, especially someone who wouldn't be all that broken up if he just disappeared. But every now and then she would walk slightly in front of him, and he couldn't help but think how beautiful she looked. She was in her late forties just as he was, but not a hint of grey hair; from a distance, she looked brunette. Out in the open, under the cover of her wide brimmed sun hat, he could see it was very dark brown. He noticed how her hair bounced when she walked. Not side to side, but almost rippled from just under the edge of her hat to the ends, when her heal touched the ground with each stride.

Her skin was pale white, not sickly, but young and fresh. She could have easily been mistaken for someone in her twenties. It was the first time Williams noticed. He was used to seeing her in the lab where the artificial lighting didn't help anyone. It was a windowless lab in the basement of a museum after all. The only windows in the place where in a set of steel doors separating labs one and two, and a small pane near the control room entrance. Still, no light from outside. He looked at his own hands. *Jeez, probably could use some sun myself.*

"I can't say that I've been to many café's here." He was trying to at least open up the walk to some sort of informal conversation.

"I go to one," she said, that's all. She goes to one. Williams assumed that meant that's where they were going, but really didn't want to push it.

"Must be pretty good then." *Nice one Nick...idiot.*

They were stopped now at a jumbled corner of different streets. Avenue de Tourville, Avenue de Duquesne, Place Joffre, maybe this is why she didn't tell him where they were going, it was just easier that way. He also didn't know what to do with himself and could see her slightly glance in his direction to make sure he was still there. So, he acted the tourist, taking in the sites, looking at what there was to see. The signal was clear, she crossed. Through the intersection, she headed to Avenue de la Bourdonnais, another street branching out through the complex intersection.

He had trouble walking next to her: one moment she was walking in a straight line on one side of the sidewalk, and then abruptly would move to the other side. He would follow, although he nearly knocked over an older Parisian.

"Pardone moi," he said, but the old woman didn't even notice. He would look over his shoulder from then on. It wasn't until they came upon a section of sidewalk that was completely shaded by a row of apartments when he realized what she was doing.

"So that's it," he whispered. She heard him, turning slightly as she walked to see what he was talking about. Williams acted as if he was referencing some piece of architecture, or the old woman, anything but Lemaire. He realized that's why she walked all over the sidewalk, she was finding shade, trying to avoid the sun. It made sense now, why she wore a light coat and gloves in the middle of the summer. And why she looked so much younger than she was.

They were walking for about twenty minutes as Williams could tell when she suddenly turned and crossed Avenue de la Bourdonnais. They must be close Williams thought, she crossed right in the middle of a bright sun lit avenue. This put Williams behind a bit as he stopped to check Paris traffic. Paris was lined with one-way streets, and if one got used to it, a two-way street could prove hazardous. It was clear, he crossed, Lemaire further ahead but in sight. He didn't want to run to catch up and tire himself out when he reached her, so he just hung back keeping his eye on her.

He didn't have to keep her in sight for long before she stopped at a small café. She took the first table outside near the corner. There were several available closer to the entrance, but for some reason she chose this one. She looked into the café through the window and smiled slightly, then looked up to see Williams.

"Not a bad walk after work, I would admit."

"Lately, it's been good to do anything after work. You can sit, Nick." She gestured with her hand at the open seat, while she tugged at the fingers of her gloves.

"Thanks," he replied, looking around at the surroundings. She positioned her chair with the back against the wall of the café, so his chair would be on the walkway. He sat.

"Nice little place. Café Alexandre. Sounds familiar for some reason." Named after Alexandre-Gustave Eiffel, Café Alexandre was a small corner restaurant and bar with a faded red awning and white stripes. A row of tables with wicker chairs surrounded the windowed façade. The mature trees lining the sidewalk and the overhead awning was just enough to keep the two of them in the shade. Exactly what Lemaire wanted. She pulled off her gloves and set them to the side, not removing her hat. Just then a waiter stepped up.

"Noisette Madame."

"Merci, Lucas. I had wondered if you saw me." Before Williams could order his coffee, Lucas was gone.

"I'll catch him when he comes around again, maybe." Williams didn't want to make it seem like he was ignored, but he was.

"He'll be back. It looks like he's the only one out here today." Lemaire said, looking back in the café through the window. "Probably had something else to do. I am here more than home, he knows me."

"Ah, then that's your usual." He was trying to make small talk again, but it wasn't coming to mind too well.

"Most of the time." She looked through the window again, but this time raising her cup and pointing a finger to Williams. They remained silent while they thought about where to start. Just before he was going to try small talk again, Lucas was back out.

"Un autre café noisettes pour le Monsieur." And, once again, before Williams could say anything Lucas was gone.

"Wow. I don't think I'll ever get used to service like that."

"It's not getting anything that you can't get used to." Lemaire took a sip of here coffee. "I already knew your name."

"Sorry, I didn't catch that?" He looked down at his coffee trying to figure out what it was.

"I knew your name was Nicholas. Legard told me before he went to America. I didn't know you prefer Nick."

"Everyone calls me Nick, it's just easier I guess. Never really got used to Nicholas." He pulled his coffee closer to take in its scent.

"It's hazelnut," she said just before taking a sip of her own.

"Kind of odd now that you think of it. I mean, people called me Nick ever since I was a kid. It's like when someone calls someone named James, Jimmy and it sticks. Everyone calls them Jimmy, even in old age. Sort of odd calling a senior citizen a kid's name. Maybe that's why we call them Mister, or Monsieur and all." *Okay, need to dial it back a bit, sounds like I am babbling.* "What about you?"

"Me?" What about me?"

"Your first name? Legard told me when we first met, but he refers to everyone as Monsieur or Madame, what do you prefer?"

Lemaire set her coffee on the table in front of her. "Marie." She held out her hand as if it were the first time they met. Williams took it. "What do you really think of our little project?"

Well, she's direct. Thought we might try small talk for a while. "I think it's interesting."

"Ha!" Lemaire laughed. She leaned back in her chair, the wicker cracking as it took the strain, and looked off down Avenue de la Bourdonnais.

It was the first thing, the word 'interesting', that came to Williams's mind. For a moment he noticed a slight smile just as it left her face. *What did I do?*

"You have come a long way to see something interesting. You could have done that at your..." she stopped for a second, "college. Surely, you think it more than just interesting. I am at a loss for words each time I enter the Musée. Each time I start the Andromeda machine." She paused. "Each time Robert drops that ball." She was looking down the avenue again.

"Is that what you all call it?"

"Call what?"

"The machine. Is that what you call it, Andromeda?"

"Yes. It's from M31." She took another sip of coffee.

"From the plans, right?"

"Yes. M31 was how French astronomer Charles Messier cataloged the Andromeda galaxy. We took our project name from that. We wanted something better than M31. Robert thought of it, he's brilliant."

"I know." He paused for a moment. "I see more than just something interesting. I can't explain it. It's probably the first time I had trouble explaining my reaction to something scientific like this. My thoughts sound like they are not too far from yours. This machine, Andromeda, it's amazing." Williams now found himself looking down the avenue too. He looked back at his coffee and took a sip. "Can I tell you something?"

"Of course. It hasn't stopped you before," she said, a subtle reference to the questions after today's test. She took another sip.

"I could hardly contain myself when François came to see me and explained what you were all trying to do. I mean, this was straight out of science fiction."

"It is, not was," Lemaire interjected.

"It is. And here was some guy I never met before, telling me he wants me to quit this awesome gig at a college where I can do what I want, when I want, and how I want. And no matter what I said, no matter how much I asked, and the impression that I thought he was full of shit, he knew I was going to do it. The moment he left I couldn't say a word, to anyone. I was at a complete loss." Lemaire looked back at him. She could see the excitement in his eyes, it was the same for her when Legard brought her in.

"It doesn't work."

"Not yet. But it will. The power problem is fixed. We got the ball to go through the field." Williams tapped the ball he still had in his pocket.

"But it didn't go anywhere."

"No. And after today's test I was just about ready to pack my bags, go back to the states, and beg for my old job back." Lemaire glanced at him, as if that might not have been a bad idea. "But then Gunter pulled up that order to Keitel. It has to be the doorway. Two officers leaving Berlin, the break-out, successful test of a transport, not vehicle, not airplane, but machine, M31. There's no doubt anymore in my mind this thing worked. I doubt we'll get it working tomorrow, maybe not even this year. But I don't think there's anyone who wants this to work more than you, but me."

"Merde. What is it we are missing?"

"I don't know. But it's right in front of us, I know it. It's hiding in plain sight."

"Your paper."

"What?" Williams asked.

"Hiding in plain sight. It was one of your papers," Lemaire explained. In the early days, Williams tried to stay away from what he called safe and traditional research topics. They were boring. No one ever learned anything. He thought most where just the same old stuff worded differently so some graduate student could get a masters. He preferred to ask the questions not many were asking.

"Ha. You read that? Oldie for sure."

"I've read everything I could find that you published. That is, once François said he recruited you." Her tone was slightly off, reminding Williams she didn't have any say in his selection. "What do you suggest we do now?"

"I've got some ideas."

"And? Are you planning to share?"

"Tomorrow. Let's pull up the plans. No more tests until we see something we think we can change. Maybe that will keep François from pulling the plug. He's going to want to see results or cost cuts. I say we give him both. He will have no choice but to keep us going if we keep giving him something, no matter how small."

"It's a plan at least. I can't just walk away from this. I can't let him shut it down, we are too close," Lemaire said with an almost lamenting tone.

"Le chèque Monsieur," Lucas said as he walked hurriedly by. He was gone in an instant but not before placing the check in front of Williams.

"I guess we're done."

"Oui. Walk me home." Lemaire stood, expecting Williams to pay the bill. She waited patiently as he fumbled with the few euro's he could find in his pocket. He was worried, being that they sat so far from the entrance, that someone would take the money when he left. But no sooner did he take a few steps away, Lucas was back to collect. The two then started to walk back toward the lab.

"Where did you learn French?" She asked. She was the one making small talk this time. "You are not French, but you understand me, and François."

"My mother. She was born in Lafayette, Louisiana. My grandparents came from France to the US just before WW1. It was pretty much the language spoken in our house, and quite a few in our neighborhood when I was younger. Have you ever been to the US?"

"No. I have had friends who have, New Orleans," she said, looking up at the distinctively French styled apartments on the street as they walked by. "They have had nothing but good things to say. Montreal, I have been there, it is a beautiful city."

"Never been there." Williams caught himself staring at her again as they walked. She was no longer wearing her sun hat, and he found himself asking those same questions. Is she married, what does she like to do? He stopped himself when he realized their relationship would revolve around their work, and that type of thing was almost always a bad idea. Getting intimate, if that were even possible, would just complicate things.

"Like Paris, but the language is French-Canadian, takes some getting used to," she explained.

"We would go to New Orleans on vacation. To a kid it wasn't any fun. We basically went from a French speaking area to another French speaking area, but with tourists. My parents liked it though, they had friends there. I always found things to do."

"Marseille."

"Marseille?" Williams asked.

"My family would take us to Marseille. We would spend weeks there."

"Do you ever go back?"

"Non," Lemaire said quietly.

"Why not?"

"Marseille isn't like it was when I was young. It is very dangerous now. I miss Marseille, but it isn't what I remember anymore. Besides, I have been working on this doorway for years now, almost nonstop. Maybe I'll find a new place when it's all over."

"You are starting to sound like me."

"That's strange." Lemaire stopped, looking over to a man standing across the street. "I could swear I've seen that man before. Yesterday, over near the Musée." Just as Lemaire stopped, the man, noticing, turned and hurriedly walked away, rounding the corner, disappearing into the crowds and out of sight.

"I don't think I recognize him. Do you think he works at the Museum?" Williams asked.

"I don't know. He was staring at me, just like now. Isn't that odd? Maybe it's nothing. Like you said, maybe he works at the Musée." They started to walk again.

"So, what do you do with your free time? Surely you get away now and again, even if it's not Marseille."

"Now I just go to the park when I need to get away. There are so many here in Paris. Or I walk around the Louvre, I can stay there for days." Lemaire's face brightened when she mentioned the Louvre and he liked seeing her that way. For a moment the two just walked quietly. Williams didn't know where they were heading; they were no longer on an avenue leading to the lab when she suddenly stopped again.

"This is where I will say good night." She looked briefly at Williams as if she was about to thank him for accompanying her home. She stopped short though, turned around, and walked up the steps to her apartment. "I'll show you everything I know tomorrow," she said before entering. "We will start new. No more tests."

"No more tests." And just as Williams waived good night, she closed the door behind her. "Well, could have been worse I guess." He started to walk again, further down the avenue. It wasn't too long before his mind was taken over by thoughts of Andromeda and the transmission to Keitel. *Successful test.* "We have to be close." Soon, he started to think about Lemaire again, their talk, Marseille, the Louvre. He stopped. "Where the hell am I?" Not paying attention to where he was headed he found himself walking down a Parisian side street. "It's nice enough out. I guess I'll either hit Eiffel or Seine sooner or later."

The sun was setting and it was just about to get dark. Williams made it down to Champ du Mars and now that he knew where he was, decided to sit for a while and watch the sun descend behind the buildings and monuments of Paris. He found a quiet spot under some trees and near a foot path where he was guaranteed to get in some good people watching.

A young man was tossing a ball to his dog nearby when he threw the ball too hard, rolling it over to Williams's feet. The dog, a Brittany, lost sight of the ball and was searching from side to side trying to find it. It's nose to the grass trying to pick up the scent.

"S'il vous plait, Monsieur?" The man asked.

"Oui." Williams picked up the ball and, taking a second look, noticed the name. HABA. "Huh, same thing." Williams looked up at the dog who was still busily searching for his toy. "Ici!" he said after a whistle and caught the dog's attention. The Brittany, upon hearing Williams, was now completely focused on his hand moving from side to side. The Brittany was off like a bullet when Williams tossed the ball over toward the owner.

"Merci," The man said.

"Je vous en prie," Williams said, waiving. It was almost dark now, so he decided he should head back to his apartment. It was only a few blocks to the east, near the lab. Seeing the Brittany in the park reminded him he still had the ball from the mornings test in his pocket. He pulled it out and began to toss it in the air to himself as he walked back home. *What am I going to tell Legard tomorrow? We have a new plan, and if Marie is on board, Gunter and Bob will be too. Probably won't be happy about not running tests, but I'll quantify that with some dollar figures. That will keep him happy, I hope. I'm going to need to see those plans, up close. There must be something they missed. Nazi eagle. Never in a million did I think I would have seen that. Transport tested successful. That had to be it. It has to work.*

Williams reached his apartment building, still tossing the ball to himself. Walking in, he checked for mail and then headed upstairs. It was still early evening, and it was very quiet on his floor. With a swipe of his room key he was inside. He opened the windows to let some evening air inside, then sat back in a chair near the balcony overlooking the museum. He tossed the ball to himself a few more times, then set it on the table next to his chair. Staring at the ceiling for a while, he tried to relax knowing what tomorrow might bring. Lemaire seemed to be coming around, but it was Legard he had to worry about now.

After a while, he dropped his head and began to look at the table next to him, the ball perched in the center. Suddenly, he straightened up in his chair. "Wait a minute," he said, squinting, "what is that?" He couldn't believe his eyes. He went over and over it in his head. He remembered what it looked like when he set it on the ramp for the test, he was sure of it. He was sure it was the same ball from this morning. He took another long look. "How could this be?" He took it in his hand, stood, then leaned against the wall by the balcony. "I don't believe it."

7. Progress

"I hope you have something good to tell us, I'm not a big fan of coming in on Saturday's." Engels was the first to get to the lab, after Williams. He left a can of Gini and a half-eaten doughnut on his console table. "What's this all about?"

"Things are changing. Can't tell you about it until everyone   is here."

"I figured. I hope Marie's okay with you calling a meeting, especially on the weekend. Sort of a French thing, not too keen on working weekends. The States could learn from that one," Engels said, making his way down to the lab.

"I'm not worried. She'll like what she hears."

"If you say so. Just to let you know, it's true about the Germans."

"Tell me about it. I still can't get over how they were able to design and build all this with 1940's technology. Amazing."

"No, not that."

"Oh. Then what do you mean?"

"They really can drink like no one on Earth. I was gone by nine, and Gunter was just starting to get a buzz. That guy is a science experiment himself." Engels rubbed his temples, no doubt nursing a hangover. Just then Williams noticed he was wearing sunglasses.

"Oh that. I'll have to join you guys again one of these nights. It's been a while."

"Probably should make it soon. If we keep screwing with this thing," Engels said as he leaned against Lemaire's console, "and not going anywhere, François will cut and run if you know what I mean."

Williams agreed but didn't say anything. He was sitting on a chair he brought down to the lab, just on the other side of the doorway. He thought the best place to explain his discovery, was where it happened in the first place.

"Guten Morgen!" Vogel cheerily exclaimed. He looked well rested and ready to go. Williams envied the mans storied ability to tie one on and still function as he was. It was a trait from Williams's younger days that he missed. The thought of it bringing back memories of some of the local hangouts he would hit in New York not that long ago.

"Gunter, dude, stop yelling, we can hear you," Engels ordered, directing his statement towards the back of the control room. "How much coffee have you had this morning?"

"I see you are in good health Bob. Maybe we should start earlier next time." Gunter smiled then patted Engels on the back.

"Yeah, maybe. From now on I am just sticking to beer. No more schnapps, that stuff is terrible."

"I was surprised to get a call from you last night Nick. Why you couldn't explain the reason for coming here today, I can only guess."

"Sorry about that Gunter, best explained in person."

"I think it could be one of two things. One, we are finished," Vogel said, looking away from the other two. "Or two, you *are* taking over."

"I think you will be pleasantly surprised. But no, I am not taking over. Nothing else until Marie gets here. I don't want to start without her."

"What did you guys talk about after we left. I assume that's why you stayed behind. You work something out?" Engels asked.

"You could say that." Williams didn't want to give too much away. He also didn't want them to get the wrong impression with his going out for coffee with Marie. At just that moment he thought of what Lemaire said about Marseille, and his going to the park last night, and then the discovery. He pulled the red ball out of his pocket, took another look, then smiled slightly. "Things are different."

"I do not see a reason we need to be here today. I thought we were going to work some things out with François before we move ahead?" Lemaire was still in her coat and hat when she entered the lab and began to make her way down to Williams.

"Hey. Come on down. I know, we do. But I found something. It's going to change everything."

"Oh? Overnight, you found something? And what did you find?" She questioned. Now standing next to him in the lab on the other side of the machine.

"Catch!" Williams said, tossing the red ball to Engels, who was far from ready. It bounced off his chest and landed at his feet.

"Uh, this isn't one of those teamwork game type things is it," he replied, bending down to pick up the ball, "because I am really bad at that kind of stuff. Now what, do I toss it back or something?"

"Nope, it's nothing like that. Take a look," Williams said through a slight smile.

"Okay. Well. It's red. It's a ball. Looks like all the others." Engels pointed to the set of balls they had in a bucket near the ramp. They kept them there because they anticipated a successful test at some point and wanted to have as many test objects ready as they could. "Do I get to chuck it at someone now?"

"That's all you see?" Williams asked.

"Yep. But I gotta be honest any kind of cognitive function is difficult right now, your turn Gunter."

"Ja, es ist rot. I would agree with Bob." But then Vogel squinted. "I got it!" He looked directly at Williams tossing the ball back to him and said, "Catch!"

"Nice try, but no. What do you see?" Not wanting to turn this into something it wasn't, Williams handed the ball back to Gunter rather than throw it.

"I don't see anything. Just a red ball. Just like all the others. And the letters. Must be the company name, ABAH, with a funny looking B," Vogel answered, shrugging his shoulders.

"What?" Lemaire questioned.

"ABAH. The company's name," Vogel reiterated.

"Let me see that," she said, holding her hand for the ball. Vogel obliged. She stared at it, walked back to Williams and asked, "What does this mean?"

"What do you think?"

"What? What is it? I don't get it," Vogel interrupted.

"Yeah," Engels added, taking a step closer to Lemaire, lowering his sunglasses, "what's the big deal?"

"The company that made the ball. It stamped its name on it," she explained.

"So?"

"This ball says ABAH." She held up the ball revealing the raised letters.

"Again, so?"

"Look at the letter B, it's backwards. The whole text is backwards. The company name isn't ABAH, it's HABA. I know because I bought them, I bought them at L'Épée de Bois." She took another look at the ball for herself. "This ball is a mirror image of the others."

"So, what?" Engels picked up one of the balls from the bucket. "I'm not getting what you guys are putting down here. It's a misprint. What does that have to do with anything?"

"Yesterday, before the test I loaded a ball on the ramp. I distinctly remember seeing HABA written on it. I even checked the GoPro, clear as day. In fact, while you guys were getting things ready, I noticed how there was a little ink missing from the H."

"Go on Nick." Vogel was piecing it together.

"We ran the test, the ball made it through the field, but not to the other doorway."

"Yeah, I remember." Engels however, still was not getting it.

"I picked up this ball, this very one," Williams pointed to Lemaire holding the ball, "on the other side of the lab after the test and put it in my pocket. Last night, I realized I still had it with me. That's when I noticed the lettering backwards. Marie, what does the H look like?"

"It's missing some ink. Just like you said."

"Could this be?" Vogel asked while Engels remained silent.

"The field. It did something to the ball. It reversed it. What we are looking at is an exact mirror image, created when it exited the field."

"Oh man. You mean this thing does work?" Engels asked.

"It does. Maybe not what we expected, but it's progress."

"What purpose would there be to a machine that would reverse everything?" Lemaire asked, turning to walk closer to the door, the ball still in her hand. "It doesn't make any sense."

"Right. Not in and of itself. It makes no sense. I couldn't stop thinking about it last night. The plans, Keitel's transmission, this ball. Then, it hit me. We have a connection problem. This doorway," Williams pointed back and forth overhead, "is not connected with the other doorway like it should."

"Non," Lemaire added.

"We said it ourselves, we don't fully understand how this works. But this is how I think it's supposed to work. Everything that enters or exits the field gets converted, sort of like a digital scan. A conversion from one state in door one, and a conversion back to the original state out of door two. But since the ball didn't make it to door two, meaning it wasn't transported, it was dumped out of door one in its converted state, a mirror image," Williams finished, taking a moment to let it sink in.

"Progress," Vogel said.

"Progress Monsieur," Lemaire said silently, still staring at the ball.

"Oh man," Was Engels thought.

"So now we need to focus on-" All of the sudden, the unmistakable hum of the power could be heard. Before the team realized what was happening, a bright light flashed, then settled into a deep blue.

"Holy shit! Is this thing on?" Engels shouted, slowly walking back away from the doorway.

"How could it be? We didn't start anything," Vogel answered.

"You guys okay? We can't see you beyond the energy field."

"What the hell is going on?" Lemaire questioned, snapping out of her thought, turning to see what was happening. She took a few steps toward the field without realizing it.

"STOP!" Williams shouted. She stopped dead in her tracks. "The field, it's generated. Look!" He pointed to the slight blue haze spanning the center of the doorway, obscuring the view into the control room.

"It is on, how could it be?" Lemaire said, frozen, afraid to move.

"You two stay there, we'll pull up the program." Engels and Vogel advised Williams and Lemaire to stay where they were. They were on the opposite side of the doorway, and the only way back was to cross directly through Andromeda. With the doorway energized, and the discovery from the last test, they didn't want to take chances. Engels and Vogel raced up to their consoles.

"What do you see?" Lemaire asked.

"Nothing, the terminals are all powered off. No way this thing just turned on with the terminals powered down like this." Engels was confused. "It's going to take about fifteen minutes to get it all up and going."

"Some residual power, from the test yesterday?" Vogel asked.

"I have no idea. I can't see how that would be possible, especially with the shutdown sequence. I need to think this through." Williams began to pace, careful to remain on the one side of Andromeda. Lemaire didn't move an inch.

"Lock out. What the hell?" Engels stood.

"Same with mine." Vogel's console was locked out too. He made his way down to Lemaire's console to see if he could access the system there. "She's locked out too. Scheiße!"

"What does that mean?" Williams asked.

"It's a safety measure. Only one set of consoles can be activated at one time. There's a dual set located in control room two, with door two. We put in a lockout so there wouldn't be conflicting commands from the different labs. It's also so we would all be forced to work in the same room at the same time."

"So, is someone doing this from lab two?" Williams asked.

"Not possible. We are the only ones who know the codes. Even if someone was in the other control room they wouldn't have a clue what to do." Engels sat again. "What now?"

"Cut the power?" Lemaire asked.

With a look of agreement, Vogel headed to the power cabinet to see what he could see. He keyed in the code opening the secure cabinet. "I wasn't expecting this. The switch has a lock. Who's got the key?"

"The switch is locked? In the secure cabinet?" Williams asked. "Uh, we might want to change that. Later. I think we'll need to shut this down some other way."

"But how?"

"What's the longest we've had this running?"

"Do you think we should be worried?" Lemaire asked.

"No, I actually don't. I mean, theoretically we fixed the power issues. I don't think it's going to over power anyway. Besides, if it did that would help us out; the doorway would shut down on its own. I just want to know when we go over the longest time, so we can see if it acts differently. Maybe there will be a clue in there somewhere." Williams started pacing again.

"Ten, fifteen minutes. Yesterday was the longest," Vogel answered, standing near the doorway just outside the exclusion zone.

"What are you suggesting, just waiting it out? Wait until it stops itself?" Lemaire asked.

"Not sure of what other options we have. We can't get into the terminals, it's too dangerous to walk through the fields." Just then, there was a disruption in the field, but only for a few seconds.

"Look, did you see that?" Engels asked.

"Yes, just like the disruption when we dropped the ball. Looks like it's back to normal."

"There, again." Engels pointed, seeing another disruption in the field. "Something's happening."

"I've got it! Auto stop," Vogel exclaimed. "Auto stop. It never activated because we never had it open long enough."

"What are you talking about Gunter?" Williams asked.

"In the initiation sequence. Part of the sequence is to initialize the auto stop. Thirty minutes after the field is initiated, it will shut down, automatically."

"Wow, you guys were thinking."

"It was in case we were all incapacitated for any reason, like the doorway explodes or something. It was never going to be something we were going to keep long term," Lemaire explained.

"But will it work? We didn't run the initialization sequence," Williams asked.

"It had to have been run. There's no way this could have started without it," Vogel answered.

"Ah, got it. Then how long have we been in here?"

"At least twenty-five. I cannot tell since the terminal will not allow me in, but if I were to guess," Vogel looked at his watch, "twenty-five minutes."

"Nice watch Gunter, you should really learn to use your-" and no sooner did Engels comment on Vogel's watch the humming abruptly stopped. The power was off, and the blue lights were dimming to nothing.

"Let's go, NOW!" Lemaire yelled the moment the blue lights were off, Williams followed in quick succession.

"I was close," Vogel said, again looking at his watch.

"That didn't make any sense." And before Lemaire could add anything else, they all heard a small pop. The doorway was no closed.

"Holy crap. Is it over, is it off?" Engels asked, slowly walking back to his terminal.

"It looks like it," Vogel answered, making his way to main power terminal at the base of the control room. "Since the power levers are all under lock and key, I'll have to do this the old fashion way, I'll unplug it."

"Oui, do it. I don't want that happening again. Robert, check control room two. It's impossible," she said, pulling a small strand of hair from the front of her face, "but I want to make sure no one was there, messing with things."

"I'm on it." Engels headed out, tapping his wrist as he walked passed Vogel. "Hey. What if someone is there?"

"Good point. Come back and get us... I guess."

"Here we go." Vogel knelt down and grasped the main power cable attached to Andromeda. It was held together by a circular electronic connector with a large retaining ring that had to be unscrewed to disconnect. After removing the retainer, he rotated the cable slightly, and with a few hard tugs, pulled it free. "That should do it. Main power is disconnected. There's no way it will kick on again."

"Good." Lemaire turned and looked at the door. "Close call," she said quietly.

"I don't think we should let François in on our discovery with the ball until we understand what happened today. What do you think?" Williams asked. He was hesitant but wanted to see if Lemaire was going to trust him.

"Agreed. I am a little shaken." She held out her hand, still trembling. "I don't think I am going to be much use today."

"Likewise. Probably best that we all go home, clear our heads, and start in on this Monday."

"Nothing," Engels said as he walked back into the lab. "The place looks like it always has. All the consoles are covered, the lights were out, I didn't see anything out of the ordinary."

"I just don't understand. Never mind. We are done for today, we are going to start back at it on Monday." Lemaire started to reach for her things, the rest of the team did the same and started to head out. As a team, they never left the lab together. Usually they all went their separate ways, mostly habit. But after today, they all felt a little more secure leaving together. They entered the elevator, not saying a word to each other, then exited out the front of the Musée.

"Weird." They were just about to exit the facility into the museum area when Williams stopped.

"What?" Engels asked.

"I don't remember those doors being painted green like that." Williams was pointing to the set of doors just outside of the walkway into the research facility. "I thought they were polished brass."

"Huh. Yeah, I guess I thought they were brass too. Weren't they? Maybe they painted them while we were in the lab."

"We were only in the lab for an hour, maybe two. Painted brass?" Vogel interrupted. "Besides, it looks worn, old. It doesn't make sense."

"Maybe not, but they're painted now. So, it had to have changed at one point. Some weekend. Man, I'm freaking out. You want a ride home Gunter?" Engels asked as he made his way through the doors.

"Yes, yes I do. Let's get out of here. I'll see you two Monday." Engels and Vogel headed to the parking garage.

"What do you think happened today?" Lemaire and Williams found themselves walking together again. He didn't mind, they didn't live too far from each other. Besides, he wanted to bounce a few ideas off her. He could tell she was still shaken; she was walking real close this time. He didn't want to misinterpret anything.

"I don't know. Every time we ran a test we had to run power sequences, initiation sequences, shut down sequences. None of what we saw today made any sense. I don't know." They kept walking, playing with possible explanations in their heads, and when something sounded reasonable, they would share it with one another.

"What about an outside influence? Do you know what I mean?" Lemaire asked.

"I thought about that two. Hackers, from another country or something. But that facility is probably one of the most secure sites I've ever seen. I think all of our network is stand-alone too. I don't even think it's possible to hack. Is it?"

"I can't stand it. It was so scary. We were stuck on the other side, who knows what could have happened if we walked through."

"We'll just have to come up with some new safety procedures. Maybe we keep the power disconnected like Gunter has it until we know what's going on. We're not running any tests anyway, at least we already decided on that. I don't think anyone will disagree."

"Oh, here we are, I didn't even realize how close we were, I was lost in it all." Lemaire started to make her way up the front stairs to her apartment.

"We'll start debugging this thing Monday. We are so close. You sure you're okay?" Lemaire was so deep in thought she didn't respond, closing the door behind her.

He started to make his way home. *Maybe I'll hit the park again. It's always good for clearing my head.* He walked, still thinking about the door kicking on by itself. He couldn't believe it was possible. He was about a block down the avenue when his phone rang.

"Hey Marie. Did you think of something?"

"You need to come back here now."

"Why?" Williams stopped in his tracks. "What's wrong?"

"I can't tell you. You just.... just come back, hurry," she said.

"Okay, I'm on my-" He couldn't finish, a voice came over the line saying the call ended. *What's wrong I wonder? Maybe she figured out why Andromeda kicked on. Where the hell am I?* Williams looked up at a street sign, 'RUE POUCHET', and just beneath it, another sign reading 'POUCHET STRAßE'. *Straße? Isn't that German? Since when did Paris put up signs in German with the French?* Just then his phone rang again. On the caller ID it read 'R. Engels'.

"Bob, what's up?"

"Something's..."

"Bob? Bob you broke up."

"Something's wrong man. I can't tell what."

"What do you mean?" Williams was about half a block away from Lemaire's apartment.

"My car. It's my car, but it's not my car, do you know what I mean?"

"You're going to have to give me more detail than that."

"I can't put my finger on it. Little things. Like, there was a tear in the seat, from wear or something, I don't know. It's been there since I bought the thing two years ago. It's gone. I never had the seat fixed, but it's gone. The millage too. I could swear I had over sixty thousand on it, but the odometer is at about fifty. It's my car though, my keys work. It's mine."

"I am sure there's a good explanation for it Bob. Hey, I got to go. Marie needed me to go to her place. She said there was something urgent she needed to show me. I have no idea what it's all about, I'm headed there now.

Just take it easy. We've had a lot of excitement this morning, it's freaking us all out."

"Okay. I guess. I'm at Gunter's house now. I'll talk to you Monday." Just as Engels hung up, Williams was turning the corner to Lemaire's apartment. He just started to make his way up the stairs when she opened the front door.

"Everything okay? You didn't sound too good."

"I don't know. I don't think so."

"Why, we're not in the lab anymore. I know it was scary, but we are okay. There's nothing to be afraid of now, is there?" Williams took a few steps up.

"Come on inside. I need to show you something." It was the first time Lemaire asked Williams to come in. Again, he was reminded of that day they went for coffee. Her hair, light skin, their talk. He was just now getting to know her better, but felt he needed to keep their relationship professional. *She's just going to show you something. Go in, see what it is, then head home. Simple.*

"Here." Lemaire led him into the kitchen.

"What?" Williams didn't see anything out of the ordinary. "Nice kitchen, you cook?"

"My kitchen doesn't look like that."

"What do you mean? You live here don't you?"

"Yes. I've lived here for ten years. This is my apartment. Those are my pictures on the wall." She pointed to the hall they had just walked down. Williams noticed one spot on the wall where there was a nail protruding. The space looked like there could have been a picture hanging there recently, but he didn't think anything of it. "This, my kitchen does not look like this. All of my appliances were old, these are all new." She walked over to a small closet near the kitchen. "Le Placard, I have not bought these things since I was in Marseille."

Williams took a moment to go over what Lemaire had just shown him. "Bob called me on my way back here. He said he was in a car that wasn't his car... but was. You are saying this isn't your apartment... but is. Something is wrong, something is different. Did you notice the German street signs outside, under the French? Where those there before?"

"No....no that is not possible." Lemaire started to walk toward the window. "What street? Paris would never do not do that."

"That's what I said. At first, I thought it was an honorary thing, we do that in the States sometimes, but it was like that on every street heading back here, and only German." Williams walked slowly into the adjoining room, then turned and sat on a sofa. "Something is wrong. I don't get it." He put his head in his hands. He sat there for a few minutes, both he and Lemaire not saying a word.

"There is something else. There's something else I need to show you. The kitchen wasn't why I wanted you to come back." Williams looked up. Lemaire was holding a picture frame and photograph in her hands facing away from him. "I saw this right when I walked in. That's when I knew something wasn't right."

"What? What is it?" Williams stood.

"It's a picture." Holding it out, but still away from him she said, "It's a picture, of two happy people." She then turned the picture around, revealing the two of them standing in each other's arms in front of Antoine's Restaurant in New Orleans. "C'est different."

8. A Changing World

"Check the logs. There's got to be something there."

"Yeah, sure. Okay. How?" Williams answered, confused. Lemaire forgot for a minute that he didn't know what to do. He was, essentially, an observer until recently. Vogel started to show him around the system, but for the most part it was all high level, nothing specific like activity logs. He could sign on to a console, pull up a test plan, maybe even results from a previous test but that was about it. The activity logs would have to wait.

"Never mind. I forgot. I'll get them," Lemaire said, apologetically. She was starting to see the results, which she regretted, of keeping Williams out of the project. His knowledge of the systems would have been helpful, especially now. "I'll show you later when we have more time." She saw an opportunity to set things right. "What are we going to say to Gunter and Robert?"

"I assume they've noticed things just as we have. To what extent I guess we'll find out," Williams said as he stood just behind Lemaire, trying to pick up a few tips. Lemaire tilted her head in response. "No time like the present," he added.

"You said Bob noticed things about his car, oui?"

"Yeah, that's what he said when I headed back to our... your place. I haven't talked to him since. I sent him and Gunter a text to make sure they would be in today."

"Good. We need them here."

"Yeah. I tried to keep it casual, I don't think it worked though." Williams started to walk down to Andromeda, Lemaire was too quick at the console for him to pick up anything. He was about half way down the aisle when he realized how quiet it had suddenly gotten. He didn't hear Lemaire, typing, talking, she was usually a presence wherever she was. He spun around to see if she was still in the room. There she was, just sitting at Engels's console in the back, staring directly at him. She had a serious look in her eyes. "What's wrong, you okay?"

"Why can't I remember?"

"Remember? What?" Williams asked.

"New Orleans." Lemaire was thinking about the picture. It was her and Williams. It was unmistakable, they were in a relationship. They were in New Orleans, the two of them together. They had proof, but neither of them could remember any of it.

"I don't know. I seriously don't. I've been thinking about it all night. That picture must have been taken within the last year. I can swear I haven't been there for at least twenty."

"I've never been there. I know I haven't. I have never even been to the States," she said adamantly. "I've only been to Canada, but I am not even sure about that anymore." She put her hands over her eyes, trying to shut it all out. Hearing someone entering a code on the control room entrance keypad made her jump in her seat. "Merde. I cannot stand this."

The door swung open, Vogel walking in as if it were a usual day. "Guten Morgen. I hope you both had a good weekend. I have been anxious to check into this power-up problem since Saturday."

"Yeah. Yeah, mine was good." Williams looked at Lemaire. He could tell she didn't want to volunteer any more information than she had too given the situation. She knew if Vogel saw her face he would start asking questions, so she hid behind a lock of her hair hanging down over her face.

"And Marie, how about you?" Vogel stopped near Bob's console, where she was sitting. "Is there anything you want to tell me? Anything at all?" Vogel smiled slightly.

"No. No there isn't." *Est-ce qu'il sait?* She was trying her hardest to avoid eye contact.

"That's a shame," Vogel added as he turned and walked to his terminal. Lemaire's tactic worked, and both her and Williams exchanged glances for a short moment. "I thought you would have spent the day in the park. It was such a beautiful weekend, I was looking forward to hearing about it. Well I hope you were able to rest up then."

"How about you Gunter?" Williams asked while walking over to his station.

"Ah. I read. I read and read and read some more." Vogel then sat, reliving the peaceful weekend in his thoughts. "Interesting thing, I found some old books of mine that I had thought were long since thrown out. I decided, after Saturday's mishap, I would not take any chances and stay in. It was wonderful. I read and read."

"Did you happen to see Bob at all?"

"No, no I didn't. He was acting strange the other day when he drove me home. He kept insisting his car was different. He drove all around Paris, passing my apartment several times. I laughed, he said he couldn't remember fixing a tear, or something. I think he overdid it Friday night, I'll have to go easy on him from now on. You Americans are too used to that watered-down stuff you call ale."

"Yeah, he called me about his car. Odd. Say, did you notice anything else different, besides those old books?" Vogel turned and looked at Lemaire when Williams asked his question.

"No. No, I didn't. But you did. Didn't you?" Vogel questioned. He stood. "What is it, what happened?"

"Well, I'm not really sure. But, I think I've seen some differences lately. Things I can't quite explain. Subtle differences."

"Some not so subtle," Lemaire added quietly.

"Bob called me about his car Friday. Like you said, he couldn't remember fixing a tear in the seat. Although to me he said he was sure he didn't. And the mileage was off."

"But what did *you* notice?" Vogel stepped out from behind his console.

"Street signs. I noticed street signs, in German, under all the French. I can't say it was everywhere, but on all the streets I happened to go down."

"I saw it." Vogel sat back down. He put his head in his hands and leaned on his console. "I tried to not believe, I tried. But I saw it too. At first, I thought I was going senile. Then I remembered Bob's car, and the books, I swear Nick, I swear I got rid of those books ten years ago. And there they were, in my living room, like they have always been there. Something happened. Something with this door, this machine." Vogel stood again, pointing towards to lab. "It has to be because of Andromeda."

"How can we be certain?" Lemaire said, trying to convince herself the two were not related.

"How can we deny?" Vogel questioned, holding his hands out, palms up, to Lemaire. She turned and faced the machine, and the undeniable.

"I suspect the same. We all remember how things were when we came to the lab Saturday." Williams was at the base of Andromeda now. "We all remember this initiating by itself. And we all remember things being different almost immediately after. It has to be something, something related to the door starting on its own."

"But it couldn't have started on its own. That would have been impossible," Lemaire explained.

"What about the logs?"

"I am working on it, it's been a while, I am not sure I am looking in the right place."

"What do you hope they will show?" Vogel asked.

"Something. Some activity, a log-on, something that will help answer what's going on." Lemaire stood now, putting her hand over her open mouth as she reacted to the tones of the keypad at the entrance once again.

"Hey, sorry I'm late," Engels said, stopping and standing at the top of the control room. He didn't move and had a worried look on his face.

"Hey Bob. Yeah, you're not dreaming. We're trying to figure it out." Williams pointed to the door.

"Holy shit, what's going on?" Engels hurried to his console. "Did we do something? Did Andromeda do something?"

"We don't know. We were just talking about the logs. That's the logical starting place. Marie believes it should tell us who kicked this thing on," Williams explained.

"Logs don't show anyone activating anything, I checked. I came in yesterday," Engels answered. "I was scared shitless after seeing some of the things I have this weekend." Lemaire moved to her console, allowing him to sit.

"Well then, we are at square one." Williams shook his head. "Damn."

"But I did notice something," Engels added.

"What? What is it?" Lemaire rushed back to his console.

"Hang on. Let me get in here." With a few key strokes, Engels brought up the archive system that retained the activity records. He searched for and pulled up the logs from Friday. "So, the logs work like this, they're continuous. If there are any actions, anything at all regarding access, system changes, anything, it gets logged."

"Only in relation to Andromeda." Vogel added.

"Yeah, right. It's a stand-alone network, segregated form anything else in the facility, so yeah, only Andromeda activity. So like, when we log in to these consoles, a line item is created with details as to who logged on, time, all that. See, here." Engels pointed to the record showing his log in on Friday morning. "There's my log on. But it also works another way. Even if there aren't any actions, a line item gets written during certain intervals of inactivity."

"What do you mean?" Williams asked.

"It's something I added, a way to make sure the logs are working properly. If there's no activity in fifteen minutes, a line item is written saying so." He pulled up the log from Friday night. "See, here. We all went home. Seven PM, boom, 'NO ACTIVITY RECORDED' system date...time, blah blah. It's a way to slow down someone trying to alter logs manually. If they tried to erase the logs, they would have to create all these inactivity entries to make it look like they were never here. It's time consuming."

"Okay? So what?"

"There are no entries like that on the log for Saturday. It's just a blank page, until about ten AM."

"So someone erased the records," Williams added, walking toward the machine.

"Oh no. The system was hacked?" Lemaire said nervously.

"No, no way. Our network is completely stand-alone. It's not even connected to the main network, totally isolated. The only way anyone could have hacked the network was to be in either of the control rooms."

"Well, we know no one but us were here." Lemaire was referring to the control room for lab one since all the team was there when the system kicked on.

"What about the cameras in room two?" Williams asked, but he already knew the answer.

"Off. We powered off all camera's, monitors, sensors, you name it, we powered all of it off when we ran the test Friday. Something in all that was causing our issues. We didn't power anything back on since."

"So that's out." Williams paced back and forth. "Unless." He stopped for a moment, his hands in his pockets, running an idea through his head. Suddenly, he started to make his way down through the lab to the hall that led to lab two, grabbing one of the cables he had lying on a table near the bucket of red toy balls.

"Where are you going?" Lemaire asked before following him. Engels logged off his console, not leaving anything to chance, and started behind Vogel. Everything was dark in lab two. Williams had to feel around for the lights before Vogel clicked them on for him. Williams looked around, under a few of the sensors, monitors, and desks arranged in the lab control room.

"Ah ha! It's right where I left it." Williams then climbed on one of the consoles, reached up, and tried disconnecting a GoPro. It was the second of two, the other in lab one, he set up prior to their test on Friday. Unlike the monitoring equipment, the GoPro had no external cables susceptible to energy interference but had a limitation of its own. "How the hell do I get this thing detached? Oh wait, it's one of these." He pulled a small lever on the mount and the GoPro fell from the scaffolding where it was attached. "Damn!" His first reaction was to reach out and grab it, but he just grazed the corner, only slowing its fall. The camera bumped the top of the vinyl covered console and came to rest at Williams's feet.

"Well, that was graceful." Engels quickly picked up the camera before it had a chance to fall to the floor.

"I guess that was the wrong lever. How does it look Bob?" Williams asked as he carefully climbed down from the top of the console.

"Looks like it's in one piece. Lucky."

"I don't know when the battery went out, but maybe it lasted until after the incident."

"Worth a shot." Engels took the camera and cable from Williams while Vogel ripped the vinyl cover from one of the consoles allowing it to settle to the floor.

"Here, use this one," Vogel said while quickly entering his log on credentials. Engels sat, attaching the cable to the console data port on the front left side, pulling up the footage.

"What exactly are we looking for?" Lemaire asked as power was restored to the GoPro, a slight flash of light displaying the menu options.

"I don't know. In fact, I have zero idea. Should only be one feed recorded. Let's try to start when the door kicked on I guess. What time was that?"

"Nine AM, yes?" Vogel said, looking at his watch again.

"Let's start then, maybe go through in five times speed, see if we see anything."

"Looks like it recorded something, still works anyway. Should almost be there. Okay, here, eight forty-five AM. Looks dark. Nobody in there."

"Let's take it slower," Lemaire said. "I can't see a thing."

"Yeah, slower. I don't want to miss anything." Williams and the team all hovered over Engels and the console displaying the camera footage.

"THERE!" Engels could hardly hold his surprise and froze the image. "Someone's there, in the dark. Just before nine AM. You guys see that? Look, right there."

"That's definitely someone. Not one of us. Let it go."

"Okay, here we go." Engels released the footage, trying to make sense of the images before him. "Their doing something to Andromeda. Someone was there."

"Keep going, real speed," Williams said, pointing to the mystery person on the screen, "let's see what they're up to."

"Oh man. They're screwing with it. They're obviously taking something apart there. I can barely see though in the dark," Engels added.

"Look, they're heading back to the console. Looks like a man, can't tell who though."

"Can you see what they are doing?" Lemaire asked.

"I can't tell from this angle, but that person knows how this all works. They are logged in by the looks of it."

"HOLY CRAP!" Engels shouted. The screen showed the unmistakable blue glow of the doorway initialized. "Look, the field. Whoever it was turned it on while we were in the other lab."

"Why would they do that? I mean, we were just on the other side of the wall?" Vogel asked.

"And how?" Lemaire asked. But before anyone could answer, she excitedly said, "Wait, is he going to do it?" The man on the screen slowly walked to the machine in lab two, the field glowing in front of him, and stopped just short of entering. She wondered aloud if he was going to go through.

"At this point, you and I were stuck on the other side of doorway one." It was starting to come together for Williams, except there were more questions now.

"And we were trying to access the terminals in room one and were locked out. That must be the reason," Vogel added.

"Wait! Freeze it. Crap, go back a few seconds and freeze it." Williams pointed to the screen. "There!"

"What is he doing?" Engels asked.

"Looks like he's sticking his hand through." Williams turned in amazement.

"He's just standing there. You sure you didn't see a hand?" Engels was completely confused.

"No, but then again I was a little preoccupied. Let it go, let's see what else he does."

"He's just standing there. Wait. Holy crap he went in!"

"He's through. He's through!" Lemaire exclaimed.

"Wow. He's gone. He didn't come out on our side. I think we would have seen him." Williams pointed to the screen again. The team watched patiently, when about a minute later, "There, there he is again. He's back."

"I don't get it. Wouldn't that have turned him inside out or something?" Engels referring to the mirror image of their test ball.

"What's that under his arm? I can't tell. Looks like a case." The man emerged from the door and walked to the console, picked up a small attaché case, then turned and re-entered the doorway. "What's he doing now?" The man disappeared once again, briefly, then re-emerged.

"His case, he doesn't have it anymore," Engels said in amazement.

"I still can't tell who that is. The light from the door makes it impossible to see." The man walked out a few paces, then turned to look back at the door. Just then, as the team anxiously awaited the man's next move it happened. In the center of the field, just as the man turned back, another person stepped through and out into the lab area. It was too dark to identify him either, but it appeared he was wearing a lab coat. He looked around, waived to the first man now standing at the console, then returned through the door.

"Did everyone else see that? Did that just happen?" Engels questioned.

"Yes. But I don't believe it," Vogel said, his voice cracking.

"I am at a complete loss. None of this makes sense now. Whoever that was did something to the door here." Williams pointed to a small metal panel on the front of the door. "They then logged on the system, effectively locking out control room one. Somehow, and this is what I cannot understand at all, they were able to start the door."

"You haven't even mentioned the part about going through, and the second guy. I mean, we were all in lab one, we didn't see any of these people. Right? Right? Am I crazy?" Engels stood.

"And that part. I don't even know where to start with that."

"Look. The field, he's closing it down." Just then Vogel pointed to the screen, the man was now sitting at the terminal. He appeared to be pulling up some system command menus, but from the camera angle and the light from Andromeda they could not see exactly what.

"He must be running the shut-down sequence. I don't know how, but that would be my guess," Engels added.

"And we are at about twenty-five minutes according to the time stamp. Just when the field ceased on our end, right?" Williams asked.

"Ja."

"What's he up to now?" The field was now shut down, the blue light no longer glowed on the GoPro footage. They could see the man head back down to the panel on the machine and pull it off again. They could not tell what he was doing in the dark. He spent a short time adjusting something behind the panel before the footage stopped.

"What's wrong? What happened?" Lemaire asked.

"Nothing. I think the battery died," Williams answered. "I think that's all the footage we have."

"That's all? I don't think I want to see any more," Engels added, sitting at another console and staring at the ceiling above.

"Why isn't any of this on the logs?" Lemaire looked over to Engels.

Engels turned and looked at the console the man was using and said "My guess is he, whoever he is, deleted all actions from the log, probably after the battery died. That's why we don't see any activity, even the," Engels made the bunny ears symbol with his fingers, "no activity entries."

"It's an inside job. But everyone who could have done this, was in the other room. We all saw it. I don't get it." Williams started to pace again.

"What I don't get is where that person went, and who that other dude was. Something looked off about him." Everyone could tell Engels was on edge. "If he wanted to deliver a package he could have used the mail, right? If this thing works why don't we know about it?"

"I don't know. I just don't know." Williams ran his hands through his hair. "Gunter. Pull up the video again. Is there a way to enlarge a section of the screen?"

Vogel looked at Williams, then to Engels.

"Yeah," Engels answered. "We have to run it through some editing software, but yeah, I can do it."

"Good. I need you to pull up the second guy. I want to see if we can get a closer look."

"Sure. It's going to take a minute, but I can do it." Engels made his way back to his terminal.

"How does this all tie in? It all has to be related. The field turning on, the changes, these two people. It all must mean something." Just as Williams was talking, Engels pulled up the section of video.

"Here. The dude should be coming through...now." Engels froze the screen. He then cropped and expanded the section of the video so it was only the one man.

"That's what I was afraid of. I thought the definition would get blurry the closer we got in. I don't recognize him, do any of you?" The team all answered no, except Vogel, who didn't answer at all. Instead he stepped back a few paces.

"What is it Gunter, do you know him?" Lemaire asked. Vogel just stood there with his mouth open, unable to speak.

"What is it Gunter? You know him?"

"No....no, I don't. But he looks like he works for the government," Vogel answered, hesitantly.

"Well, that would explain a lot. I wouldn't put it past the government to put their hands over all of this. From all we know they've been spying on us the whole time."

"No Bob. Not this government."

"You mean, not French?" Williams squinted while looking at the screen to try and get a better look.

"No. Unlike any government, today."

"What do you mean?" Williams went in closer, and that's when he made it out. "Oh no."

"What?" Engels was starting to get worried. "Would someone please explain to me what's going on?"

"What is it Nick? Tell me." Lemaire was looking at Williams, who had now stepped away from the console and was walking closer to the doorway.

"It's what's on his lab coat, isn't it Gunter?"

"Ja, Herr Williams."

"What's on his coat? I can't tell." Engels tried to get a better look. Lemaire was now by Williams's side. He then ran back to the console to try to pull up an image on the internet.

"You can't Nick, it's not connected to the network," Lemaire explained.

"Damn. Come on." Williams jumped up from his seat and made his way to the exit, heading down the hall that lead to the elevator, and up to the museum. After the short trip, they were topside, no one saying a word. They took a few steps out from the elevator doors when Williams stopped. He spun around, walking backwards, taking a look over to the brass doors that had at some time had been painted, then headed in to the museum. It was still early and the crowds had just begun to queue up. "Follow me."

"Nick, slow down, I cannot keep up." Lemaire was wearing short heels and could not keep up with Williams's pace. Vogel walked slowly. He knew what was on the coat. He knew where Williams was running.

Williams stopped just outside of the Leclerc Room. He took a brief look around, then found what he was looking for. Walking slowly, he stopped in front of what it was he wanted to show the team.

"I can't believe it," Williams said, almost out of breath. Engels and Lemaire were right behind him, Vogel, a few steps behind them.

"It's what is on his coat," Vogel said.

"It's what is on his coat. I can't believe it." Williams was standing next to a display of a small banner from world war two. Williams turned to look at the team. "That person knew how to fix the door. They knew how to start it. But it's not what we thought it was."

"What 'what' was? The door? What is it?" Lemaire didn't believe it, she wanted to hear it from Williams.

"That person, who came though. It's a Nazi Eagle on his coat. He's a scientist, for the Nazi's." Williams pointed to the red cloth banner hanging behind a large piece of glass, with a white eagle perched atop a black swastika in its center.

"I told you he looked off," Engels added.

"M31, the machine, Andromeda. It was never a doorway from one place to another. It's a doorway from one time to another."

9. Mystery Man

"This isn't happening. No way, this isn't happening." Engels was sitting back at his terminal, his left hand over his eyes.

The team, who had collectively walked back down to the control room, said nothing to each other after what they had just seen in the museum. It was unmistakable.

"I want to believe you, but it IS happening," Vogel followed, slowly taking his seat at his terminal.

"Arrêter!" Lemaire barked. The team was surprised by her tone. For the most part, since her and Williams were trapped on the other side of door one, she stayed reserved, scared, confused. She was being cautious about everything from how she spoke to how she acted in the lab. Now it seemed like that all had changed. She was back to her normal self and Williams welcomed it. She took charge again, and part of him was relieved because that meant he didn't have to. "We need to keep our heads together. All of us. We need to focus. We need answers, and I intend to get them."

"This just isn't what I signed up for," Engels said, trying to keep it together. "I mean, I never would have-"

"I know. But we aren't doing ourselves any good by losing control. We have to face the fact that what we've been working on is something different entirely. And, as evidence suggests," Lemaire paused, looking for the right words, "it screwed things up."

"I can probably think of about a hundred things I don't understand about all of this," Vogel said while he stood and then walked to the large screen at the back of the control room. He pulled up the schematics to Andromeda for all to see. "One thing jumps out at me."

Williams followed, careful to see what Vogel was pulling up.

"That man, who worked on door two, to get it started. How did he know what to do?" Vogel asked.

"He obviously had help," Engels added. "He had to have had some working knowledge of this thing. There's no other way to explain it."

"That may be true, but then why are we here? I mean it this way. If you already know what you need to do, why involve the three of you?" Williams said, referring to the other three members of the team before he joined. "Why spend five years of trial and error, then get me involved from half way across the globe?"

"I don't know."

He couldn't tell if she was answering the question in the whole, or just the part about him. He finished. "Then one-night sneak into the lab, make some changes and start the thing up. And, even more, why break it again and cover your tracks?"

"Maybe that Nazi scientist helped him," Engels hesitatingly added. As impossible as it was, he thought he was reaching.

"No," Williams answered as he started to pace again, "that would be impossible."

"Why?"

"It's a Paradox."

"Yeah? How so?"

"So, if the scientist helped him open the door, it implies he opened the door to get the help. He couldn't open the door to begin with, which would mean the scientist couldn't help him. One couldn't happen before the other," he explained, then suddenly stopped pacing. "Unless."

"Was ist es?"

"Well. Our assumption was based on the idea of this doorway involving two doors, right?"

"Oui. One to send and another to receive. That was the whole basis for the project," Lemaire explained.

"We know the mystery man opened *one* of our doors, or at least *used* only one, right?" Williams asked.

"But both were on, no?"

"Yes, both were on, we know that. We witnessed door one from the other lab, and we have GoPro footage at the same time for door two. But, from what we can see only door two did anything. Those two men, both moving in and out of door two and none of it seen on our side, at door one."

"Sure, but what does it mean?"

"There's a third doorway." The team were completely silent upon hearing what Williams just said.

"I am officially going to be sick," Engels whispered, putting his head into his hands.

"A third doorway? But how?" Vogel asked.

"It's the original doorway. It's the first one the Nazi's created back in Berlin." Williams was getting excited, racing around getting a clear view of Andromeda, then back to the monitor in the control room. "Holy cow this is amazing."

"Where could it be? It could be anywhere," Vogel said.

"Here's the part that's going to blow your minds. It doesn't matter."

"What do you mean it doesn't matter?"

"It's irrelevant. In fact, it doesn't even matter if it still exists anymore." Williams smiled. "Maybe it was destroyed or dismantled twenty years ago, still doesn't matter."

"It would have to, we saw the two men, it would have to exists for that to happen." Vogel was adamant. "Where else would he go if Andromeda connected to this… third doorway?"

"We did see them, but if I am correct, Andromeda is a time doorway. On Saturday the other door was opened and connected to the one that was created in 1945." The team was again silenced by Williams statement.

"But wouldn't your paradox still happen?" Engels asked.

"No. Because of Keitel's transmission."

"What does that have to do with anything?"

"Pull it up Gunter," Williams ordered.

Vogel, already at the back of the control room, pulled up the copy of the intercepted transmission, displaying it on an adjacent the screen.

"There. It says the test was successful. Here's the genius thing about all of this. They only needed to open their doorway once."

"What? Why? You mean this is it?" Lemaire asked, confused.

"No, no. They only needed to open the doorway once, then get the plans out of Berlin, to someplace safe. See, the whole concept relies on two doorways. The part that doesn't matter is when the second doorway is created, and, subsequently opened."

"I must be getting stupid or something, I didn't follow any of that," Engels said, still with his head in his hands.

"It's like this, an example. You create doorway A, right now, in 2018. Right? You then start it up and run it for, say, a week. You follow me?"

"Yeah, I think."

"Okay. Now then let's say you give the plans to your son who builds doorway B fifty years later. You give him everything he needs to know, including how to turn it on and all that. In 2068 you are long since dead, but your son isn't. He builds and turns on door B. It wouldn't even matter where; Germany, France, America, doesn't matter. He steps through, and voilà as Marie says, he is back in 2018, having a cold one with his dad."

"Of course! Of course! It makes sense! The Nazi's created a doorway in 1945, that order proves they turned it on. They then had orders to get the plans out of Berlin so another doorway could be built somewhere else, at a later time. It is genius." Vogel could hardly hold his excitement. "Pure genius."

"So, we're the second door, we've opened it, or that other dude did. I still don't get why, what for?" Engels asked, apparently with enough strength to lift his head from his hands.

"So they could bring back anything they wanted from our time to 1945. The possibilities are endless. They would have all the time in the world to do it too. The only thing that mattered was that the first doorway, in Berlin, was open long enough to get anything through and to use it to their advantage," Williams followed.

"They wouldn't even have to do anything now. They could wait another hundred years," Lemaire added. "Because any time the second door opened, it would link to the one in Berlin, in 1945, wouldn't it?"

"All the technology they could bring back, oil, and weapons. They could bring back designs, designs to anything so far advanced they would be unstoppable, in 1945." Vogel's excitement soon vanished. "Oh no," he said, his tome changing. "Oh no."

"What? Gunter? Man, I don't like it when you say that." Engels said, making his way to the back of the lab, purposely not looking at the screen.

"The differences. The things we see now, after the door was opened here. They were already given something. That attaché. Whatever was in it, it changed the past." He sat, unable to stand after his realization.

"I don't like it, but I'm thinking the same thing," Williams responded. "Whatever it was, it probably altered something. That means the very first doorway was open long enough to be useful."

"But what about us?" Engels asked, calmer now that it had all sunk in. "You're saying he, or whoever, had everything they needed, so again why involve us?"

"That's why." Williams pointed to the picture of the tattered remains of the plans Vogel had pulled up on one of the screens. "These plans, the schematics. You all said a full set was never found, right? Whoever that was in lab two, they knew how this would work, but they needed us to fill in the gaps, the missing pieces of their M31. I suspect we accomplished their goal last Friday."

"What about the brass doors?" Lemaire asked. "We all remember them being polished, not painted. The street signs too. Why do we remember things, the way they were before? If the past changed, wouldn't that mean *we* changed?" Lemaire again had a sincere yet cautious tone to her voice, the realities of the situation setting on.

"Yes. Yes, that would have to be true. We were as much a part of the past, this past, as anyone else out there. It would be impossible for the past to change and people, including us, not remember it that way. Short answer, I don't know." Williams turned and looked at door one. "But I'm going to find out. Let's have a look at that panel."

He started to make his way to lab two with the rest of the team following. He was cautious, for whatever reason, to make sure no one else was there. The team walked in, looked around to make sure it was all clear, then walked toward the panel. "Okay, stupid question, just checking, this thing is unplugged, right?"

"Ja, I made sure.

"Do you guys have any idea what's behind this?" Williams asked.

"Yes, but we don't really know what it does," Lemaire answered.

"I don't mean to be rude, but didn't you guys build this?"

"Yes and no," Engels stated.

"You're going to have to enlighten me."

Engels looked at Lemaire as if he were asking for permission to fill in the blanks. It was habit.

"Go ahead, no secrets," Lemaire said, approving.

"When we were brought on, most of the work done was analysis. You know, what does this thing do, what does that. That sort of stuff. We built some parts, but mostly the consoles and control equipment."

"So, who actually built this thing?" Williams asked, pointing to Andromeda. "Not you guys?"

"It wasn't just one company. We knew, or I should say we thought we knew, what we were building. But we didn't want anyone else to know. We also didn't have the material to support something like this by ourselves."

"So, you outsourced it? Maybe that explains our mystery man." Williams crossed his arms not believing that something so important as this was built by an outside company, maybe even the lowest bidder.

"Sort of. Like I said, we didn't want anyone to know its purpose. The work was broken up in sections and sent to five different companies, mostly in western Europe. None of them knew the other was part of it. Some of them weren't even the same industries. And as an added safety measure, each individual piece they were working on was a paper weight by itself. Couldn't do anything. You couldn't even power it on until all parts were together."

"Okay, I feel a little better, still don't have a clue who that guy is then. After everything was built, who put it together?"

"The three of us, that's where we came in, we just didn't build the major parts," Vogel added.

"What about this section. What do you know about it?" Williams was standing next to the area where the panel was located, where the mystery man made changes.

"It's the crystal," Lemaire spoke up.

"Crystal? What crystal?"

"Lemurian quartz. It's part of how we think this all works. It's a crystal, an oscillator. There is no oscillator as big as the two we have anywhere."

"Like an electronic circuit, a sine wave, that type of oscillator?"

"VCO," Vogel answered, "voltage-controlled oscillator to be exact."

"Industrial strength," Engels added.

"This is where the mystery man was working. There's something about that oscillator. Let's take a look. How do you get the panel open?" The location of the panel was clear to everyone in the room, however it lacked any sort of fastener or access method. Williams felt around looking for anything he could that resembled some sort of latch or opening mechanism.

"Here." Lemaire slightly nudged him out of the way, she pushed on the left side, top and bottom of the panel and it clicked open. She carefully slid the panel cover to one side. This was the first Williams would see of the inner workings of Andromeda. It was like nothing he had ever seen before. The oscillator itself was about ten inches long, and was secure lengthwise into the machine, almost as if it were plugged in to a socket. There were bright brass or copper looking cables that spanned out from the oscillators perch. Williams couldn't see where they went, just that they disappeared into other areas secure behind the machine's panels.

"What do those do?" Williams asked.

"The theory is they react with the vibration from the crystal oscillator, into a..." Lemaire stopped, "we don't even know. There's some relationship between the oscillator and the ports surrounding the center of the door. It's way ahead of its time, even to us. We just know it's what creates the field when the door is active."

"Does this look like it's all there?" Williams asked.

"Oui."

"And what happens if the oscillator is removed?"

"Nothing, nothing at all," Vogel answered. "We tried that, at the beginning. Without the oscillator nothing happens, we cannot even run the initiation sequence. A giant paper weight, as Bob said."

"So, it rules that out."

"What?" Engels asked.

"I thought maybe he took out the oscillator. But if the door doesn't work at all, then I would guess he did something else."

"We even had to try other crystal-based oscillators until we found this. Everything else didn't have the right frequency," Engels added.

"Say that again?" Williams turned to face Engels. "What did you just say?"

"What? That we had to try other oscillators to find the right frequency?"

"Yes, that. How many did you try?" Williams was on to something.

"All of them. I mean, we tried every crystal type on the planet, no lie."

"And what happened?"

"Most did nothing, and I mean nothing. Complete waste of time. A few caused a light or something to flicker, the quartz-based was the only one that actually created some sort of a field." Engels watched as Williams just stared at him, waiting to see if there was more. "That's all there is to it."

"He must have swapped out the oscillator. He had to have. He opened this up, swapped out the oscillator for something else, and when he delivered whatever he did, he swapped it back. Once he was done he went back and erased the logs, covering his tracks. Does that make sense?" Williams asked.

"I guess it is possible, but for one thing," Vogel added. "We tested every crystal-based oscillator known to man in this machine. François even had, I cannot remember his name, from the..." Vogel tilted his head, trying to remember where the man was from.

"The natural history museum," Engels finished.

"Ah, ja, the natural history museum. François acquired his help. He brought us dozens of sample crystals from all areas of the world. We created and tested oscillators from each type he was able to supply. It took months."

"Maybe the mystery man had something he didn't," Williams added.

"Something we've never heard of before? I would not believe it." Vogel turned and walked away.

"Would you believe Paris would hang street signs in German?" Vogel stopped and turned upon hearing what Williams just asked.

"I guess I..." Vogel started. His face wearing a long look, the kind that said he really had no answer. "I guess I would have to believe. We worked so long trying everything imaginable. The quartz was the only material that even made a difference. There was nothing else."

"It has to be something different." Williams lifted his index finger to his bottom lip. "Something else that we don't know about."

"Even so, this doesn't explain the street signs. We still have memories of things before they changed. If something was done to alter the past, why do we still remember?" Lemaire asked again, hoping a look at the panel would provide some clues. Williams looked up at the doorway, then back down at the tape separating the control room and lab.

"You said the oscillator creates the field, somehow anyway, right?"

"Oui. It's frequency," she answered.

"Maybe the field has something to do with it."

"But how?"

"We were all pretty close to this thing when it started, right? When the field was generated?"

"Yes, yes we were. Do you think that somehow shielded us? Protected us from the outside world?" Lemaire said, stepping closer to Williams.

"It's a theory. Not much to explain all of this, but in theory, it makes sense," Williams answered.

"But then that would mean..." Vogel stopped.

"What, what does it mean Gunter?" Engels asked.

"Our friend, the mystery man. He was within the field too, albeit in lab two."

"So?"

"So, he would remember too. He would be unchanged."

"Yes! Yes, he would, he would be just like us."

"Is that a good thing?" Engels was reacting to Williams's excitement.

"He doesn't know."

"He doesn't know what?" Engels tossed his pen from his lab coat in the air. "You guys are going to need to start explaining this better."

"He doesn't know that we are unchanged too. Don't you see? He is completely unaware that we know he turned on the machine." Williams started to smile as he pulled a small table closer to the Andromeda machine, near where the field would be generated, and set a chair on top of it.

"So he thinks he got away with, I don't even know, got away with whatever he did," Lemaire added.

"Exactly. I don't see how this could be anything other than an inside job. You all said it yourselves. You barely know the interior of this thing." Williams stopped and looked up at the machine again, then took a few steps back. "This guy knew too much, he knew what to do, he had help, probably from information he had from the Nazi's he's held onto for all these years. We got the project to where it needed to be, unaware of what we were actually working on. Now it's his turn, his turn to help them."

"What can we do? He's already given them something, that attaché," Lemaire pleaded.

"True. And there's no doubt it would ease my mind a bit if I knew what was in that case. But for now, we'll just have to go without. I've got another theory how we might be able to fix this, but first we need to get some information from our friend."

"How are we going to do that? We don't even know who he is," Engels asked.

"Right. But I suspect he's not done using this thing. Saturday was probably not the last day he planned to turn this on. And, are you ready for this?"

"Here we go again, what?" Engels asked.

"Last Saturday might not have been the first time he's used it."

"No way! We would know. We remember how things were." Engels didn't want to believe it.

"Yeah, but only if we were within the field. If he turned this on a month ago, we would be like everyone else, our past changed and not even know it. He would be the only person with any knowledge."

"The logs."

"The logs? Okay Bob, now you've lost me," Williams said.

"If he's done this before and did the same stuff he did Saturday he probably deleted the logs. Maybe they're intact, somehow, just like the other day. The consoles are close enough to the machine. I bet there're missing entries."

"Now that's worth looking into. Wouldn't know what changed, but at least we would know how long this has been going on."

"Okay, I'll check it out." Engels started to make his way back to control room one. "It's going to take some time."

"I'll help you. Maybe I can work with this footage and try to see if I can get a clear picture of who we are looking for." Vogel followed Engels. Once again Lemaire and Williams were alone. The looked at each other for a moment in silence.

"I don't get something," Lemaire said, sitting now, looking over the plans on the monitor.

"Just one thing?"

"If what we did this last weekend was the one thing that, whoever it is, needed to get Andromeda fully functioning, how could he have used it earlier?"

"Normally I would say that's not possible, but I've seen a lifetime of not possible in a few short minutes today alone. Things changed out there, which means, theoretically anyway, so have timelines."

"Merde."

Williams could see today's events were starting to wear on her. "You okay?" he asked.

"I don't know. I just don't see why anyone would do this, what would they have to gain? France is free, Europe is free. What this person is doing threatens all of that."

"No doubt. We have to find him. I think once we do we can get some real answers. We have an advantage, he was counting on no one else knowing." Williams reached into the pocket of his lab coat. "It's fully charged."

"What are you going to do with that?" Lemaire asked.

Williams then climbed on the table and chair he set up a few minutes prior, and reaching up, clamped the GoPro to an inconspicuous spot out of sight. "We can't stay here forever, close to the machine waiting for the field to kick on."

"And?"

"Theoretically we won't be protected if he turns this on when we're not in the lab. If he does, the past changes, our past, and we forget all about this. I'm banking on Bob noticing the wiped-out logs again. If we are smart enough, we'll come looking for this."

"What good will that do?" Lemaire asked.

"From this angle, tell us something about the past we're not supposed to know."

10. A Familiar Face

She stepped out from her bedroom, walking gently on the wood floor, barefoot, trying not to wake him. It was early and he was still asleep on the couch, where, given their new living arrangements, he agreed to stay. It was a lot for both of them to accept, just a week earlier being alone, and she thought, happy, for the most part. But now there she was, sneaking out of her own house. It wasn't that she wanted to hide anything, she just needed to get out, she needed her life to be what she considered normal. A morning walk in the park and a café noisette would do the trick.

She knew he wasn't going to be asleep for long, the sun was already starting to creep in. Walking slowly, she stayed near the picture wall of the hallway trying to keep the wood floor from creaking underneath. All old Parisian apartments where like that, it added character. She stopped for a moment, caught by her picture, the picture of her and Williams in New Orleans now hanging back in its place. The wall looked unfinished without it, so after a few days she put it back.

Reaching the front door, she slowly turned the bolt lock with one hand, pushing the door handle down with the other. As she pulled the door open slightly she looked over her shoulder to make sure she didn't wake him. "À plus tard," she said. *See you later.* She then slinked through the narrow opening and closing the door behind.

After taking a moment outside to slip on her shoes, she walked down the steps of her apartment, stopped, and took in a deep breath. She could smell the linden trees in the air, and for a moment forgot about everything.

Taking a few steps, she surveyed the landscape, just to make sure it was what she remembered. She took another deep breath, soon realizing she was doing so unconsciously and made a mental note to not do it again.

"Merde," she said, and then continued down the sidewalk, trying to stay out of the sun. The park was not far and to the west, so she headed in that general direction. She didn't take her normal route on purpose, wishing for a quiet walk, away from the hustle and bustle of the boulevards.

The crowds had already started to fill up the streets and into the chain coffee shops before a day of site seeing. "Merde," she whispered, it appeared like everyone had the same idea. But before she knew it, she was under a tree lined pathway in the heart of Champ de Mars, taking a long route to her café. She walked slowly, her eyes to the ground, purposely trying not to think of anything. It was impossible, an image of the street signs kept finding their way in. It wasn't why she was there, she wanted to see the things she remembered. She would make her way to her fountain.

For Lemaire, going to the park was best done in the early morning. It was close to Eiffel, and that meant there would undoubtedly be tourists. She didn't necessarily mind them, it was a way of life in Paris. But today she didn't want to be bothered, so she headed to her favorite spot. Just out of the way from the open grassy area of the park, hidden near a patch of Horse

Chestnut trees and Elder shrubs, was a small white fountain. Most of the time it wasn't running, but that didn't matter to her. The small square area around the fountain was framed by green park benches, and in the morning, they would be covered in shade. It was undiscovered by most. Perfect.

"Voilà," she said, as she rounded the corner of the pathway, Rue de Maréchal Harispe, the edge of one of the green benches in sight. There was no one else near the fountain when she arrived, so she picked one of the benches off to the side to take in the summer morning's air. With her legs crossed, she sat sideways, holding up her head with one of her arms resting atop the back rest of the bench. Once again, she tried to think of anything but the last few days. Andromeda was working, but not at all how they thought it should. There had to be answers, but they weren't where she was looking.

Slowly, she started to think about Williams. At first, she despised him. Legard made a decision that he would be brought on the project, her project, without her say so. She didn't need anyone meddling in something she spent so much time working on. But it wasn't that which was getting to her. He had been living at her place for a few days now, a result of something in the past that had changed. She was starting to like it. He genuinely wanted to see Andromeda work, almost more than she did, and that was getting her attention. She found herself thinking about him more and more.

"New Orleans," she whispered.

"Bonjour Mademoiselle," a voice said from one of the benches near the fountain. Lemaire jumped slightly. She was so lost in thought she didn't see or hear anyone step up. "It's a beautiful morning, isn't it?"

Lemaire looked over. "Bonjour," she said. He was a tourist, she thought, or at least he looked it, exactly what she didn't want or need right now. "Je ne parle pas anglais." *I don't speak English, now get lost.*

He looked directly into her eyes and smiled slightly, as if he hadn't seen his old friend in a long time. "I will have to admit, our meeting here isn't just by chance, Marie. May I call you Marie?" The man stood, walking closer to the bench where Lemaire was sitting. "May I?"

Confused as to how he knew her, and knew that she understood English, she answered. "Please, be my guest," allowing the man to sit next to her, "have we met before?"

"That's better. I will have to apologize for my rather unorthodox method of meeting with you, but, given the circumstances, this is the safest, for both of us." The man sat, closer to Lemaire than she was comfortable. "No, we haven't met before, and you don't know me. But I, we, know you." The man then looked out into the park as if to see what Lemaire had before he walked up. "It is a beautiful day today, isn't it? Paris is always wonderful during this time of year, wouldn't you agree?"

"Who are you, and what do you want?" Lemaire was starting to worry. *This is the safest way to meet? Who the hell are you?* She sat straight against the bench, and out of the corner of her eye she started to look for a way out of the alcove, even if that meant jumping over the hedges and into the park.

"Andreas. You may call me Andreas. Please Marie, I mean you no harm. I must be brief," he said, slowly pushing himself away as if to give her space, then looking around to see if he was being watched.

"What do you want?" Lemaire asked again.

"Very well, of course. I represent an international organization working on behalf of the government. I wonder if you might answer some questions I have about your work?" He held up a small identification card, far enough away so she couldn't make out anything. Just as she tried to get a batter look, he put it away.

"International organization? Check with the Interior office. They can answer anything you want to know. I cannot comment on such things without approval, and certainly, not here."

"I am afraid it's not that easy Marie. It's the interior we are investigating. Specifically, François Legard. Do you know him?" Lemaire's heart started to race when she heard Legard's name and that he was being investigated. *The ID, is he INTERPOL? I think so. That would make sense, especially if the Interior was being investigated. Still, it's very odd to meet like this.*

"Yes, what is this about? Is he in trouble?" she asked.

"No, no, I assure you he is not. We would just like to ask you a few questions about him... if you don't mind. You don't need to tell us anything that would compromise any agreements you have made regarding confidentiality if that would put you at ease."

"I suppose so, what exactly do you want to know? Why do you need me?"

"Can you tell me how long have known him?"

"For about five years or so. He recruited me from the university, to work on a project for the Interior. I don't see how that could be useful to you."

"Has he ever talked about his past to you, or to anyone you know? Specifically, where he is from?"

"His past? I think so, I mean, he's talked about where he had worked before, where he received his education, normal things," she answered, starting to wonder where this was going. "Nothing that isn't publicly known, I think even on the Interior website."

"Has he ever talked about his personal life, his mother or father?"

"Not particularly, though I think he mentioned his father before." *That's an odd question he asked, what about his family and what did that have to do with the Interior Ministré?*

"His father? What about his father?" he questioned, getting very excited by her mentioning it.

"What is this all about? Why do you want to know such things?" She started to feel uneasy again, something wasn't right. Legard was in a high position with the Interior, so it wasn't all that unusual for her to be asked about his professional background at some sort of event or lecture. But the man was asking about Legard's father, and that didn't make any sense. She started to push off from the bench with her hands as if she was going to leave. "I have to go."

"Please Marie, just a few more questions. What can you tell me about his father?" he asked, moving in closer to Lemaire. "Did he ever mention the resistance? Does he belong to any clubs, social or otherwise?" he added, getting even more excited with each question.

"I am leaving," she breathed, standing now, looking frantically for a way out from her secluded fountain.

"Does he have friends in positions of power? Please Marie! In banking or government?"

"I have to go, please." Lemaire started to walk away. The man stood, and for a moment Lemaire thought he was going to reach out and grasp her arm. She quickly started to move away, heading down the foot path. "Please, leave me alone."

"Marie, do you know what it is capable of?" Andreas asked loudly. She acted as if she didn't hear him, chills running down her spine. She didn't look back, making her way to Avenue Gustave Eiffel. The crowds were just now starting to gather around the tower, it would be safe there she thought.

"Merde," she breathed.

"We'll talk again Miss Lemaire," he said, turning to head into the park. "We'll talk again." He walked in the opposite direction of Lemaire, disappearing out of sight.

"Quel salaud," she whispered. *'It', what 'it' is capable of. How could he know? And why is he asking about François? I shouldn't have left Nick. Merde.* She started to walk faster, every few blocks looking back behind her to see if she was being followed. *How will I know?*

After a few blocks she came up to one of the chain coffee shop she passed on the way to the park. There were now a lot of people there, and she knew she would be safe for the most part until she figured out what to do. She reached into her pocket, realizing she didn't bring her cell phone with her when she left her apartment silently only a short time ago.

"Merde!" she barked, catching the attention of a few onlookers. She just stood, working out what to do in her head as she waited near the back of the café. After a few moments, she felt her only option was to get back to her apartment as soon as possible. She made her way to the terrace near the entrance, taking a brief look around before starting out. Her sun hat fell from her head slightly, getting caught in the air rushing past as her walk turned into a run. She quickly pulled it to her side and tucked it underneath her arm. *All those questions about François. Could he be the man who used Andromeda? There is no way he was from INTERPOL.*

Another few blocks from the café, Lemaire rounded the corner to her street. Out of breath from her run, she stumbled up the stairs. But before she could reach for the door, it opened, causing her to jump slightly.

"There you are. I started to think maybe something changed again and you were not around anymore. Crazy I know. It wasn't until I realized you left your purse. I called your cell, but it rang in your bedroom. Then I just didn't-"

"Oh Nick, it was a mistake, I should have stayed here," she said, falling into Williams who was standing in the doorway. She quickly pushed him aside and slammed shut the door behind.

"What do you mean? What's wrong?"

"I went out for coffee, I couldn't stand it and had to get out."

"Hey I'm not going to get in your way, this week's been a mess."

"A man approached me in the park. It was terrible."

"What? What happened? Who? Did he try anything, are you okay?" Williams started to look her over, just now noticing her hat at her side, crushed under her arm. He took it and placed it on the three-legged coat rack she had standing next to the entrance. "What did he do?"

"It wasn't like that. He stopped me in the park, out of sight by a fountain I sometimes go to. It was like he knew I was going to be there. He said he worked for some international organization for the government."

"The government? You mean the Interior?" Williams asked.

"He flashed some badge, I don't know." She took a few steps in, leaning against the wall in a corner of the apartment still trying to catch her breath.

"What did he want? What did he say?" he asked.

She said, holding her left hand in front of her eyes, "He started to ask me about François. He was polite at first, but then started to ask about his father. The man, I remember him saying his name was Andreas, he got very excited. He just kept asking question after question, I couldn't answer even if I wanted to. He just kept pushing."

"François? Why would he want to know about François?" Williams started to pace. "The government? Why wouldn't they just check with... themselves?"

"I thought he was with INTERPOL, the way he sounded, but he just wouldn't stop." Lemaire took a deep breath, remembering her mental note from earlier. "I think François might be in danger. We need to talk to him now," she commanded, making her way to her bedroom. After a moment she emerged, holding her phone in front of her desperately trying to unlock it.

"Hold on! Hang up, stop dialing, whatever, but don't call him."

Lemaire looked up, dropping her arms to her sides, no longer searching for Legard's number. "I want to argue with you but I am so scared. Why not?" she asked.

"What if, that Andreas guy, he didn't actually say he's with the French government, or INTERPOL, right?"

"No, no, he didn't, and I couldn't see his identification to be sure."

"What if he's trying to get François to make a move? To do something. Maybe their trying to get information about Andromeda and were using you make that happen."

"Quel salaud. Do you think they're spying on him? Do you think he's in danger?" she asked.

"Probably. To both of those questions," he said, pointing to her phone.

"Merde," she replied, then gently placed her phone on a side table that she was now standing next to. "Do you think so? But that means-"

"That means we're probably in the same boat."

"Merde," Lemaire said as she sat on the couch Williams had been using for a bed the past few nights.

"Did Andreas say anything else?"

"I think he said we'll talk again. Oh Nick, what are we going to do? I am so afraid."

"I don't know. We need to talk to Gunter and Bob. Maybe we can talk to François Monday, too. At least one thing is for sure."

"What's that?" Lemaire asked.

"He isn't dangerous, at least not yet. If Andreas wanted to do something he probably would have already done it, this morning, in the park."

"That's it. I am not leaving here. I am not going anywhere. I'll only go to the lab where it's-"

"Where it's safe? It still is, I hope," he said, finishing her sentence. "That's probably not a bad idea, not going anywhere, at least not alone." Williams started to make his way to the kitchen. "I need coffee. Did you have anything?"

"I had.... no. No, I was on my way to the café when I stopped in the park. I talked for a moment then I ran home."

"I'll make us some. It won't be as good as that café, what was the name of that place we went to, near the Eiffel? I can't remember."

"Alexandre. Café Alexandre. And I don't care, anything will be fine," she said, still weak from her unexpected run. She could hear Williams working away in the kitchen. She felt useless, so she leaned back on the couch looking up at the ornamental plaster ceiling. After the mornings excitement she only had the strength to sit on the couch. Every noise she heard outside she assumed was someone spying. No matter where she sat she felt as if she was being watched. "How long do you think he's been following me?"

"No telling," he said as he emerged from the kitchen holding two coffees, handing one to Lemaire.

"Merci."

"I don't want to worry you more, but he's probably been tailing you for a while. You said for yourself, it was as if he knew you would be there. For all we know, he, or them, whoever they are, have been watching all of us, waiting for the right time to start asking questions."

"That's it!" Lemaire sat up. "I knew I've seen him before. I saw him when we went for coffee, at Alexandre. You reminded me when you asked about the name of the café. I saw him when we were leaving, do you remember, he looked away. And another time, by the Musée."

"That answers that I guess." Williams took a sip of his coffee. "Not bad, for an American."

"There's something else. Something else he said."

"I was afraid of that." Williams pushed over a few pillows and blankets, not yet putting his things away from his night on the couch, then sat next to Lemaire.

"I felt scared, so I started to run." She put her head in her hands again, her eyes starting to tear up. "He said something, something that upset me, even more than the questions about François."

"What, what did he say?" Williams asked.

"He asked me if I knew what it was capable of."

"So that's out," Williams said, pacing back and forth. "Unless." He quickly started down through the lab to the hallway that led to lab two, taking one of the cables that was lying on a table near the bucket of red toy balls.

"Where are you going?" Lemaire asked, her and the rest of the team following close behind. Williams stopped just inside lab two, pausing for a moment, then searched for something above. He peered under the sensors, cameras, and monitoring equipment near Andromeda, puzzled.

"Weird. I don't see it. I swear I put it right here before we ran the test." He kept searching, walking near the opening of the machine, looking up between all the scaffolding and sensor equipment. "Huh. There it is. I don't remember putting it this close. I thought I put it back there, where I could get a good view of the ball coming out of the door." He then pulled a small table near the machine, balanced a small folding chair on top, and precariously climbed his impromptu ladder to retrieve the GoPro.

"Don't drop it," Engels warned as he moved to position himself underneath where Williams was climbing.

"I think it's just this.... damn!" Williams pulled a lever and the GoPro slipped from its mount. Before he could react, he looked down to see Engels holding the camera in his hands.

"Told you not to drop it."

"Yeah. Yeah you did. Nice catch." Williams slowly made his way down from the make shift climbing apparatus to the floor below. "I don't know when the battery went out, but maybe it lasted until after the incident."

"Worth a shot," Engels said as he made his way over to the center console, trying to affix the adapter cable to the camera. "Hey Gunter, can you log on?"

With a whip of his arm Vogel quickly slid off the vinyl cover from the terminal and entered his sign on criteria. "You should be good to go," he added as he cleared the way.

"Cool. Let's see what we can see."

"What exactly are we looking for?" Lemaire asked.

"I don't know. Maybe we should start around when the other door kicked on. What time was that?" Williams asked, looking to Vogel.

"Nine AM, yes?" Vogel said, looking at his watch he pulled from underneath his lab coat.

"Let's start then, maybe watch at an accelerated speed, until we see something."

"Okay. Should be almost there." Engels worked carefully to scan the footage to where they wanted to start, every now and then stopping to be sure he didn't go over their target. "Okay, here, eight forty-five AM. Looks dark. Nobody in there."

"I swear I put the camera over here, right above the console," Williams said while pointing above the center console. "I have no idea how it ended up over-"

"THERE!" Engels interrupted. "Someone's there, in the dark. Just before nine AM. Look, they're screwing with Andromeda. I can't tell what, it's too dark."

"Looks like whoever it was did something to that panel. But what?" Lemaire spun around to get a better look at Andromeda and the area she saw from the footage.

"Look, they're heading back to the console. Looks like a man, can't tell who though." Williams and the team continued to watch the video feed, and witnessed the man enter the field with an attaché. They watched in amazement as he emerged empty handed and were completely caught off guard when they saw the scientist walk through.

"Bob, any chance you can zoom in to a certain area on that footage?" Williams asked.

"Sure, it's going to take a minute, what do you want to see?"

"That guy, scientist or whoever. He's got something on his coat. I want to see what it is."

Engels pulled up the video again and zoomed in to the man standing just in front of the door. Vogel was standing off to the right of the team, not looking at the footage. He knew something but couldn't believe what he was seeing. Williams went in for a closer look.

"Is that? Oh no. Gunter, is it?"

"What?" Engels squinted, trying to get a batter look at the section of the footage he had just zoomed in on. "Can someone please explain to me what's going on. I don't get it."

"What is it Nick, tell me," Lemaire pleaded, looking directly at Williams, the grasp she had on his arm slipping as he slowly walked away from the console and headed closer to Vogel.

"It's what's on his lab coat, isn't it Gunter?"

"Ja, Herr Williams."

"What's on his coat? I can't tell." Engels tried to get a better look. Lemaire followed by Williams's side, who then ran back to the console to try to pull up an image on the internet.

"You can't Nick, it's an isolated network," she explained.

"Damn!"

"Hold on guys? You need to see this."

"What, Bob? What is it? Were you able to get a clearer image?" The team all gathered around Engels.

"There's like, about another thirty minutes of video on this thing. But it's not him I want you to see." He rolled his chair back so Williams and the rest of the team could get a good look.

"What's going on here?"

"That's you. What are you doing on the video feed after this guy opens the door?"

"I have no idea. Wait, look!" Williams pointed.

"It's....us." What's going on?" Lemaire asked.

Vogel simply stood, still speechless.

"Look, he's...I mean I, am taking video of the ceiling. Hey, that's where I put the camera for Friday's test, I am sure of it."

"What's that you're showing us in your hand?" Lemaire asked.

"Is the volume on? Why can't we hear anything? Stop the footage for a sec."

"Yeah, should be, it's pretty simple, plug and play." Engels picked up the GoPro to inspect the device when he noticed a small scratch and dent on the corner of the camera. "Huh. Did you drop this when you set it up? Looks like the mic is busted. You almost can't tell."

"Not that I remember. I guess that explains why we don't have sound. Can you go back a few seconds?"

"No prob." Engels reversed the footage to show Williams holding up something in his hand. "Any of you guys read lips?"

"Nope. Looks like he's...looks like I'm holding a key. Damn I wish we had sound. I don't know what I'm saying."

"I caught a few words, it would have been better if you spoke German," Vogel answered, now standing behind the others. He paused as if waiting for agreement to his statement. "You said it's a key to the cabinet, and something about a list. But that's all I could get."

"Hold on. Check this out. You just gave the key to Marie." Engels pointed to the screen, freezing it at the point where Williams handed the key to Lemaire.

"Appears that way. You don't have any idea where..." Williams stopped mid-sentence as he turned to look at Lemaire. Her head was down, her eyes fixed on a small key in the palm of her hand.

"It's the key you gave me. I found it in my desk a few days ago. I had no idea what it was for and thought nothing of it, until now."

"And I don't remember giving it to you. Well, what do you say we find out which one it belongs?"

Lemaire agreed, then walked to the section of wall where there were about five steel cabinets. "Here goes," she said, slowly reaching out her hand, ready to try the first lock.

"It's not that one," Engels interrupted.

"What?"

"It's not that one. It's the last one. It's right here, on the footage. I guess we left ourselves a shot of it, for whatever reason."

Lemaire pulled back her hand, then walked to the end of the row of cabinets. She inserted the key and twisted her wrist. "Voilà," she said as she turned and looked at Williams who was now standing by her side.

"Yeah. Open it. Let's see what's inside." On Williams's suggestion, Lemaire pulled on the doors of the cabinet. It was almost completely empty, except for a one small item lying on the shelf.

"It's just a trashy notebook."

"It's Bob's. Look at the coffee rings on the cover. I noticed that the first day I met you all," Williams explained, leaning over to get a better look at the new discovery.

"Guys, there's something else, it doesn't stop. There's footage from... this angle." Engels pointed to where Williams stood earlier, atop the table and chair where they found the GoPro just a short time ago, then looked over to Williams and Lemaire. "Hey, is that my notebook?"

"Look at the date-time stamp. That's not until next week," Vogel added, looking over Engel's shoulder.

"That's not possible. Do you think someone messed with the date and time?" Engels asked.

"It would have to have been us who did it, right? I mean, we taped ourselves, we set up the camera, Marie's key."

"Yeah, Gunter, and I don't see any reason why we would do that. Let's see what's on it."

"Eight forty-five AM again?" Engels asked.

"Why not," Williams answered as he stepped up behind Engels and Vogel. Lemaire was busy flipping through the pages of the recently discovered notebook.

"Jeez. Looks dark again." Engels rolled his chair closer to his console. "I'll move it up, slowly. Holy crap, look."

"Can you bring it up a few minutes," Williams asked.

"There, done. That looks like the same dude, right?"

"Yeah, sure does. I still can't get a good look though. Do you guys recognize him?

"Nope. Still too dark. Whoa, wait a minute, that's no attaché, that thing's a crate. What do you think he's doing?" Engels asked. The man in the footage was wheeling a large yellow plastic crate through the activated field, disappearing through the haze.

"I wish I knew, it's a lot bigger than that briefcase. What does that notebook say? Anything useful?" Williams asked, directing his question to Lemaire. She didn't respond. "Marie?"

"Hmm? Oh. I'm not sure." She was lost looking through the pages of the notebook, standing close to the machine. "What is this? Did I write all of this? It's my handwriting."

"What does it say?" Williams asked. He, Engels, and Vogel were all still hovering over the console.

"It says someone started door two when we were in lab one Saturday. But it says it happened a week ago."

"A week ago? I guess that explains how this thing kicked on. But a week ago? We just started to see things differently, since last Saturday when we were trapped."

"Does it say who those people were, or what was in that attaché?" Vogel asked.

"Non. Merde. It says we were wrong about the purpose of this machine."

"Nick, what's this about 1945? What is all this? There must be pages and pages here." Lemaire handed the notebook to Williams who, after a glance, handed it to Vogel.

"I can't believe it. Once I saw the scientist's lab coat, I knew." Williams added, pacing again.

"I told you he looked off. That was a Nazi eagle on his coat, wasn't it?" Engels asked.

"The machine. It was never a doorway from one place to another. It's a doorway from one time to another. The future versions of ourselves on the GoPro found that out, and for some reason, and somehow left this information for us to find."

"How is that even possible? How did we know all this stuff? It was just turned on last Saturday, right?" Engels asked.

"That's the reason!" Williams exclaimed.

"What?"

"That's the reason we left this. Andromeda was opened a week ago, by the looks of it. At least that's what the first part of the footage shows us, that and what we taped of ourselves."

"Okay guys, I'm lost again." Engels pushed back on his chair, pausing the video not wanting to look at the console images anymore.

"The first time that guy went into the door with the attaché, that was a week ago. A week ago, we came back here, looking for the GoPro, and we found it. We found it right where I left it, over there." Williams pointed to the area back by the rear of the lab where he originally planned to cover the door.

"Okay, I'm still with you," Engels added.

"We set up the GoPro again, maybe to get a better look at who's using the door, or if they tried again. We even left us some information on this notebook locked in that cabinet."

"It looks like they did. They did try again, didn't they?" Lemaire asked.

"Yes. Yes, they did. And whatever was in that yellow case, or whatever the other guy on the other side of the doorway did with it, changed our past. That's why things aren't as we remember them. And by looking at the footage, it's at least the second time it's been done too."

"But why are things just now different?" Vogel asked.

"They're not. Not just now."

"What do you mean?"

"Things changed a week ago too. We just don't remember." Williams slowly walked closer to the machine in lab two. "I have a question for you. What happened Saturday that hasn't happened before?"

"Andromeda powering on by itself. Or I guess the mystery man powering it on," Lemaire answered.

"Right, in a way. And, where were we?"

"Standing about where you are, but in lab one."

"Yep. We were in lab one, close to the field generators. Gunter, do we tell ourselves anything about what led up to coming to the lab that Saturday a week ago?"

"I don't see any mention.... wait, here's something. It says, I don't believe it."

"What does it say?"

"It says Saturday...it's dated last week, we were going over what you, Nick, noticed about the lettering on the ball, when Andromeda turned on by itself. The four of us were in lab one, you and Marie on the other side of the field, trapped."

"Hold on, that just happened two days ago. Didn't it?" Engels asked.

"Yes. And a week ago."

"How? How is that possible?" Lemaire asked.

"The field, the field created by Andromeda, that shielded us somehow. It kept us from being impacted by anything that changed in the past."

"But if we are not near the field..." Lemaire started.

"My guess is that we found the footage with that man and the attaché a week ago. However, since then, he used Andromeda again, but we weren't here. That changed everything. That caused the past to be altered in such a way that the ball didn't change until last Friday, a week later. All according to events on this new timeline."

"Which made it so we didn't come in to the lab until a week later," Vogel finished.

"Precisely. The GoPro and notebook tell the whole story because they've always been in the lab, protected by the field. The field is the key, it has an effect on everything within a range of the machine, an andromeda effect."

"So wait. We remember how things were before because we were near the field?" Engels asked.

Williams nodded in agreement.

"But the way we remember everything to be as of Friday is actually different than how things actually were a week ago?"

"On our original timeline, yes."

"I think I am going to be sick. What makes you so sure?"

"It's here."

"What is Gunter?"

"It's here. We left a list for ourselves. It's in a section of this notebook, 'CHANGES'. It lists all the...all the things we noticed that were different a week ago. You drove a BMW Bob."

"What? I did? Not my VW?"

"Yes, you noticed it didn't have a tear in the seat and had less miles. Imagine that."

"My VW is in good shape, and they can drive forever. Was my Beemer a 3 series or better?" Engels asked.

"I am sorry Bob, you were not detailed enough in the past to mention it. Me however, I got back a few books I threw out." Vogel stopped reading and glanced over to the team. "Why would I have ever thrown out books? Who does that?"

"So things are different, even from what we remember. All because this person," Lemaire pointed down to the console that had the image of the mystery man paused as he was in mid stride, "started the door when we were not here."

"Yes. We don't remember our past anymore. And if he does it again and we are not here, we'll think everything we find so strange today is normal," Williams finished, walking back to the table and chair he still had set up near the machine.

"Oh wow. It's true."

"What is Bob?" Vogel asked.

"The logs. I went back and checked them from last week. I can't believe it, it's the same thing. One week ago, today, completely blank. There's absolutely no entries. The rest of the week is fine until last Saturday."

"What about our tests this week?" Vogel asked.

"All there, just two portions are wiped out, but I see our tests from last week, and me and Gunter logging on a little while ago. That guy's really done this before," Engels added, pointing to the logs he now had up on the console.

"Well, he's consistent, whoever he is. He's deleted logs during the same timeframe for two Saturdays. I wonder if he'll do it a third time?" Williams questioned.

"What else does it say Gunter?" Lemaire asked.

"There must be at least a hundred pages here, it will take some time to go through."

"They...I mean, *we*, must have taken some time to put it all together," Lemaire said.

"Here's a section titled 'SAME', what do you suppose that means?" Vogel asked, spinning around in his chair to look at the rest of the team.

"One way to find out?"

"Right! Let's see, aha. Descriptions, places and things around Paris. Why would we need to know about that?" Vogel asked.

"Maybe in case they are different now. Let's hear one."

"The Louvre."

"Never heard of it," Williams said.

"Le Musée National d'Art Classique. Hasn't been called The Louvre for decades," Lemaire added.

"You suppose it was the Louvre until last Saturday? Could it have been something that changed?" Williams questioned.

"What else is there?" Lemaire went on.

"The Eiffel Tower."

"Nothing new there, that hasn't changed." Lemaire sat now at one of the open consoles. "I was in the park this morning. This is so strange talking about things as if they are not real."

"Here's one, it looks like it is an entry for you Marie. A place called Café Alexandre, down Bourdonnais straße, near Eiffel. Do you know it?"

"No, I don't go that way much. What does it say about it?"

"Corner place near Eiffel with whicker seating surrounding the terrace. There is a red and white striped awning, and you know a waiter names Lucas. It says you go and have a café noisette almost daily."

"Café Rostov? That's near Eiffel, and on the same street. I don't know a Lucas though, and the service is terrible. They don't have a red and white awning either, it's green and-" Lemaire suddenly stopped, wondering if she really did go to Café Alexandre daily. She realized now that the past had changed, she wouldn't know.

"Maybe that's enough of the comparisons for now," Williams interjected. "We should probably think about our next steps."

"We have to destroy it. Before he opens it again and screws up something else. The way I see it, I am down a Beemer, that's got to stop," Engels argued, not holding back his thoughts on Andromeda.

"Yes. We need to blow it up, or something. There's no telling how much has changed that we didn't write to ourselves. What if.... what if it was free?" Vogel asked.

"What are you saying Gunter?"

"What if we didn't need papers Marie, identification, to walk around Paris before last week? What if people didn't have to watch what they say?"

"Stop Gunter."

"I know we shouldn't talk about it. I am the last, you know that. But what if? There's no mention of these things in this notebook. We have to ask ourselves these questions."

"I don't think we should destroy Andromeda," Williams added.

"Why not? You see the footage, you see the documents in that notebook," Engels said, standing now, his hands out questioning Williams's statement. "This guy, who we don't even know, has screwed up things, big time. Why shouldn't we?"

"He's giving that Nazi scientist, and who knows who else, information. If I were to guess, probably info that changed the outcome of the war in Germany's favor. For all we know, before last week, it didn't end in a stalemate. Maybe Germany lost?"

The team looked around at each other after what Williams just said.

"All the reason more to destroy it."

"Robert!" Lemaire barked. "You're talking about destroying something we've been working on for over half a decade. I will not let that happen."

"Look at the evidence. What if things weren't this way before?" Engels asked.

"We can't," Williams interrupted. He pulled down the chair he used to retrieve the GoPro, set it next to the table and sat.

"You're going to have to do a better job at convincing me. At this point I don't see any other choice," Engels said, turning to face the console once again.

"Why not Nick?" Vogel pleaded.

"If things were different, better maybe, and I am inclined to think they might have been, if we destroy this machine," Williams pointed to the doorway, "we destroy any chance of setting things back."

"I can't believe this," Engels moaned, now holding his head in his hands.

"Do we say anything about this in that notebook?" Williams asked Lemaire, who was now looking over the notebook again, anxious to see if there was anything else she knew that had now changed.

"Yes, yes we do. We say we can't destroy it. We would be forced to live our lives in this reality."

Williams got up and made his way to the void in the middle of Andromeda. "So we'd be stuck here."

12. Business as Usual

"So what do we do now?" she asked, everyone now back in control room one.

"On the surface act like we're just doing what we always do," Williams answered, assuming his position near Engels's console. "Bob, do you see anything planned, a test or anything?"

"Yep. Looks like we have one scheduled in about ten minutes."

"Wouldn't that be useless, dangerous even given the circumstances?" Vogel asked.

"Maybe so, but until we get some answers we will have to spin our wheels a while. If it says we have a test planned, then we should run a test. Most likely, whoever turned it on knows what we have planned."

"What if it isn't useless? I'm not in any hurry to screw anything else up you know," Engels added.

"I don't think we have to worry about that."

"How do you know? I mean, seriously?" Engels countered, clearly worried.

"We don't have the right oscillator, or whatever it is, that I think made this thing work to begin with. The only thing we did was power off the externals, all the sensors and such. That's where we should be anyway, according to the footage. As a matter of fact," Williams stepped down closer to Andromeda, "we should power all that back on."

"But you said it messed with the field, what good would that do?" Lemaire asked.

"Nothing. It won't do any good. In fact, I am hoping it will interfere with the field enough to cause a failure."

"Very good Nick. That should buy us some time, I agree," Vogel said, hurriedly bringing his console to life to prepare for the test.

"Right. Then we'll spend the rest of the afternoon trying to figure out more on our mystery man."

"Why should we even bother then. Why not just try to figure out what happened?"

"I'm with you Bob, but I suspect this to be an inside job. I don't see any other way around it. It could be anyone with any knowledge of Andromeda, and that doesn't leave too many. They don't know we were caught in the Andromeda field, so we have to play along, at least for a little while. You got it?"

"I guess. Still don't like the idea though."

"We should do our best to act ignorant," Williams said with a smile, making sure to look over to Lemaire to get her reaction.

"Well, I think we have that covered," she replied, a rare quip before she walked back to her console.

"If we have a test planned for nine AM, we should probably get started," Vogel interrupted.

"Oui, right, you know what to do. Let me know when we are at the one-minute mark." Lemaire started to pull up the initiation sequence on the terminal, clearing a strand of hair from her face.

"All sensory equipment is powered on, all IR and motion detectors initialized just for good measure."

"Good. We'll need all the help, lack of a better word, we can get." Williams took up position near the ball bucket as was his usual station before things started to change.

"Initiation in one minute," Vogel called out. "We're just going to turn this on and then off right? We're not actually going to try anything else, are we?"

"Yes. We just want it to appear that we tested, whether or not a ball goes through doesn't matter, it's the sequences that will be logged," Lemaire answered, diligently typing away on her console.

"Cameras on, blah, blah." Engels was going through the motions. The team did everything they would normally do, logging on, running sequences, calling out their commands, all of it. They didn't want to take chances of whoever was responsible for using Andromeda finding out they know something about it.

"I'm ready to run the sequence. At zero."

"You are okay to start Marie," Vogel called out, letting her know they were at the zero mark.

"Okay, here goes. I'm activating." She clicked on the icon she had pulled up on her console. The machine, as they knew it anyway, hummed to life. The familiar flash of light, followed by the blue glimmer, they could see the field was on.

"It's energized. The field, the field is fluctuating, as we suspected," Vogel added, turning to look over to Lemaire.

"Well, at least we confirmed our suspicions about the interference of the monitoring equipment, didn't we?" Lemaire said openly.

"Yeah, thought the same thing. Still progress I guess," Williams added, his back still to the rest of the team, watching the field glow before him.

"Okay Robert," Lemaire called out, "go ahead."

Engels pressed the release for the ball, but Williams never loaded it. They weren't going to go that far. There was no point. No one would know anyway, the only action recorded in the logs was Engels hitting the release, and that's all they needed.

"And the ball…" Engels made the bunny ear gesture again, "is on its way."

"I'd say that's good enough." Williams turned and headed to Marie's console. "Might as well shut it down."

"Running shut down sequence," she replied. She clicked the icon from the menu she pulled up the moment the doorway turned on. She wasn't going to wait any longer than necessary. She didn't want to risk anything.

"And… there it goes." Engel pointed to the blue light fading. With little excitement, the light disappeared, the humming stopped, and the field was no longer active.

"Let's hope they still call it Paris," Williams joked.

"Don't say such things," Lemaire whispered. "It will always be Paris. That's the least of our concerns."

"It's less exciting I would say, knowing what this is really for. Almost uninspiring," Vogel added. "Part of me hoped that scientist from the footage would pop through, just so we could ask him some questions."

"Not me. If I go the rest of my life without actually meeting a real Nazi, I'd call that a win." Engels leaned back in his chair while his backup was running. "Storing backup in the usual place, blah, blah."

"What would you ask him Gunter?" Vogel's comment made Williams curious. He thought the same thing, almost as soon as he saw the image of the scientist peer through the doorway, but he wanted to hear what Vogel would ask.

"And not if he knows your dad or anything Gunter, that would be lame," Engels joked.

"I would first ask him his name. Of course, not just to see if we are related," Vogel anticipated Engels next jab, "but to see if I know him. All of this, all of this is a direct result of German research of the 1940's." Vogel started to walk closer to Andromeda. "It would be hard to believe someone who could pull this off would be unknown, both then, and now. He would have to have been in some sort of science literature of the time, and, presumably if he made it through the war, now."

"I doubt we could deny that. Von Braun, Schwesinger to name a few. Who knows, maybe that guy was part of Operation Paperclip."

"Operation Paperclip? What's that? The US's effort to keep things nice and tidy in Europe during the war?"

"Nice try Bob." Williams eyed over in Engels's direction, reminding himself of Travis back home. "It was their effort to recruit former Nazi scientists and other useful people for an advantage over the Soviet Union after the war. They were our ally against Germany, but everyone knew that would be different once the war ended. And it was. My guess is that scientist was on the list of personnel to relocate, unless of course the Soviet's got him. That would be a different story altogether."

"I would ask him why he thinks changing the past is a good idea," Lemaire added.

"Ah, but on the contrary. From his perspective, he's not changing the past. The farthest back one could even go with this is 1945, when they first opened their door. Anything earlier than that, their past, wouldn't have changed. It was the future they were concerned about."

"It would be no different."

"No, to us it wouldn't, but we all try to alter the future, with almost everything we do, right? The difference is, with this," Williams pointed to Andromeda, "they will know the outcome of their decisions, we won't".

"Well then, what would you ask him?" Lemaire turned to face Williams, which caught him off guard.

"Well, I guess I would, I-" Just then, a beep from the key pad interrupted Williams mid-sentence. The door to the entrance of lab one swung open slowly and a man entered.

"Bonjour all," Legard said. "Ah, I see you are wrapping up another successful test. I must have missed it, again. I will have to make sure I catch the next one, it has been too long."

"I don't know if we can call it a success, at least not yet." Vogel started to head to the back of the control room.

"I am sure Gunter, you are on the right track. News of a breakthrough is due any day now, I know it."

"Well, then you are a little more optimistic than I. It's nice to see you today anyway."

"You all have made great strides with this project from the beginning, and I suspect more to come. I would however like to suggest some changes in the near future. Perhaps we can meet tomorrow to discuss?" Legard looked at Lemaire and them Williams, who then looked at each other.

"Ah, sure, I don't see an issue, Marie?" Williams asked.

"No, if we have time we will meet tomorrow." It was what she didn't need. Someone used Andromeda and changed the past, and now Legard wanted to make changes. It was going to complicate things.

"That will be fine. I will make sure Adriane schedules some time. I am sorry to have disturbed you after your test, however I have an important meeting this weekend for which I must prepare and this was the only time I had available to see all of you." Legard turned to look at Andromeda. "It truly will be marvelous, wouldn't you say? The thought of being able to travel in an instant to other parts of the world. Truly marvelous. Anyway," he finished. He waived his hat in the air as he turned to the exit saying, "Adieu," then made his way out of the lab.

"That was odd. I don't think I ever heard him say anything about us getting anywhere on this. I thought for sure he was going to complain about the budget or something again," Lemaire questioned.

"Yeah me too. I wonder what tomorrow's meeting is about?" Engels asked.

"He's probably going to push me aside. I can feel it."

"Maybe. I have no clue what he would want to talk about." Williams took a few steps closer to where Legard stood. "He's acting on behalf of a timeline that changed though, so it could be anything."

"I don't wish to be sidelined no matter the timeline." She turned and sat. "He's still a bastard."

"There was something else about him. I can't quite put my finger on it," Williams added while walking over to the door where Legard had just exited. "I don't know what it is. Anyway, it seems he still thinks it's a teleporter."

"Or he is just playing the part," Lemaire added.

"Yeah, that too."

"He looked weird. Glad he didn't stay long," Engels said.

"He seemed kind of chatty. Maybe it was just the way he addressed us all. I can't seem to think of it." Williams then started to walk back down to the lab when he stopped. "Wait." He turned and looked back at the entrance. "Something I can't put my finger on. Bob, you've got that backup footage from the GoPro, right?"

"Yeah, at least I think it's still here. I remember it at least, so that means the past hasn't changed again, right?"

"Pull it up. There's something I want to see again, something I want to check." Williams made his way to Engels's terminal.

"What? Did we miss something?" Vogel asked. "I went over that a hundred times. There's nothing but shadows and that scientist, and you can barely see him."

"Pull the footage after we see ourselves, the second time the doorway was opened. That should be the one with the better angle."

"Okay, here goes. One sec, got to skip past all this other stuff. Okay, I think this is the first time, the one none of us remember which is crazy by the way." Engels was forwarding through the footage at ten times speed. "Here's us again. Still can't get over that either. Okay, should be almost there, I'll slow it down."

"Okay. It should be here, somewhere. Where are you?" Williams was clearly on to something. "Can you slow it down, I think it will be there for only a second or two?"

"What are you looking for?" Vogel and Lemaire were both behind Williams now at Engel's console.

"Something I noticed, but it didn't strike a bell until a few minutes ago." Williams had his arms crossed, tapping his fingers against his side. "There! Stop. Rewind, go back, back it up a few seconds and stop."

"No problem. Don't see anything but darkness, maybe a shadow. I don't see the scientist yet, maybe he's back in his time again."

"Right there." Williams pointed to a small section of the footage. "What is that?" Williams tried to move his head to get different angles to identify what he was look for. "Any chance you can enhance this area? Maybe contrast the lighting?"

"Don't see why not. Give me a second," Engels responded.

"What is that? And why did he…. I'll be damned."

"What? What is it? I can't make it out." Engels pulled a closer image of the object on the screen.

"It's a hat. It's the brim of a fedora or something similar, resting upside down." Williams got out of the way so the team could get a closer look.

"That's a hat alright. Now that you mention it I can make it out," Lemaire said.

"Not just any hat, and not just anyone's hat."

"You are losing me again. What do you mean?" Engels questioned.

"He had it with him, just a few minutes ago. He waved goodbye to us with it as he left."

"François? What would he be doing with the hat in this...." Engels stopped and rolled his chair back. The rest of the team stood silently, making the connection, not sure what next to do.

"I can't believe it. I just can't believe it. It's him. It was an inside job. It all makes sense. François is the mystery man, and he stood there and lied to us," Lemaire finished.

"François is the mystery man, certainly looks that way." Williams started to pace.

"He *could* access all of our data, all of our notes. That would explain so much," Lemaire said, now crossing her arms. "The bastard."

"Why would he have to? If he had notes on almost everything from the Nazi's?" Engels added.

"Because he didn't have everything."

"What do you mean? He had everything," Engels reiterated.

"He didn't have it all. Remember, the schematics, the plans never made it to Keitel because the Russians invaded Berlin. And whatever ended up in Russian hands were incomplete and partially destroyed."

"Soviet," Vogel correcting.

"Right, Soviet. If I were to guess, I don't think the plans were even intended to go to someone like François.

But somehow, he knew of their existence and knew what to do once this thing was fired up."

"Do you think this is all part of something bigger?" Lemaire asked.

"It would have to be. There's no way one man could have persuaded any government body to create all this without help," Williams said while pointing to Andromeda, walking closer to get a better look. "Maybe that's what was in that attaché."

"What? I don't see," Lemaire asked, confused.

"François handed over an attaché, from the camera footage. Someone was waiting for it, they knew François was going to deliver it. Maybe they didn't expect François, maybe they thought it was going to be one of Keitel's men."

"I am sure of it," Vogel added. "From the intercepted order."

"Right. But it was François, and I suspect he handed them something important, something they could use. Maybe government secrets after the war, something he got his hands on from other members of his organization. That could be anyone, even people who hold sensitive positions throughout European governments, positions of power."

"And the Nazi's used this information to their advantage," Vogel added, walking near where Williams was standing.

"They used that information to change timelines. Each transfer was enough information for that to happen. We weren't supposed to know."

"Exactly Marie. Because of the andromeda effect we traversed timelines. That was an accident." Williams sat again.

"What do you think would happen if someone finds out?" Lemaire asked, worried.

"I would suspect they wouldn't take it too lightly," he joked.

"We would disappear," Engels added.

"Oh Bob." It was one of the few times Lemaire called him Bob.

"You kidding? You heard Nick, it would have to go higher than François. No doubt. High level government stuff, shadow ops and all that crap. We weren't supposed to know anything. We were just supposed to get this thing running, then someone would change the past and we would forget all about it. But something went wrong. They never intended us to know, so what do you think they would do to fix that?"

"Merde." Lemaire was the one who needed to sit now.

"Yeah, totally. What do we do now?"

The team was quiet. Vogel was now sitting at his console, his eyes fixed on Williams. Lemaire was sitting at hers, head down afraid to look up. Engels was leaning back in his chair, not sure what else to ask. Williams on the other hand, was thinking. The door has been opened more than once, the future manipulated, and there was a man, agency, government even, leading the effort. It was a very real possibility that if the wrong people found out, their lives would be in danger.

"He said he had an important meeting this weekend. Bob, can you pull up the logs again?"

"Yeah, Saturday again? Why?"

"It's been used at least twice in the last two weeks. Is there any consistency? I mean, was it on Saturday both instances? Was it at the same time?" Williams asked.

"Sort of, if I remember. It was on Saturday both days, but different times. The first one was around nine AM, the second way earlier, around six," Vogel answered.

"Do you think he's going to do it again this weekend?" Lemaire asked.

"It's starting to look that way."

"We have to stop him! He can't keep doing this. Everything is changing out there." Lemaire stood, clenching her fists. "The bastard!"

"I agree, but if we straight out confront him we may just as likely disappear. You're right on that Bob." Williams looked at Engels. "And we may lose our opportunity to fix things."

"Then what do you propose we do?" Vogel asked.

"We let him start it up."

13. Alone in the Dark

"You ready?" Williams asked. Both he and Lemaire were walking to the lab, this time before sunrise, and once again on Saturday. They agreed to get there before the earliest instance from one of the logs, six AM, well before curfew ended. It wasn't a sure thing, but it was their best bet and they didn't want to miss anything. They planned to meet Vogel and Engels, take cover in the darkness, and spring out when Legard, if it was him, tried to start Andromeda.

"As much as I can be, I guess. What time is it?"

"Yesterday," Williams replied, smiling.

"That's not funny," she answered as she slipped a dark shirt over her head, fitting her arms through the tangled fabric. She looked at herself in the mirror hanging by the front door, then took in a deep breath.

"Sorry, gallows humor." Until that moment he realized he's never seen her in dark clothes; he didn't know she owned any. He had always seen her in light, airy, and soft colors, but today was different. Today they were going to use the dark to their advantage, an off white or salmon color wouldn't do. "We should go before we get stopped. You have your papers, right?"

"Oui, I almost forgot them. I am exhausted, I didn't sleep at all last night."

"I know," he replied. It was his apartment too, now, but since the two of them couldn't remember details of their new life, this timeline, they slept in separate rooms. He heard her pacing throughout the night behind her bedroom door.

She looked at him apologetically.

"There was no way I was sleeping either," he added.

After peering through a slightly open door, the two quickly made their way down the apartment steps and into the shadows of the street. They headed in the direction of the Musée stopping across from the park. Surveying the openness before them, they took cover near two large planters and in the recessed entrance of a small restaurant. It wouldn't open until well after curfew.

"Is it clear?"

"Looks like it. We have a pretty straight shot. We'll cut through the Esplanade, better chances staying in the dark of the park. We'll be at the back entrance a minute after we come through the trees."

"Okay. We better get going." Lemaire started to walk, Williams followed. They made it across Rue Fabert without seeing a sole. They relaxed a little, but still stayed behind a large tree on the corner. They had a valid excuse to violate curfew, working for the Ministré, but they still wanted to avoid any unwanted attention. Even with an excuse, there would undoubtedly be an interrogation and Legard would certainly find out what they were up to if they didn't make it in time to catch him using the machine.

"Now!" Williams lunged ahead, heading for a break in the trees. Lemaire was right behind him. She crouched, almost as if she were hiding behind him. It made her feel invisible. The two made it through the outer boundary of the park, framed in large trees that seemed to cast a dark shadow even in the dark. They stopped for a moment to survey the landscape. "Nobody. Looks like we are doing okay so far. Let's keep going. We'll keep it slow now, okay."

"Okay. You lead the way." Lemaire again stayed close. As they broke into the middle of the park, the trees gave way to an open grassy plain. She noticed his shadow from the moonlight cast on the ground in front of her. She worried they were walking out into the open where anyone could now see.

"ARRÊTER!" A voice said. Williams and Lemaire couldn't tell what direction it came from, and both stopped dead in their tracks. "ARRÊTER!"

"Nick... what do we do?"

"Shhh, hold on. Don't move." The two stood frozen as if statues in the park.

"ARRÊTER MAINTENANT!" The voice screamed. This time Williams and Lemaire could see the source. It was a police officer, walking hurriedly on the parks paved path near the street on the other side of the trees. He was chasing down another person, walking under cover of night, steadily moving away from the officer. Williams could barely make out the man, wearing what looked like jeans, a sweater, and tennis shoes. The man turned slightly and revealed a tired face that seemed out of place.

"It's not us. He doesn't see us," Williams said quietly. He looked around to see if there were any other officers coming to lend a hand. "Let's go. Stay in the middle." The two began to move again. It wasn't long before they found themselves crossing the oval shaped stone throughway and in front of the iron gates of the Musée. They both leaned against the stone pillar that held the gate in place, looking back to make sure no one followed them, and breathed a sigh of relief.

"I think we made it."

"Yeah, I think so." The two of them then stayed close to the shrub lined walkway. They wouldn't be seen that way. "Look. It's Bob and Gunter." The two men were standing close to one of the entrances where they agreed to meet, hiding in the shadows.

"What took you guys so long?" Engels asked. Even in the darkness he was wearing his sunglasses.

"We almost got stopped, in the park. Had to wait it out a bit. How did you guys do?" Williams replied.

"No problems. Stayed at Gunter's house. We didn't see anyone," Engels answered, taking off his glasses.

"We'd better get moving. I assume François will be here soon so we don't have much time to get ready." The three entered through a service entrance near the back of the building. They wouldn't be questioned from this point on; the small number of security officers during the overnights had better things to do. The team made their way down to the lab and began to get ready.

"What happens now?" Lemaire asked as the team found themselves in the control room. It all seemed like a good plan, hiding in the lab, waiting for Legard to show up and try to start Andromeda. But she didn't know what would happen, what they were going to do to keep him from going any further.

"Good question, and to be honest, I don't know. I was thinking of a few possibilities, but."

"Why don't we just corner him and tell him we are on to him?" Engels asked. "Tell him he better fix everything."

"He would just deny it all, tell us he doesn't know what we are talking about," Williams countered.

"Yeah, I guess there's that."

"Besides, if we have him, here, on a weekend when no one is supposed to be here, and we witness him doing whatever he does to the door at that panel," Williams pointed to the panel that was opened when they first discovered someone turning on the machine, "it would be hard to deny. Not to mention we might find out what he is using to make this work."

"But once we confront him, present the evidence, what then? We simply can't go about our lives, can we?" Lemaire asked, still unsure of their plan.

"Probably not. But maybe we can find out how big this is. Maybe he'll tell us who else is involved, and most importantly, why. Only then will we be able to figure out how to make things right again... if we can. Hey Bob, you got those GoPro's set?" Williams asked.

"Yeah. Should have all angles covered." Engels started to make his way up to the top of control room two. "I've got the entrance, and two angles near the door covered. Maybe we can get an idea who that scientist is too."

"Good. That will help determine everything he's doing down there. Well, you guys ready?" Williams asked.

"As I will ever be," Lemaire answered.

"Okay, by my guess, he should be here soon. We should take positions." The team nodded, then moved to carefully disguised locations throughout the lab. Engels took a spot in one of the metal closets near the back of the lab, leaving the door open slightly to get a good look. Lemaire stayed off to one of the sides behind a dry-erase board and desks, unseen in the dark. Vogel and Williams both knelt behind some of the storage cases near the door below. They all waited quietly for Legard, and secretly hoped he would be the only one coming.

"Nick?" Vogel whispered.

"Yeah, what's up?"

"Do you really think the past, or maybe the future, has changed that much? Do you really think they will change even more?"

"Judging by what we remember from last weekend, yes and yes. Based on the information we left for ourselves, I would say the past has changed a lot more than we even suspect. I don't see any reason it's not going to change even more. Now that he's got a system here, and can open the door relatively easily, I think he's going to move more and more material that will change the past drastically."

"There's something I just can't understand. Why would Legard do this? He is French. I've known him for many years. He is quintessential French. His father was part of the resistance in Calais. Yet, everything he's done, whatever he's provided the Nazi's, has been in their favor. It doesn't make any sense. It's as if he would have rather had Germany, Nazi Germany, have control over France."

"I thought about that too. I can't see any reason myself. It makes no sense. There's got to be something for him to gain."

"Hey!" Engels whispered loudly. "I can here you guys all the way up here. You're going to scare him off."

"Sorry," Williams answered. "We should keep quiet Gunter, wait him out."

The team then waited patiently for their guest. They all huddled in their chosen spots, adjusting every now and then to relieve the stress from sitting in awkward positions and in confined spaces.

"Jeez Marie. I am sure he could hear that sneeze from down the hall," Engels said.

"Sorry," Lemaire whispered, just after sneezing from behind the board.

"Gesundheit," Vogel responded, then they all waited in complete silence for about an hour before they heard anything.

"Wait."

"What is it Nick?" Vogel asked.

"I think I hear something. Footsteps." Just as Williams said that, the tell-tale beep was heard from the badge scanner at the door of the control room. The lab lit up momentarily from the light coming in through the open door. Williams ducked back behind the crates to keep from being seen. The door closed behind, and a pair of footsteps could be heard turning around. The shade that was partially covering the small window on the door of the entrance was pulled down completely blocking out all remaining light.

"What's he doing?" Vogel whispered.

"Shhh, I don't know. He might hear us." Just then Williams could see a glow from a small flashlight stream over the top of the crates. Both him and Vogel ducked behind, then didn't even breathe. The man started to walk down to the console closest to the machine; with him, two small cases. He then took a step down and using his small flashlight to sweep back and forth throughout the lab, made sure he was alone. He propped his light on one of the cases, then walked down to the panel the team investigated the previous week.

"Voyons," he said as he slowly pressed on the corners of the panel, releasing and pushing it to the side. "Voilà."

Williams waited silently, thinking about when he should come out of hiding. It was then he realized they didn't discuss who was going to come out first and when. Williams was sure Vogel and Engels would stay out of sight until he sprung forward, but he wasn't sure about Lemaire. He hoped she would wait until the man finished at the panel.

Hold back Marie. From his vantage he could see the man place the other small case next to him as he knelt on the floor. There were two clicks, then the man pulled it open. Williams watched as he slowly pulled the oscillator from inside the panel slightly releasing it from the machine. Setting it aside, he pulled out another oscillator from the case, carefully holding it with both of his hands. With a slight fitment, he slid the new oscillator into position.

"Voilà," he said, closing the panel and then heading back to the console.

"Did he swap it out?" Vogel whispered.

Williams could see the man stop, taking the flashlight from the corner of the console, stepping up and then sitting down. He could no longer see what the man was doing, his view obscured by the cases and the console. He could hear typing, and after a moment, the control room lit up slightly from the glow of the monitor in the console.

"Ah choo! MERDE!" She couldn't hold it back any longer. The man now knew he was no longer alone.

"Bonjour Marie. What might I ask are you doing behind the chalk-board?" The man spun around in his chair and shone his light in the direction of the sneeze. "Why don't you come out here and join me?"

"What are you doing here François?" she asked.

"Perhaps the rest of the team would like to come out of hiding and join us, Monsieur Williams, Gunter, Bob?"

Williams and Vogel stood slowly, the light from Legard's flashlight revealing their faces. Near the back of the lab, the sound of a metal door from one of the cabinets could be heard, prompting Legard to look over his shoulder at Engels stepping out.

"Hey François."

"Answer me!" Lemaire demanded. Just then Engels clicked on the set of lights that covered the doorway and the first console, where Legard was sitting.

"Please, why don't you join me, and come out from the dark," Legard suggested. Williams wanted to ease into the conversation, but it appeared Lemaire wasn't going to let that happen.

"Don't you know what you've done? What are you giving them?"

"Please Marie. Why don't you relax. There's plenty of time to talk. This excitement will help no one." Legard then reached down to open the other case sitting on the console.

"NO! Answer me!" Lemaire started to make her way toward Legard when he abruptly stood, reached into his case, and pulled out a Glock 17.

"MARIE STOP!" Williams called out. Lemaire stopped moving. She was frozen, just standing there staring at the gun.

"Holy shit François, what are you doing?" Engels asked from the top of the stairs.

"Get down here now Bob. All of you, stand over there, by the crates."

"Easy François, we'll do what you want. No need for any of this, we just wanted to ask you some questions." Williams tried to keep everyone calm. Lemaire still didn't take her eyes off the gun. Engels slowly moved down toward the others, his hands up and in the air.

"Ah Monsieur Williams, I don't intend on hurting any of you, although you see, I will not let you stop me either. Just stay where you are and everything will be okay."

"How could you do this François? What you are doing is changing the past and the future. This isn't France anymore," Lemaire pleaded, still focused on the gun.

"I should hope not Marie. I should hope not. Although, I don't know how you knew. Perhaps you could tell me?" Legard pulled up the gun slightly.

"We were caught in the field. Undoubtedly you knew about the effects of the field on everyone and everything within a certain radius. We call it the andromeda effect," Williams answered.

"What? When?" Legard asked.

"We don't know. It looks like two weeks ago, but you opened the door since. Whatever you gave those people,"

Williams pointed to the machine behind him, "it changed things. We only remember getting caught in the field last week."

"But how? I made sure no one would be here," Legard questioned.

"It was something I noticed about one of our tests. A change, progress. In my excitement we all came in Saturday morning to discuss it."

"Ah ha, a most intelligent and engaged team. Saturday. Ah yes. I was stopped by the police for breaking curfew. Most unfortunate. I told them who I was and they let me on my way, but it delayed me, and as it seems caused a small problem." Legard smiled, still not lowering the Glock. "If I weren't stopped I would have been as early as I am today, and you would not have any idea."

"We were standing near door one when you initialized the systems. Still don't know how you did that."

"A benefit of being in my position Monsieur."

"We had a camera set up on door two which captured you turning it on. Whatever you gave them, it changed things, but since we were caught in the field, we remember the alternate timeline. You know about alternate timelines, don't you?"

"Ah, Monsieur, oui."

"You bastard!" Lemaire let out.

"It was an error that you were in the field, and I am sorry for that inconvenience, c'est la vie. I'll make sure you are nowhere near the machine next time, you will only know this new and wonderful world we are creating. You won't question a thing."

"You bastard," Lemaire said once again. Legard motioning with his gun as if to say, 'what can one do?'

"Why are you doing this François?" Vogel appealed.

"You wouldn't understand, I assure you."

"Try us." Williams leaned back against the wall. Legard looked around briefly.

"Most intelligent indeed," he said, lowering his pistol.

"Why them, why the Nazi's?" Williams asked.

"Charlemagne Monsieur, Charlemagne."

"I don't get it. What do they have to do with you?"

"My father, he was a member of the unit. He was one of thirty men who made it out of Berlin in 1945, chased and nearly executed by those barbarians in the East. But he made it out. He regrouped with other French fighting against the defeat of Germany, and more importantly, for Vichy France. He was fighting for a way of life, a French life!"

"You said your father was resistance?" Vogel asked.

"A lie, here and there, you can understand." Legard raised his pistol again. "The Germans had no use for France, none. It wasn't part of their goal to reunify French territories. And France was simply Churchill's stepping stone to Germany, his pawn to use as he saw fit for the benefit of England." Legard sat, resting his pistol on the console, he started to pull up the menus and sequences for Andromeda.

"So you're using the door to change the outcome. To make sure Vichy France, and incidentally Nazi Germany, come out ahead."

"Precisely Monsieur Williams. The Nazi's developed the door, and we are now using them to protect our way of life."

"What way of life? Under Nazi control?" Lemaire questioned.

"Marie, Marie. A French way of life. France for the French. Germany for the Germans. Europa! That is what we are trying to accomplish here." The hum of the doorway started and the blue light began to come on. "You can remember, can't you? Europe is slowly being erased. Culture, way of life, we are looked upon as degenerates if we exhibit the slightest hint of national pride. How long until we don't speak French?"

"It's progress, isn't it?" Vogel asked as he looked over to see the blue haze of the activated field.

"Progress? A country's own people offering up their culture... their identity to be sacrificed on the altar of change? Immolation, nothing else."

"You can't believe that François," Lemaire pleaded.

"I am one of many who have dedicated their lives for this moment. To change the future of Germany and France of 1945."

"How, by information?" Williams wondered.

"Exactiment Monsieur, with data, design, and outcomes. Everything to give the Nazi's and Vichy the advantage. Like this." Legard held up a small packet in his hand as he stood from behind the console.

"And that is?"

"Names Monsieur. Names, the French resistance."

"You can't be serious?" Williams stepped closer.

"I am Monsieur." Legard stared to walk to the doorway with the envelope. "Names of the French resistance in 1945 that will soon be eliminated. Now, I am afraid I am late delivering my package, you will excuse me."

"I won't let you!" Vogel lunged toward Legard, but just as he started a shot rang out piercing Vogel's side. He fell to the floor gasping for air. Williams and Lemaire both looked up at the door to see a German officer who had just stepped through the blue haze. He was holding a Luger, a small column of smoke seen rising from its barrel. Engels, who thought it was Legard who fired, started to run to the exit. The same German officer spun around, aimed and fired one round into Engels back. Engels stopped and stumbled as he tried to make his way out of the lab only to fall backwards onto the floor.

"NO! How could you?" Legard yelled to the officer. "I had them under control!"

"I cannot take chances Herr Legard. The names. Give me the names." The officer held out his hand, motioning for the package. Legard stepped closer, but seeing Gunter lying on the ground, he threw the envelope to the floor.

"Why did you shoot? I had them under control!" Legard exclaimed. Williams, seizing on the opportunity, rushed behind Legard and pushed him into the officer, who, along with Legard, fell back through the blue haze of the doorway and out of sight.

"Marie! Kill the power!" Williams yelled. He could see her just standing there in shock. "Marie! The power, kill it!"

"What?" Lemaire just stood looking at Vogel on the floor.

"Emergency shut down! Hit it!" Williams yelled. Lemaire snapped out of it, turned around to face the emergency shut down switch located near the side of the doorway.

"Got it!" She pulled down the switch as fast as she could. The humming abruptly stopped and the blue light completely faded.

"It's off. Help me," Williams said, running over to Vogel to check his condition.

"Nick... I didn't see that coming, I can tell you," Vogel gasped, then his eyes glassed over.

"Shit. He's gone. What about Bob?"

"No.... I can't believe it." Lemaire knelt next to Engels, a pool of blood forming underneath his body, lying on his back half way across a tiered level of the control room floor. "He's gone too. Nick, what happened?"

"I don't know. But we need to get out of here. Legard is not alone. Someone else will power this up and he will be back. We can't stay here."

"What are we going to do?" Lemaire asked.

"Take this." Williams handed her the package of names Legard slammed to the floor. "No sense leaving it behind. Everything he walked in with, take it." Williams then made his way over to the panel.

"What are you doing?" She asked.

"The oscillator. They can't do anything without it. I don't know if they have more, but maybe we can slow them down. I'm taking it with us." Williams slowly pulled the oscillator free of its attachment point in the doorway. He gently laid it in the case Legard brought with him when he arrived. "I've never seen anything like it. Have you?"

"No, no I haven't," Lemaire said, standing next to Williams. "Let's go. Someone had to have heard those shots."

"Damn, you're right. We need to get lost." The two immediately ran to the exit, turning off the lights behind them. "No alarms. Let's go." Williams stood for a second before making his way through the secure doorway and out through the museum exit.

"What are we going to do? If he was not alone someone is going to try and find us," Lemaire said while trying to keep up with Williams.

"I don't know. We need to get out of the city. We need to be off grid while we sort this out."

"East. I know a place, there's cabins in the woods. No one will ever find us there," she said.

"Great, how are we going to get there?" The two started down the street unsure which direction to go. Just then, a man stepped out in front of Williams and stopped him. He had a look on his face like there was something important to talk about. He was slightly shorter than Williams, and wore a small cap. He wore a short beard and longer mustache, which Williams noticed only up close.

"Nick Williams?" The man asked, his hand in his jacket.

"Shit. How did you guys-"

"Come on. We need to get out of here," The man said.

"What? Aren't you-"

"Come on, both of you. We don't have much time. They will be after you any second now." A van with no side windows pulled up and the door opened. "Come on, get in. I'll tell you more once we get moving." Reluctantly Williams and Lemaire jumped in. The driver started to make his way away from the museum.

"Who are you? What are we doing?" Williams asked.

"I'm with the resistance, Mr. Williams. We've been watching you for the last several months."

"Resistance?" Williams looked at Lemaire. "How did you know we would be out there?" Williams asked.

"We've been watching you. One of our men made sure that officer in the park chased him, and not you this morning."

"You were out in the park?" Lemaire asked.

"We knew you were on to something. What happened to the other two on your team?"

"They're dead. They were shot," Lemaire answered.

"Shot? What exactly happened in there?"

"What's your name? You have any identification?" Williams was worried. He didn't know who to trust now.

"You can call me Hugh, but that's all I'll tell you. It's better for you, better for me. You'll just have to trust me."

"Why should we trust you? Two of our friends are dead?" Lemaire asked.

"And you are not, and we are helping you get away. That should be enough, don't you think?" The man turned and faced Lemaire and Williams as if waiting for an answer.

"I guess that's a good enough reason as any," Williams answered, leaning back in his seat.

"Besides, we can move freely during curfew, our plaques are delivery."

"Where are we going."

"We're taking you someplace safe. We are just delivering you to someone else."

"Who?" Williams sat up. "Who are you delivering us to?"

"Someone who needs you. Someone who says you can help us."

"Are they part of the resistance?" Lemaire asked.

"No. We work for them from time to time. That's all I can tell you here. You might as well get comfortable, we are going to be in the van for a while. Here." The man passed a small envelope back to Williams and Lemaire. "Your papers."

"Our papers?" Williams asked, opening the envelope. It contained four books of papers with an unmistakable white cross imprinted on the front. "We're swiss."

14. Alpine Summer

"What do you mean?" Lemaire reached out and took one of the passbooks Williams still had held out in front of him. They were identification documents, needed to move between France and neighboring countries. "It's my picture."

"Mine too." He held up his set. "There's also one for Bob and Gunter."

"They won't be needing theirs. Please." Hugh turned and reached for the books meant for their two team members unexpectedly shot in the lab. There was to be no trace, nothing to link Bob and Gunter to the resistance. The papers needed to be destroyed. "Frankly, I am surprised you made it out."

"Why do you say that?"

"We intercepted some chatter over..." Hugh paused, "over the network about your team. We didn't understand what it meant. You and Marie were mentioned specifically, but not Robert and Gunter. We thought it best to tail you, but of course, we couldn't follow you inside. I guess it worked out."

"What happened to the man from the park this morning? The one who kept the officer occupied. He was out during curfew."

"The one who made sure you weren't interrupted? He was wearing a disguise, he got away. The officers have heavy hands when in arms reach, not so much when they have to run-" Hugh suddenly stopped. They were driving for about a half hour when he noticed they were not far from a checkpoint.

"What's going on?" Williams asked, pulling himself up by the back of the passenger's seat to get a better look through the windscreen.

"Checkpoint. They're all around the city. It shouldn't be a problem. Just don't say anything, we'll take care of it." It was morning, and there was the usual curfew approved traffic entering and leaving the city. Although it all happened a short time ago, Williams was worried someone would have found Vogel and Engels in the lab, and he and Lemaire would be wanted. He settled back into his seat, crouching down as if to hide.

"What if they are looking for us?" Lemaire asked.

"Please, be quiet. You will put us all in danger if they suspect anything out of the ordinary. Don't say a word." The van pulled up slowly behind a few cars that had already queued up, patiently waiting their turn. Eventually they pulled up next to the guard station, only taking a few moments before being waved through.

"Voilà," The driver said.

"See, I told you we would take care of it. It's busy, they don't have time to search everyone, unless there's a reason. Our vans go through here regularly, so they don't even ask anymore."

"Where are we headed?" Williams asked.

"The Swiss border. I can't say it will be as easy to get across there as going in and out of Paris, but that's the plan."

"What happens when we get there?"

"We don't know," the man answered. "Just relax if you can, we will be driving for a while. You'll know more later."

"Can't you at least..." Williams pleaded, but Hugh tilted his hat over his eyes and settled into the seat of the van as if to take a nap.

They weren't more than twenty minutes out when the driver noticed something odd. "Nous sommes suivis," he said.

Lemaire looked over her shoulder through the window in the back of the van. "Merde," both her and Hugh said in unison.

"Are you sure?" She asked.

"Oui," the driver responded.

"What did he say?" Williams asked, missing what the driver said. He was caught off guard while looking out the window, thinking about Andromeda.

"Pull over at the next station. We'll check then. You two stay back there, no matter what."

"What is it? What's going on?" Williams asked again.

"He said we're being followed," she answered. "We're going to pull over."

"Here. Pull over here," Hugh said, motioning to the service station at the side of the road. The driver slowly turned in. Once stopped, Hugh got out and quickly headed inside. The driver then purposely pulled to the far end, the following car did the same. The driver couldn't make out who was inside.

"Merde, there they are. What do we do?"

"Nothing, he's going to check it out. We'll know if we need to go." A few minutes went buy, and Williams could tell the driver was getting nervous, a bead of sweat rolling down his temple. He was just about to pull the van away from the station when the passenger side door opened. Both Lemaire and Williams jumped slightly.

"It's nothing," Hugh said while climbing back into the van. "Pensioners. Older than Napoleon. It was a coincidence. Let's go."

"Merde," the driver said, pulling the van away, heading for the Swiss border.

The long morning was catching up to all of them. Every few miles Lemaire would slowly fall towards Williams's shoulder as sleep took hold, only to wake again from a bump in the road or a swerve of the van. Williams for his part couldn't sleep. Thoughts were racing through his head. *What are we doing? Where are we going? Will we get through this alive?* He caught himself daydreaming once and again as the pastures gave way to mountains, the Alps off in the distance.

"The border," Hugh called out, waking Lemaire. "There's no reason we will not get across. Don't say a word, not even if they ask you anything. Hold on to your papers. Only give them if they ask."

"We don't speak German. How will we know?" Williams asked.

Hugh turned with a blank look on his face. "He'll ask for his," he said, pointing to the driver, "and probably mine. If he asks for yours I'll reach back for them. Just don't say anything, we'll take care of it all."

"Merde," The now awake Lemaire said quietly, picking herself off Williams's shoulder, then fixing her hair while holding her forged papers in her teeth.

"Yeah, I'm not too happy about this either. Don't really have a choice I guess." There were only a few cars in front of the van, and it seemed they were moving at a good pace. The guard even let a few cars go without stopping. The van pulled up, and the guard raised his hand asking them to stop.

"Tag. Papiere bitte." The guard held out his hand for the driver's papers. "And his too," he said, pointing through the window to Hugh. Both men complied and handed over their documents. Unlike the forged papers of Williams and Lemaire, the other two were the real thing. The guard stepped away slightly, checking the two ID's. He then held out a small scanning device and pressed it up against one of the documents. A recurring beep could be heard, followed by a constant beep that abruptly stopped. The guard handed the booklet back to the driver, then took another look at Hugh's picture before handing it back to him. "Where are you going?"

"The University Hospital, Zurich."

"Who are they?" The guard asked, pointing to Williams and Lemaire in the back of the van both attempting to be as casual as possible. Williams kept his eyes fixed on the man in the passenger seat, while Lemaire kept her eyes fixed on the guard post ahead.

"Doctors. They are returning from an assignment in Paris. We work for the hospital and were assigned to drive them back." The guard hunched over slightly peering through the driver's window to get a better look. Just then he straightened out and took a step back. "Their papers please," he asked.

Hugh briefly looked at the driver, then started to reach back for their passenger's documents. But just as he had them in his hand, the guard raised his, prompting Hugh to freeze. The guard took a step backward, then looked behind the van to see an oncoming car with blue lights flashing.

"What is he doing?" Lemaire whispered.

"Get ready. If we have to we will floor it and break through. There's not much they can do once we are on the other side. Damn. We are almost there," Hugh whispered as he looked back through the rear windows.

"What is it?" Williams asked.

"Police. By the looks of it. Coming fast. I don't know how they could have known we were here."

"What do we do?" Williams spun in his seat to get a better look. He could see the guard turn and look over the van, then pull out a small radio he had tucked in the belt of his uniform.

"Shut up. I told you not to say anything."

Just then, the guard stepped up to the driver's window. "Emergency vehicle. We are going to open the gate, once we do, drive through and clear the way. Get moving."

"Okay, I'll follow him." The driver pointed to the car in front of them. The gates opened, and both the car and the van sped through and pulled to the side. An unmarked car, which looked similar to a police car but with no markings, sped through the gate and out of sight.

"Huh," Williams said to Lemaire. "Not for us."

"He's lowering the gate," The driver said while looking at the guard through his mirror.

"Then get going before he realizes he didn't check them." The driver turned back on the road and started off, purposely not looking in his mirror in case the guard realized his mistake and tried to waive him down. "We have people in the documents office who prepared these for us." The passenger handed the booklets back to Williams and Lemaire. "We've been through before, but sometimes the guards get nosy and that's when we have problems." The passenger lifted his window slightly and turned to look at the scenery.

"So, we're going to a hospital?" Did I catch that right?" Williams asked.

"You didn't need to understand German after all, did you? No. No, we are not going to a hospital. That was just our cover story. If he didn't believe that we were going to bust through the gate and chance it."

"Would that have worked?" Lemaire asked.

"It hasn't yet," Hugh recalled. "There have been previous attempts, but it was always a last resort that almost always proved fatal."

"How long has the border been like that?" Lemaire asked, prompting Hugh to turn and look at her.

"They said you would seem strange to us in some ways. I would have to agree."

"What do you mean?" Williams asked.

"The border has been that way since the war. Everyone knows that," Hugh answered.

Williams and Lemaire looked at each other, wondering if it was another change as a result of Legard's actions. "Where are we going then?"

"A safe place."

"You said that before, but where?" Williams asked again, needing answers.

"Le Locle. We leave you here. We don't know where else you will be taken, and I don't want to know." The van turned down Rue de France, a street in the small town of Le Locle, just over the border Switzerland shares with France. "Get ready. We are almost there," Hugh said as they made their way down to where the street branched off to Rue Daniel-Jeanrichard.

"To the safe house?" Williams asked.

"No. We are going to pull up to the Hotel-De-Ville. Listen to my instructions carefully." Hugh turned in his seat so half of his body was facing Williams and Lemaire. "There is a restaurant in the lobby, you will go in and stay there for at least five minutes. No less, understand?"

"Five minutes, yeah."

"Take a menu or something and kill some time but don't order anything. You must make sure you stay for five minutes. We will drive the van around to the other side, which will signal the others that you are on your way."

"Others?" Lemaire asked.

"Please, listen to me. You will find out about everything once you are out of here, but until then, it's not safe. You must do exactly as I explain. After five minutes, leave, exit through the doors opposite from which you entered. Do you understand me?" Hugh asked.

"Yeah, yeah, we got it. Enter, five minutes, leave from the other side. Easy."

"Waiting for you outside will be a woman and a man standing next to another car on Avenue du Technicum. Once they see you they will get in their car, so don't ask questions, just get in after them. They know who you are and what you look like."

"They do? Oh yeah," Williams said, holding up his passbook, "you have been watching us, I forgot."

"They will take you where you need to go." The man spun back around, trying to see if he could see anything out of the ordinary. "Good luck, now go." The van came to an abrupt stop next to the hotel, blocking the street.

"Thanks, thanks for your help."

"Get going," Hugh said, pointing to the hotel.

Williams and Lemaire exited the car and headed in. The van immediately sped off. Williams was surprised at what he saw at first, it looked very old world from the outside, but once inside it was a mix of historic and modern. He almost forgot to make note of when they stepped in.

"Where should we go?" Lemaire asked.

"Here, let's just stay over to the side. Grab a menu, like he said. I forgot to see when we entered. Probably has been two minutes, hasn't it?"

"I don't know. I guess. Where do you think we are going?"

"I have no idea. Any place is better than Paris at this point. I wonder if they found Gunter and Bob yet?"

"Let's not talk about it, I can't keep myself together." Lemaire turned her head and started to read over the menu, her eyes watered as she fought off the urge to cry. "C'est français, it's in French."

"Sorry. Anyway, better to be out of there with everything that was going on. We have no idea how wide François's group can reach. You think it's been five minutes yet?"

"I don't know. I don't think so."

"I don't want to miss it. Let's get out of here." Williams took the menu and placed it back in the holder near the front door, then turned and walked into the lobby. He briefly searched for an exit, not remembering which one they stepped through. He took a guess and started to walk through a set of double doors and then to outside. "Crap. Where are we?"

"I don't think this is it," Lemaire said while looking over a small grass square just outside of the hotel. She stopped for a moment, a small fountain reminding her of where she liked to spend time in Champ de Mars.

"Look, it's them." Williams pointed. He could just make out a man and a woman standing near a small car. It was parked in the street near the exit on the other side of the hotel, the exit they should have used.

The man and woman immediately turned and got into the car once seeing Williams and Lemaire heading in their direction.

"Let's go. I want to get out of sight," Williams said, hurriedly making his way to the car and climbing into the back seat.

"You two are early," The man in the driver's seat said.

"Sorry, didn't judge it right."

"No problem. I want to get out of here anyway."

"That make's two of us," The woman said.

"Make that four," Lemaire added.

The driver cautiously started to make his way out of Le Locle. The car was basic, nothing fancy, and blended right in to every other car. He first made a series of turns down side streets, stopped, looked to see if anyone followed, then did it again. Williams and Lemaire didn't ask why, they just sat back exhausted by the day's events. Eventually, the driver started to make his way away from the small town and head South-East towards the Swiss Alps.

"It's okay. It won't take long. I just had to make sure you weren't followed. I am Andreas, and this is Katia," The man said, looking back at his passengers through the rear-view mirror.

"Hallo," Katia said, turning slightly to glance at the pair.

"I suspect you know us," Williams said.

"Yes, Nick, and you too Marie. And your two friends in Paris, Gunter and Robert. I guess they will be joining you soon."

Williams and Lemaire looked at each other. "How much do you know of what happened in Paris?" Williams asked.

"Not much. With what we do, we don't get much information, only what we need to know. And today, it was to pick up both of you."

"They didn't make it," Lemaire added. Andreas and Katia looked at each other, then were silent for a while.

It was getting late now, with the sun setting behind the mountains. At some point Lemaire fell asleep again against Williams's shoulder. She didn't try to fight it. His arm was falling asleep as he held the case he took from Legard in his lap. He looked over the seat and could see Katia was fast asleep as well. Andreas didn't move, he just kept on driving, looking in the rear-view to make sure no one was following.

"Andreas?" There was no answer. "Andreas?"

"Oh, sorry, I get in a trance when I drive. I don't fall asleep, but I don't do much else but drive."

"Can we stop. It's been a while since I used the bathroom, maybe we can get something to eat?" The chatter started to wake Lemaire.

"What are you talking about?" She asked.

"We will be there in about twenty minutes. Can you wait?"

"Yeah, where are we?" Williams asked.

"It would be best that you don't know," Andreas answered while looking in the mirror.

Williams could tell they were in the mountains, in the alps. He had no idea where. He slept for a little while too, unable to fend it off. He looked around and could see they were in a heavily forested area, very remote. Every now and then he caught a glimpse of light from a town or city in the valleys below, only for it to be blocked again by the thick trees. Some of the mountains in the distance were covered in snow.

Lemaire was awake now, unable to sleep while the car bounced and pitched on the rugged terrain. "Is this it?" She asked as they pulled up through a clearing and started to drive toward a large cottage with large overhanging eaves.

"I don't know. Looks like a chalet. I always wanted to stay at one."

"You'll be here for a while. You'll be safe here. There's food and drink inside. Katia will lead you in with your things. I'll pull the car around, out of sight." As Andreas was speaking, Katia started to get out and open Lemaire's door. The three exited the car and started to head inside.

"Follow me. Let's get inside. I'll make some coffee." Katia reached for a set of keys and opened the front door.

"I can use some, it's been since this morning. I have a headache," Lemaire answered.

Williams walked up the front steps, turned to look out through a break in trees across a clearing to the towns in the valley. "Should be peaceful anyway," he added, following Katia and Lemaire inside.

From the outside it looked like a typical Swiss chalet. There were long overhanging eaves, decorations in the wood along the railings, a shallow pitched roof, and it wasn't all too different from the inside. Once in though, Williams noticed another set of doors beyond those on the front of the chalet. Katia then reached into her bag and pulled out an electronic keycard. She raised it up against a bare area on the wall and held it there for a moment. *CLICK*. Katia then pulled the door open.

"Secure," Williams acknowledged.

"It's safe here. Come inside. I will show you where you will stay," she said.

"When do we find out more about you?" Williams still held the case he took from Legard close to his side. He didn't know what it had to do with the people he's been traveling with but didn't just want to hand it over.

"You mean why we got you out of France?" Katia turned and faced Williams.

"You could say that. This last week has been unlike anything I've ever been through, and that's not even counting today."

"We work for MI6, British intelligence, as part of a special projects unit here in Switzerland," Katia answered, standing near a large window to the rear of the chalet. Williams could tell, by the slight blueish tint, that it was bullet proof glass.

"British? Not Swiss?"

"The Swiss don't know we are here. And if they do, they tolerate it. They are neutral, but even they question Germany's ambitions so they don't stop us as long as we keep it quiet."

"So, you want to know what we have been working on, in Paris." Williams looked over to Lemaire who looked up from a sip of her coffee.

"We already know. We need you for our project."

Williams heard what Katia said, and immediately thought about Operation Paperclip. *But why? The war was over. Why do they need us? Why were we smuggled out of France? Why would we even need to have been smuggled? Couldn't we have just hopped in the car and left?* "Your project? What project?"

"We call it Cassandra. You are familiar with Greek mythology yes?" Katia asked.

"I can't say that I am, sorry."

"Cassandra could see the future. You see where I am going?" Katia walked over and poured herself a cup of coffee. Lemaire offered Williams one as well.

"You stole our plans." Lemaire stated.

"No, no it wasn't like that. It would have been so much easier if we could have. We wouldn't have had to get you out of there, would we?"

"Good point. But we are working on the same thing, right?" Williams asked.

"Your project is based off plans from a German officer, correct?"

"Yes, but how could you have known... never mind. Yeah, as far as we know."

"Ours were discovered on a German soldier who fled Berlin in an attempt to deliver them to the Alpine Fortress," Katia said.

"What's the Alpine Fortress? Is this it?"

"No, this is just our safe house. The Alpine Fortress was an area where high ranking German military officials could retreat should Berlin fall. It was starting to look like that was going to happen, at least until May of 1945."

"Who were they going to, do you know?" Williams asked.

"Keitel, at least that's what the soldier said during interrogation."

"We know of him." Williams looked to Lemaire. *The orders.*

"We found that the documents were at one point in the possession of Brigadeführer Zeigler. He was wounded and died leaving Berlin. The soldier then attempted to carry out Zeigler's orders, and failed. He was captured instead. The documents he was holding where then moved to a facility here in Switzerland."

"We had anther set. A partial set," Lemaire added.

"Almost immediately after their capture, things started to change in Berlin. It was inevitable the city would fall by May 1945. But suddenly, there were reports of the Soviets being unable to break through."

"Andromeda," Williams said, again looking at Lemaire.

"They reported the German's were one step ahead of every move. They even had superior firepower, weapons no one has even seen. There was one report of an entire brigade of Soviet soldiers eliminated by a few members of Volkstrum. Berlin would not fall after all. Germany slowly began to take back what they had lost, and even pushed back through to France."

"Wait, it's still going?" Williams asked.

"Of course not. But if it were not for the London Treaty, there would still be hostilities today."

"London Treaty?" Lemaire asked, not taking her eyes off Williams. They were confused, having never heard of this before. It was the first wide spread impact of what Legard had done that they had seen. The war didn't end, Legard was responsible, things had changed drastically.

"It was signed in 1952, a result of mutually assured destruction."

"What do you mean, mutual destruction?" Lemaire was beginning to wake from her coffee.

"Mutually assured destruction. There was evidence both sides had nuclear weapons. The US detonated an atomic bomb in July 1945, Germany followed suit in Africa soon after."

"They got it, my word they got it," Williams said quietly.

"All sides knew the first to get a functioning atomic weapon would win the war. After each side learned of the others nuclear capabilities, the war remained a conventional one and dragged on for seven more years."

Lemaire sat quietly after hearing what Katia had said. "Merde. I can't believe it."

"As part of the treaty, Germany regained all control of land lost from the Treaty of Versailles. As a result, they gave up land acquired from hostilities, namely all of France and Belgium.

"Wait, they gave up France and Belgium? Why all the security? Why were we so worried about getting out of France?" Confusion was setting in. Williams was getting a history lesson like he had never heard, and one he could barely believe.

"Although France was declared independent once again, they were under the control of the Vichy government. This was a major reason Germany went through with a withdrawal. The Vichy government is a strong ally to Germany, and therefore acts on their behalf. One can now travel between countries, but you are always watched." Katia took a sip of her coffee. Just then Andreas stepped in.

"Ah, coffee," he said.

"These plans, the machine. They are the key to why Germany didn't fall," Katia said.

"It's what François sent them. He used our machine, Andromeda."

"François Legard? We know him. He's high in the interior," Andreas added.

"He changed the future for Germany. Whatever he's been sending them, it's apparently working." Williams leaned up against the wall, lightheaded as if he were going to pass out.

"It does work!" Andreas shouted. "And it is a portal, yes, to 1945?"

"Yes. We thought we were working on a teleporter. Some way to move things from one place to another quickly. Some of the team spent years putting it all together but couldn't get it to work."

"But you must have? There's no other explanation," Andreas insisted.

"A week ago, we came to a point of near breakthrough. That's when we learned the true nature of what we were working on. We were talking over a recent discovery when Andromeda kicked on. We were all standing within the field generated by the doorway when it happened. After a minute or so, it all shut down. That's when we noticed changes. We were protected by the andromeda effect." Williams went on.

"What changes?" Andreas asked.

"Subtle changes at first, street signs were different, that sort of thing. Then later, presumably after Legard opened the doorway several times, more substantial. We only discovered it because the effect protected some footage we left for ourselves. We tried to confront him-"

"That's when things went bad," Lemaire finished, looking away, hiding her eyes from view.

"He opened the door again, when we tried to catch him in the act and confront him. This time a German officer came through from the other side. He shot two of our people, Gunter and Bob. I managed to shove François into the officer and back through the doorway. Marie shut it down before he could come back."

"But what's to keep them from opening it again and getting him back?" Katia asked.

"We took something." Williams held up the case he has been holding since leaving Paris. "Without it, Andromeda is useless."

"What is it?"

"It's an oscillator. It's unlike anything we have ever seen. It's the only one that will get the frequency modulation right. It's the only one that will keep the field stable."

Katia and Andreas looked at each other. "I need to show you something." Katia put her coffee down. "Follow me."

"Where are we going?" Lemaire asked, following Katia to an almost bare wall at the far end of the room. Lemaire thought it unusual that there was only a single painting, about twenty by twenty centimeters hanging on the wall at about eye level. Katia stopped and stood about a meter away, and that's when Lemaire realized it wasn't truly a painting at all, but a proximity retinal scanner. She watched as Katia stood, looking directly at the disguised scanner, while the security software compared her retinal map to that on file.

"Retinal?" Lemaire asked.

"Yours are calibrated too," Katia answered, referring to the retinal map of Williams and Lemaire, already on file. Without any sound, a small keypad and scanner unfolded from the wall, just under the painting. Katia took her badge and held it up to the bare scanner. The wall pulled back about five centimeters, then slid down into the floor revealing an entrance and stairs that led below. She quickly walked toward the stairs and made her way down, the rest following.

"It's a lab," Lemaire said openly. "I would have never guessed."

"It was a bunker, built in the mid-forties. Switzerland was neutral, but that didn't stop them from fortifying. We converted it to suit our needs."

"What needs are those?" Williams asked, keeping up from behind. Katia and Andreas didn't answer.

The four kept walking until they came to the end of the stairs and a heavy steel door. Katia once again held her badge to the scanner on the wall, and the doors slowly unlocked and opened. The group stepped through the doors and stopped on a landing just before a smaller set of stairs. Just on the other side of the hand rails was what looked like a control room similar to that which they worked with in the Musée.

"What is this?" Lemaire asked. "I can't believe it." She stepped just past a set of control terminals, then stood to look at what was in front of her. "Is this Cassandra?"

15. Finishing Touch

"You have you own. It's almost exactly like ours, Andromeda," Williams said, at almost a whisper, amazed at what he was seeing.

"Theirs now," Lemaire added. They could never go back to the lab in Paris, it was no longer her project.

"It looks almost exactly like it." He walked closer to get a better look. "It's identical, right down to the panel."

"We've been trying to get on the inside to find out how it works and what it was used for." Andreas took a step closer. "We are no closer to figuring it out."

Williams pulled his case closer to his side. "Let me guess. It doesn't work."

"No, it doesn't, despite all efforts. We've tried for years. We know it's the key, it's how they were always one step ahead. If we can open the door, we can stop them before it's too late."

"Too late?" Williams asked.

"Over the past year, there have been a number of our operatives that have simply vanished. All worked on our project in some capacity or another. We have no idea how they were exposed. We believe whoever is responsible is close to finding..." Andreas looked over to Cassandra. "Once they find this machine, and us, we are done for."

"How do you know you can stop them? The damage has already been done. France is no longer France," Lemaire questioned, almost to the point of crying again.

"France has not been France since 1952," Andreas answered, immediately. He could tell his statement had Lemaire thinking and forgot for a moment that he didn't know the France she remembered. "We think we have identified a weakness. Something we can exploit."

"How so?" Williams turned to face him, curious as to what he was getting to.

"One of the men captured heading to the Alpine line was interrogated by British intelligence. He was a guard in the Berlin lab, with a Doctor... Henke I believe, where they were running their tests. He witnessed the door opening, seeing a man walk through; a well-dressed man, with a French accent carrying a small briefcase."

"François," Both Williams and Lemaire said at the exact same time.

"The visitor returned through the door from which he came, only to emerge a few seconds later, with a larger case. It had only been a few seconds, but the man was wearing an entirely different set of clothes."

"That's because he opened Andromeda on separate occasions," Williams added. "Hold on, that's it."

"What is?" Lemaire didn't put it together. "Nick, je ne comprends pa."

"That guard Marie, he saw Legard come though his end in 1945, but to him it was as if it were only seconds between appearances. We know from our footage that Legard made several visits, and they spanned weeks."

"But what is the significance? He still changed the timelines."

"It means the doorway in 1945 must always be open, in some sort of idle mode, a listening state, waiting for a future doorway to connect. Any visits to that door will be mere seconds from the last. We can stop them." Williams spun around.

"We can stop them? You mean we can set things back?" Lemaire questioned, a glimmer of hope in her voice.

"I think, theoretically. Weeks, maybe months have passed since Legard started up Andromeda, but maybe only a minute has passed in 1945. If we opened it up right now and walked through, we would see François and the officer picking themselves up off the floor."

"The bastard," Lemaire added.

"Which means we can stop them from using the information he gave them. It's only been a few minutes to them, it hasn't even left their hands. That's what you all suspected, isn't it Andreas? What do you propose we do?"

Andreas walked over to a small storage area of the lab. In front of him was a small crate covered in a white canvas cloth. "We destroy it from their end. The machine, all the data they've obtained, all the scientists who know anything about it. Everything."

"But how. He's got the German Army on the other side of that door. We take one step in and we're toast."

"We don't go in. We send this." Andreas pulled back the canvas cloth to reveal their solution. It was about a meter wide, and another meter high. It was strapped to a large steel frame on castor wheels so it could be more easily moved.

"Is that what I think it is?" Williams took a step back. Arranged on the steel frame were about fifteen large blocks of a material stacked in three rows of five blocks each. The individual blocks were wrapped in a green plastic covering and marked with 'CHARGE DEMOLITION M112 C-4'. Detonators protruded from each block with wires that fed into a timer assembly on the top of it all.

"It will have a complete effect," Andreas answered. "If we can get this door to open," he pointed to their machine, "we set the timer, roll it in, and shut down our door. Anything and everything in their lab will be vaporized."

"Including François," Lemaire added with a smile.

"Legard, the scientists, any military officers, everything."

"Then they never get the chance to use the information François gave them. They won't even be able to use the door again. Everything will go back to how it was. If only we knew what that meant." Williams stepped closer to the bomb, wanting to get a better look.

"But it's impossible unless we can get our door working." Andreas turned, looking at Williams and Lemaire.

Lifting his small case in front of him, Williams said, "Well then, I think you're going to need this."

The team made their way to a table near the bomb crate on the side of the lab. Williams didn't say anything else about what he had in the case. Instead, he gently placed it on the table, clicked the tabs securing the cover, and opened it for Andreas and Katia to see.

"That's the oscillator, what you took from Paris? I've never seen anything like it," Andreas said, moving to the side to let Katia get a better look.

"It's the key to why you can't get Cassandra to work. I think it's what you are missing."

"What is it made of?" Andreas asked.

"I presume you were trying some quartz crystal-based oscillator, as per the plans? It's what we did. We didn't know if had to be this, whatever it is. I am guessing it came from one of Himmler's expeditions."

"Yes, yes, we settled with quartz, that's when we started to see progress. What expedition?"

"Something like Schäfer's expedition to Tibet. It was one of Himmler's escapades. He was many things, among them an occultist who sponsored expeditions that traveled the world researching ancient mythology." Williams turned and began to pace. "All of them were under the guise of anthropological explorations, but all had the same goal, to secure mystic objects that might be used to give Germany an edge."

"So, this came from Tibet?" Andreas asked while peering over the open case.

"Hard to say exactly. All I know is that no one who's seen it has ever seen anything like it. And somehow," Williams stopped and looked at the machine, "it makes it all work."

"I'm going to go topside. They're going to want an update soon," Katia said, quickly turning and heading out of the lab. "Let me know if you need anything."

"Where's she going?" Lemaire asked.

"We need to give an update to headquarters about the mission. They'll want to know if you made it. We also need to arrange our extraction. If we don't get this working, we need to get out of here. That bombs going off one way or another." Andreas pointed to the cart, the white canvas cover draped over one side. "They're not going to get anything from us."

"Good idea. Let's hope we can do something."

"So, what's next? Do we turn it on and see what happens?"

"No. No, I don't think so. Like I said, when we turn it on it will bring us back to Germany to the point just after I pushed François through. If that's the case, then there will be an angry officer waiting with presumably more guns. I think we need to finalize our plans with that," Williams added, pointed to the bomb. "We'll only have a small window."

"Agreed. We only need to set the timer and attach the cover. That way no one will have time to deactivate it. We just roll it in. Once we close the door it will be finished."

"So let's get it closer to the door." Williams made his way to the bomb, pulling the canvas off to the floor.

"We're going today?" Andreas asked.

"There is no reason to wait," Lemaire answered as she started to walk to the panel on the doorway. She knelt down and pried it open, just as they did on their machine in Paris. "It's exactly the same."

"Okay. I don't see why not. What do we do with this?"

"Hand it to me. I'll swap it out with your quartz. It should fit exactly. It's what François did to start ours." Lemaire reached out her hand. Andreas stopped.

"You said it's what François did to start yours."

"Oui, and?"

"Nothing. I just had a thought. What if they were capable of turning on this machine as a result?" His question caused Lemaire and Williams to look over to each other.

"I would like to say that's impossible. But lately, I've been proven wrong." Williams turned back at the bomb.

"Yeah, I wouldn't see how either. Just a thought."

She reached in and firmly grasped the oscillator plugged into the machine behind the panel and with a slight tug, pulled it lose from its attachment point and set in gently on the floor. Andreas carefully handed her the new oscillator, and with some adjustment, she fitted it into the machine.

"That should do it." She stood, taking the old oscillator back to the table and placing it in the case. "Show me the controls." She snapped the tabs closed, then followed Andreas to a single terminal at the corner of the lab.

"We've made this extremely simple since there are only a two-person crew here at one time. We only have an open and close function, everything else is automated. Power, system capacity monitoring, all of it automated. I just hope it works." Andreas logged on and showed Lemaire the controls.

"Simple," she said.

"Good. We'll only have one shot at this," Williams added while attempting to wheel the heavy cart closer to the door. Andreas walked back to get the yellow plastic cover. Suddenly, he stopped, hearing a sound coming from outside of the lab, in the chalet above. "What was that?" Williams asked. "What is it?"

"I don't know. It sounded like an explosion. Two explosions. I can't be certain, it was dampened from the walls of the bunker."

"Explosions? How?" Lemaire asked. Just then one of the heavy steel doors swung open and Katia stumbled in, wrenching in pain. She collapsed, hanging on to the corner of one of the steel doors.

"Katia!" Andreas ran to her aid. "What happened?"

"They found us. I don't know how but they found us. You must... you... get out of here." Katia had blood coming from her mouth and ears, the result of the explosive concussion above. Her head fell back and she was gone.

"We must get this going now!" Andreas screamed. He dragged Katia's lifeless body clear of the doors and onto the landing. He then hurriedly worked to close the two steel doors separating them from the entrance above. "They are at the outer doors. We will have little time before they break through." Andreas ran directly to the bomb and began to set the timer. "We either get the door open and send it through, or it goes off in here."

"How could they have known? How could they have followed us? There was no chance of it." Lemaire looked around. She then thought about the case, the oscillator they took with them. "NO!" she screamed. She ran over to the table and opened the case, tossing the old ceramic encased crystal to the side allowing it to slide off the table and tumble to the floor. She didn't see anything at first, so she pulled back the foam padding to get a look under the lid. Seeing nothing, she ripped out the foam that held the oscillator in place, then gasped in disbelief.

"What is it?" Williams asked, walking over to her. She held up a small electronic device.

"They've been tracking us the whole time. It was in the case with the oscillator. François, you bastard!"

"Get the door open!" Andreas screamed. Lemaire dropped the tracking device on the floor and crushed it with the heal of her shoe. She raised her hands to her head, not knowing what to do.

"I said get the door open, we haven't much time!" Lemaire then looked directly at Andreas as if she didn't understand him.

"The door!" Andreas commanded getting Lemaire's attention.

"But what about François and the officer?" She asked running back to the console. She knew if the door was open long enough, they would be at risk of Legard stepping back through, and this time with more German military.

"It's too late. We have to get this through, even if we don't make it." Andreas was busy with the bomb. He flipped open a cover on the detonator, and gently began to enter data on the keypad.

"I think I have the sequence up, it seems ready. The field will be energized when you give me the go ahead."

"Okay, I'll set the timer for three minutes. I don't think we'll want any more time than that. There's no way they will be able to disarm it at all."

"Then what? We just push it through?" Williams asked.

"Almost too simple, isn't it?" Andreas answered as he closed the key pad of the arming device and reached over to the cover sitting next to the bomb. "Help me with this."

The two men worked tirelessly to secure the cover, knowing it would be one more layer the Nazi's would have to get through to disarm the bomb. "There, all set," Williams said, taking a step back.

"Damn!" Andreas exclaimed, after fastening the last of the straps securing the yellow cover.

"What, what is it?" Lemaire asked.

"I can't remember. DAMN! I can't remember if I set the detonator for three minutes, or thirty."

"Does it really matter?"

"I don't what to give anyone time to disarm it. Help me take the cover off, I'll reset the detonator."

"No time to reset." Williams pointed to the terminal where Lemaire was sitting. "Get the door open Marie." Just then, a few loud banging noises could be heard from outside the lab, followed by what sounded like a few gun shots.

"I think they are here," Andreas said. "They have to be right outside the steel doors. We better hurry."

"I hope this works." Williams uttered.

"Yeah, me too. Let's get it moving." Suddenly a loud explosion blew open the heavy steel doors from outside. There was smoke everywhere, and debris flew throughout the lab. The three of them were caught in the confusion for a moment. Andreas instinctively ran to a metal case against the wall and began to key in a code. Without delay, the two metal doors sprung open. "Get Ready!" he screamed.

"Initiating!" Lemaire announced, taking cover behind the large control terminal. Andreas peered over to the steel doors, smoke pouring from under the header. Taking little cover from his position, he reached for one of the weapons stored in the case, a SIG SG 553. He slapped in a loaded magazine, took a look at the fire selector switch, and pulled back on the charging handle. Before he took aim at the intruders, he emptied a small wooden crate into a canvas bag and slung it around his shoulder. "A little treat for later. Now come on."

"I'm definitely in the wrong place," Williams said, kneeling, taking shelter behind the now covered bomb in the middle of the lab. "There has to be about a hundred better places to be right now."

"There you are," Andreas whispered. A second later, a few men charged through the lab doors, the sound of their gunfire filling the air. He took aim and opened fire, taking out the first two, one falling on the body of Katia.

"It's open!" Lemaire screamed.

Williams peered over the side of the bomb and could see the unmistakable blue light from the field of the open door. "Just like ours."

"Get it through Nick! Get it through!" Andreas screamed between three-shot bursts aimed at the armed men coming through the door. Lemaire stood, now that the door was open, to try and make her way to Williams to help get the bomb through. Running behind Andreas, still shooting at whoever came through the now open steel doors, she immediately fell to the ground. One of the intruder's bullets had pierced her thigh as she ran. Crawling, she struggled through the pain and noise, stopping for a moment to look over to Williams who was still crouched behind the bomb. She smiled slightly, when a line of bullets ripped through her chest.

"NO!" he screamed, wanting to run over to her. He could see she was gone, blood pooling on her side. He was pinned down behind the bomb.

"Get it through! Get it through! I'll cover you!" Andreas screamed.

"How the hell am I going to do this?" Williams asked himself.

"Get going!" Andreas stood, taking aim at anyone who came through the blown lab entrance.

"Here's to the future!" Williams stood and got directly behind the cart and started to push it toward the open energy field of the door. "Dammit, this thing weights a ton." He struggled, but Andreas's shooting kept all eyes off him. Williams kept pushing, once spinning around so he could push with his back. He caught a glimpse of Lemaire, laying on the floor. "It's not supposed to be like this." He was closer to the door now; he could see Andreas reloading his rifle in between shots from a SIG pistol. Andreas stopped for a moment, making eye contact with Williams.

"Good luck," he whispered, springing up to resume firing at the intruders.

Williams was still pushing the cart when he witnessed Andreas being hit in the shoulder, falling backwards to the floor. "Dammit. Andreas?" he called out.

The armed intruders began to filter into the lab, one of them stood near Andreas, kicking away his SIG pistol. After checking Lemaire's lifeless body, the remaining intruders took aim at Williams and started to fire.

"Oh shit," he whispered, still pushing the cart as hard as he could, ducking down low when a bullet would whiz past and pierce the metal fixtures on the far wall. Almost the instant he was enveloped by the blue haze, all the sound, all the smoke, all the commotion was gone. He felt the bomb cart give way and fell with it into the field.

"Pretty simple," Andreas said witnessing Williams disappear through the blue haze. "Pretty simple." He lay on the floor, taking a moment to survey his wounds. It was just a matter of time now.

"Hände hoch!" A voice screamed. Several of the armed men made their way to Andreas, who was now holding his bloodied shoulder, the canvas bag lying next to him. He could hear the sound of crunching glass beneath someone's feet walking slowly and purposely. The other armed men lowered their weapons and moved to the side. It was their commander.

"Where is it?" The man asked. Andreas did not recognize him, but presumed he was with Legard somehow.

"I don't know what... what you are talking about." Andreas was starting to feel the effects of his wounds.

"You are the only one alive," the man looked around. "so, I will refresh your memory." He pulled out what looked like a trench knife. It had a cast handle similar to brass knuckles and a long sharp edge. He held it in such a way that the blade was pointing down. He squatted next to Andreas and made like he was going to thrust it into Andreas's knee. Just as the man raised his arm, ready to strike, he caught a glimpse of the empty oscillator case on the floor and stood. "Where is it?" he asked again, walking over to the empty case, the knife still grasped firmly in his hand.

"I don't know what you're talking about," Andreas replied, turning his head away. The man quickly ran back to Andreas, putting the sharp edge of his knife under his chin, just enough that skin would break under the slightest move.

"The oscillator! The one that was in that case! Where is it? I want it now!"

"There." Andreas, lifting his injured arm, pointed to the panel where Lemaire inserted the oscillator they stole from Legard in Paris. "It's in there."

The man quickly put his trench knife away and headed over to the panel. "Shut it down. Shut it down, we'll get it when it's off." The man motioned to the terminal where Lemaire was once sitting, then pointed to the case. "Bring it to me."

"You won't get away with it," Andreas coughed.

The man, amused, turned and walked back to him. "What makes you so sure? All your people are dead. I'll soon have what I came for." The man reached into his holster and pulled out a pistol. He slid back the slide on the gun and took aim at Andreas.

"Because," Andreas answered, displaying his other hand. Dangling on his index finger was the pin from one of the six grenades he stashed in the bag at his side. "Because you'll be dead."

16. Setting it Right

"The Führer has explained to General Krukenberg, and hence to me, that there will be no more delays. The German people and the Führer himself have been put through great sacrifices to see to it your..." Lieutenant Haas looked around the bunker at all the equipment and personnel, "project is completed. Frankly I believe it to be gross misappropriation. Military resources should be used for military purposes. Not chasing around fairy tale crystal powers and folk lore. Wouldn't you agree Doctor Henke?"

"Of course, Lieutenant," Henke said, sweat forming on his forehead. He knew Haas, and Böttger for that matter, resented having to look after his project, which the two officers considered a waste. Böttger envisioned Tempelhof as the central command of the Luftwaffe, serving long range bomber units beating British and Soviet forces into submission in their own territory. His dream would never materialize. Haas on the other hand, couldn't be trusted in any critical capacity. Tempelhof was all but officially shut down, a perfect place to keep a communications officer out of the way. If it weren't for his family's contribution to the Nazi Party he would have long since died in a Russian winter.

"None of this will ever help Germany."

"You would have to agree, Lieutenant, that the Führer has a solution for an overall victory for Germany, wouldn't you? And that his belief, sacrifice as you say, in this project is part of that? Wouldn't you?" Henke stepped out from behind his control panel. Although the two men disliked each other, they both knew M31 had the backing of the Führer. Any chance to remind Hass of that fact, Henke would take.

"Carry on Doctor." Haas turned and started to make his way out of the bunker. "I will be outside to see if I can lend some assistance to Brigadefuhrer Krukenberg."

"Very well Lieutenant," Henke added. "I will carry on with our scheduled test." Hass stopped, turned slightly, then walked out. Henke looked over to some of his colleagues and smiled, relieved Haas was gone. Another one of Henke's aides took a few steps, stomped his feet, turned, and did it again. The rest of the team was amused at his representation of the tightly wound Haas, even a guard smiled slightly.

"We should be ready to test now Doctor," One of the scientists said. He turned and faced one of several control panels near a large cement wall, each maned by another scientist. They were all preparing to start up the machine, or M31 as they knew it.

"Fine. Fine. Our gross misappropriation of military funds should soon pay off." Henke reached down to his desk retrieving a pair of goggles, which he slowly pulled over his head and covered his spectacled eyes. "Everyone, please, your goggles. It will get very bright and I need all of you to be able to see your work stations."

With his direction, the remaining scientists donned their own goggles, adjusting them so as not to distort their view of the readouts, instruments, and alerts that made up their areas of responsibility. The guards, realizing they were without goggles, looked at each other, then pulled their helmets over their faces.

"Power," Henke commanded. The scientists then began to work diligently to power on their machine. The lights in the lab dimmed to near blackout with the power loss, the voltage surged and could be heard humming through the walls, panels, cables running along the floor, and lastly, to the M31 itself.

"Full power Doctor, the field should generate any moment," One of the scientists called out, with his back toward Henke, continuing to monitor his gauges.

"Very well." And with a small pop, a bright flash illuminated the lab. It was followed by a deep blue haze, the machine was operational, the doorway was open. Henke gazed at the field for a moment, then decided to take off his goggles. "It's fine. It's stabilized, you may take off your goggles." The team all took a brief look at the blue field emanating from the machine, then they all slid off their goggles and began to monitor their terminals.

"What now Doctor?" One of the technicians asked. Before Henke could answer, a sound of static emitted from the machine, drawing their attention to a person's hand piercing the blue haze.

"It works! It must be one of Keitel's men, from the future. It has to be. Get word to Lieutenant Haas, he must contact Vistula, they must send communication to Keitel! If we don't, none of this will happen."

One of Henke's men, working at the back of the lab, rushed up the stairs and out the blast doors in search of the lieutenant, Henke eyed him as he ran making sure he was on his way. Just as he turned to face the blue field again, the visitors hand pulled back through the door and was no longer seen.

"I suppose they wanted to make sure everything was okay?"

"Yes. Yes, I would assume so. Keep it open." Henke expected a soldier, someone from the Wehrmacht to walk through the door but was puzzled by what he saw next. "What is this? Who are you?"

"Allow me to introduce myself Doctor Henke. My name is François Legard. I don't have much time to explain. I am here to provide you with as much information on your future as I can, to help Germany win the war. But we must act fast."

"Where is Keitel? Where are the soldiers, reinforcements?" Henke asked.

"Keitel never received the plans. They were captured."

"Captured? By whom?"

"The Soviets. The Soviets take Berlin in only a few short hours." Legard started to walk closer to Henke.

"Soviets?" Henke took a step back, and a guard with a Machinenpistole 40, or MP-40, took up aim at Legard.

"Please Doctor, allow me to explain. You expected Keitel to create a doorway and send in troops and supplies to aid in the protection of Berlin, yes?"

"Where is Keitel, the troops?" Henke asked again.

"The plans were captured Doctor. And if you don't do exactly like I say, Berlin will fall."

"Who are you? Where are you from?"

"I am with Vichy supporters from France. The plans didn't make it to Keitel. Instead, they were captured by the Soviets. The Soviets didn't know what they had, and eventually I was able to secure them," Legard reasoned.

"When are you from?" Henke asked. It was no longer who. Henke expected someone from the German army, someone from around 1945. After hearing Legard's story, he began to question exactly how long it was.

"2018," Legard answered, expecting Henke and his team to be shocked. "From where I came, Berlin will fall. The soviets will gain control unless we act now."

"How? We need troops, supplies," Henke whispered.

"I have something for you, information, but I needed to make sure I was going to the right place." Legard turned and went back through the doorway, back from whence he came. Henke stood, motionless, still working through the brief bit of information that was given him.

"Doctor?" One of the scientists said trying to get Henke's attention. He was holding the long arm of the main power lever, ready to kill it on Henke's command.

"No. No, let's see what he is talking about. Keep it running."

A few seconds later, Legard emerged from the blue haze, and with him a small attaché under his arm. Legard walked slowly over to Henke and handed him the case.

"What is this?" Henke asked.

"Results. In this attaché is every move the Soviets make in the next few days that seal the fate of Berlin, and, ultimately Germany. This must get to high command immediately. With this information you can stop the advance with minimal troops and supplies."

Henke just stood, holding the fate of Germany in his hands, unable to say a word.

"France, Spain, Italy, they will all be under Germany's control within weeks."

"I, I... how did you get this?" Henke asked, struggling for the right questions.

"Monsieur, I am from the future," Legard said, patting Henke on the shoulder. He stepped back, turned and started to walk back through the open field. "Keep this open, I will be back with more useful information and supplies." Legard disappeared.

"Doctor, what is this?" One of Henke's men asked, standing close to his terminal.

"I don't know. Take this." Henke, eyes fixed on the blue haze, handed the attaché to a guard standing close by, then started to walk through the doorway. Emerging on the other side, in the lab that housed Andromeda, he expelled the deep breath he took in before entering. This caught Legard's attention, who was now making his way to the center console in lab two. He turned and faced Henke, now standing at the platform, getting a good look at where he just entered. Henke waived, not sure what else to do.

"Let's not do that again, it could prove to be too dangerous. Not everyone here, in my time, is on our side."

"Of course, Herr Legard, I understand. But you must see, I had to get proof." The small size of the consoles caught Henke's attention, and for a moment he just stared.

"Of course. You must go back through I am afraid Doctor, it is much too risky for me to maintain the machine open here for too long. We will be in contact." Henke understood, held in a deep breath, and made the return trip back to 1945.

Upon seeing Henke walk back through M31 and into the Berlin lab, the scientists, still holding the attaché Henke handed him before venturing into the future asked, "Herr Doctor. Where did you go? You walked in and immediately came back out here."

A guard was busy making his way closer, his MP 40 pointing at the doorway.

"It's real. It's very real." Henke said. "Get Haas!" Henke screamed.

"He is here Doctor." One of the scientists pointed to Haas, standing with his mouth open by the entrance to the lab. Krukenberg dismissed him, reminding the lieutenant once again he had his orders. Haas simply stood, just having witnessed everything.

"Did you see Lieutenant? Did you? What do you think of our misappropriations now?" Henke rejoiced.

"I don't believe my eyes. I can't, it's impossible," Hass said, not moving an inch.

"It is real Lieutenant. I saw it, from their time."

"You were…" Just then, the unmistakable static of the field could be heard from throughout the lab and a figure emerged from the haze, wheeling in a large yellow crate.

"Herr Legard. I didn't think it would be-" Henke stopped. He soon realized Legard, who had again stepped through the doorway, wasn't wearing the same clothes he had on just a few seconds prior. "That's impossible, you couldn't dress yourself differently that quickly."

"Monsieur, it's been one week?" Legard questioned.

"Of course! Of course. As long as we keep our door open, you will always come back to the point you left. I would suspect the same would be true if we were to traverse through your door, much like I did. Presumably, you shut your doorway down, hence the lapse in time and the change in clothes. Amazing."

"Here," Legard said, "help me with this."

"Unbelievable." Henke once again just stood there, mystified at the machine's potential.

"Quickly, I haven't much time." Legard stopped and stood.

Henke snapped out of it and ran to help, getting some of his scientists to follow.

"I promised you more. These are M134's. They can fire 6000 rounds per minute." Legard opened the crate to reveal two guns. "No Soviet will even be able to cross the Spree before being obliterated."

"Who has such power?" Hass asked, leaning over to get a better look at the weapons in the crate.

"There is more, I have more crates with ammunition and instructions."

"Quickly, get this moved," Hass ordered, motioning to the scientists who were enlisted to help make room. In total, Legard was able to move four crates of ammunition before he hurriedly walked back towards the blue haze.

"It's been too long. I must get back and shut down my side. This should be enough to protect Berlin. I will have information next time that will help destroy any resistance in France. That is the reason I am here." Legard turned and started to enter the field.

"More military tactics and equipment Herr Legard?" Haas saw an opportunity to try and elevate his status among other military officers.

"No," Legard said as he started to enter the field. "Names."

"Names?" Haas questioned. His queries prompted Legard to stopped, half way between the two fields.

"Yes, names of people operating in France as part of the resistance. Names, resources, hideouts, escape routes. You will be able to shut down the French resistance overnight. That should allow Germany to operate freely, and therefore defend France."

"I will be a hero of Germany," Hass said, standing at attention, giving a Nazi salute.

"Until next time," Henke said, while motioning to the supplies that were left behind as Legard disappeared into the static and the haze of the machine.

"Well Doctor. I see I was wrong about your project. Perhaps it will serve me quite well after all," Hass added.

"Serve Germany." Henke's answer seemed to run Haas the wrong way.

"Of course, Doctor. But there is nothing wrong with personal gain at the same time. Our new-found friend is going to see to that." Hass began to walk closer to the doorway.

"What are you doing Lieutenant?" Henke asked, walking closer to Hass and the doorway. "Lieutenant, don't get any closer, you're almost in the field."

Hass turned and gave Henke a look, much as a child would when he was about to disobey a parent. "Get this ready for General Krukenberg." Hass signaled his men, pointing to the crates and the attaché Legard delivered. "Inform him I will see him in a moment and that he should be waiting for me."

Henke could see the power already starting to go to Haas's head, giving orders to a general. "I beg the Lieutenant's pardon, but wouldn't it be a better idea to deliver these items to him yourself, Lieutenant Haas?" Henke wanted to keep Haas from doing what he thought he was going to do by reminding him of his lower rank. "I would be willing to say Herr General might even put you in for a field commendation, with such information."

"2018. It would be a glorious Europe." Haas took a step closer to the door.

"Yes, I know it will be, but please, stay out of the field. It's much too dangerous," Henke pleaded. Hass ignored him, turned, then stepped through the haze into 2018.

"Glorious Eur... "

"NO!" Henke screamed as Haas disappeared.

"Lieutenant!" One of the guards shouted, quickly running to get closer to the machine. He looked back at the group in the lab, wondering how they were going to explain the disappearance of the lieutenant. He then decided he would have Henke do the explaining and ran toward the steel doors and out of the bunker to find a superior officer.

"What is Haas doing?" One of the other scientists asked.

"Being a fool. François said not everyone in his time is on our side and that-" Just then, Henke was interrupted by a loud crash. He looked back to see the lieutenant and Legard falling backward though the field into the bunker. Once again, Legard was dressed completely different. Haas's Luger echoed as it bounced on the cement floor behind him.

"What have you done! I told you I had them under control! Why did you shoot them?" Legard screamed. Haas, unphased, picked himself off the floor.

"He was going after you, and I needed those names!" Haas brushed the dust from the floor off his uniform, then walked over to retrieve his pistol.

"You won't get them now! They are turning off the machine as we speak. If we try to go back now we will just be in the listening state. You fool!" Legard, kneeling, could not believe what he just witnessed.

"I did what I had to do for Deutschland."

"Today was for France," Legard said, sitting on the floor with his head down, lamenting at the opportunity lost. "You have what you need for Germany."

"What happened?" Henke asked, seeing the two men come through the door the way they did, and Legard mentioning Hass shooting.

"He shot two members of my team. I told you, I told you not to go through, it was too dangerous." Legard picked himself off the floor and stepped closer to Henke. He turned and looked behind him at the blue field of the machine, realizing he was now trapped in 1945.

"I know Herr Legard, I tried to tell him, but he is a pigheaded fool."

Hass sneered at Henke but said nothing.

"It's done now. It may very well change. You need to get this information to your superiors, you can handle that, Oui, Herr Lieutenant?" Before Haas could answer, the bunker loudly erupted in the sound of static once again. From the doorway another large crate, slightly different from those Legard had brought through, came rolling out from the blue haze. It came to a stop as it crashed against one of the boxes of ammunition not yet cleared out of the way.

"Holy hell," Williams said. He fell in behind the crate that he struggled to push through from the machine in Switzerland. He took a moment, laying on the ground, gasping for air. He realized it was silent, there were no more explosions, no more gunfire, he made it, and so did the bomb. He quickly felt his body for any wounds, then coughed from the smoke and dust left from the chalet. He slowly sat up and started to look around. He immediately noticed the features of the bunker, the large phosphorous lights, the cement ceiling, no windows, and of course, the M31 doorway still buzzing with blue light.

"Well. Bonjour monsieur Williams," Legard said. "I would have to say I didn't expect to see you again, at least, not here."

"Hey François." Williams turned his head to see Legard. "I did expect to see you here, wherever here is."

"Put that away!" Legard said, speaking to Haas who was leveling his Luger toward Williams on the floor. "He can't do anything here, and I won't have any more bloodshed by your hands."

Haas took a look at Legard, then to Williams, lowering his pistol. "Very well," he said, motioning to a soldier holding an MP 40. "Watch him. If he tries to go anywhere, shoot him."

"Jawohl Leutnant," The guard said, clapping his boots together.

Williams remarked at how young the soldier looked. "He couldn't be more than sixteen," he whispered.

"Monsieur Williams is not partial to our cause. He and his team would rather Europe throw away their culture, their history, their identity. He is anything but a threat."

"I seem to remember his forcefully pushing us through that door," Haas said with a smirk.

"I seem to remember you shooting everyone," Williams added.

"Easy monsieur. I can't keep you from suffering the same fate as Gunter and Bob."

"And Marie."

"Marie?" Legard asked.

"Yes, Marie. She's dead too."

"Merde. Why did you have to be there? If you were not in the lab you would have never known, they would all be alive."

"Believe me, we all asked ourselves that same question." Williams looked around. "At least I now know what you were sending them. I can only imagine where you got those guns. If I were to guess, people sympathetic to your cause."

"You are quite right. Our reach is all over Europe. All branches of service. All departments of state. We can get almost anything at any time. What you see here is just a small representation of what we can obtain. I was counting on your team being out of the picture, not the way it happened you understand, but not part of the project anymore. That's when we would really increase our efforts."

"So what happens now?" Williams asked.

"I would have hoped it would have went differently as you can imagine. I, that is we, shouldn't be here. I presume, by the haste with which you came though, something wasn't right on the other end. Would I be correct in my presumption?"

"You could say that. We took the oscillator and left Paris the moment I pushed you and, whoever that guy is," Williams thumbed in the direction of Lieutenant Haas, "through the door."

"You took the oscillator?" Legard questioned.

"Yes. And that little tracking device that came with it."

"Ah, a necessity, should things have gotten out of hand. And you used it in another door, oui?"

"Yep. That's where I came from. Got to say, your people didn't give us much time before shooting up the place." Williams again motioned to Haas and added, "Worse than him."

"We had suspected there was another, we don't know how, and until you fled Paris, we didn't know where either."

"Zeigler's plans, the British found them with one of Zeigler's staff, escaping to Switzerland. I guess that hasn't happened yet now that I think of it. Anyway, the British helped us out of Paris which was extremely dangerous thanks to your handy work."

"To get better, sometimes things must get worse. It doesn't matter anyway, they have what they need." Legard pointed to the information, guns, and crates he provided. "You are too late."

"You sound so sure."

"While we are sitting here monsieur Williams, I am keen to the fact that you did bring another crate through with you. It's obviously not one of mine. What is it?"

By this time Williams realized Andreas didn't set the bomb for three minutes. He looked at his watch. He needed to buy time so the bomb would go off at the thirty-minute mark. "It's nothing. I just hid behind it while your friends tried to kill me."

"I wish I could believe that. You had time. You left Paris. You purposely came through the door when you knew I was stuck here. Why?"

"Just wanted to get away, that's all."

"Open it!" Haas ordered, demanding to see what was inside.

"It's nothing, just some-"

"Open it!" Hass motioned for the guard, who quickly took aim with his machine gun.

"Okay, okay. It's going to take time, I don't know how it works."

"You have five minutes, then we shoot," Haas ordered.

"Okay, well, I better get started then. I can work faster without that thing in my face." Williams sat with his hands in the air. The guard didn't lower his weapon. "Okay, I'll just see what I can do."

"What could you be up to monsieur Williams?" Legard asked.

"You really should call me Nick. Just saying." Williams clicked open the two retaining tabs on the bottom of the yellow crate, then stood, pulling the cover off in one motion.

"SCHEIßE!" Haas exclaimed, not recognizing the explosive charges, but assuming by the timer it was a bomb of some sort.

"Foolish Nick," Legard joined. "Very foolish. We'll all be killed."

"Disarm it, now!" Haas ordered. The guard took a step closer.

"I can't it's-" Williams lunged. He was going for the young guard's MP 40 but was unable to wrestle it away. As he pushed and pulled, the gun went off spraying the lab with gunfire. A bullet pierced Haas's side causing him to fall to the floor. Two of the scientists were killed instantly, while another was wounded. Henke, not a victim of the errant gunshots, darted for the steel doors in an attempt to escape.

"Herr General!" Henke yelled as he made his way up the stairs as fast as he could. He stopped briefly when he heard two more gunshots, most likely putting Williams's fight to an end. He looked down at the steel doors below, still open from his escape, and realized he wouldn't be safe from the bomb blast. As he turned to try to get out, he tripped over several tins of nitrocellulose film. There were spools and spools of it that had been stacked up all around the corridor, left over from aerial reconnaissance flights that had stopped months ago. He picked himself up realizing he was standing in a corridor full of the extremely flammable film. "No! No!" Terrified, he started shouting. "I must get out! Help! I must get out of here now!"

By this time the Soviets had begun to shell the area; Elektror L1 air raid sirens effectively muted out any sound coming from the bunker. Outside, General Krukenberg was getting ready to pull back. The shelling and recent intelligence told him the Soviets had crossed the Spree, he needed to get his troops out of harm's way and back to the center of Berlin. "Get moving, we need to leave now!" Krukenberg ordered his men.

"General, what about the personnel in the bunker, the Lieutenant, and Doctor Henke?" One of the men asked.

Krukenberg pointed to the two troop carriers on the road ahead. "Tell them to get back to sector Z as fast as possible. I will take Haas and Henke's team with me."

"Jawohl!" The soldier clicked his heels and ran to the two troop carriers, waiving his hand in the air signaling them to start moving.

"General Krukenberg! General Krukenberg! We must get out of here!" Just as Henke could be heard beyond the steel entrance doors, he was torn apart by the blast from the inside of the bunker. Krukenberg was thrown to the ground, thinking a Soviet shell scored a direct hit right in the doorway. When he picked himself up off the ground, he realized Henke and his team were gone. There was nothing left, the bunker spitting flames from the nitrocellulose film ignited by Williams's bomb. The military plans, the guns, and the ammunition Legard brought through Andromeda was all destroyed. The Nazi's wouldn't get to use any of it.

"Get going," Krukenberg ordered, the carriers stopping to see what happened. He looked around making sure no one else was left. In the back of his Kűbelwagen, a long round container caught his eye. He hopped in and started to make his way to sector Z. "I must get these plans to General Wielding."

17. Once Again

"Arrêter!" It was a Paris police officer. "Arrêter! Arrêter!" The officer didn't stop running while at the same time blowing his whistle. He would get close to the objects of his pursuit, a middle-aged man and woman, only to slip on the stone walkway and tumble to the ground. "Merde!" he said as he rolled on his back trying to catch his breath. He could hear the running steps of the man and women of his pursuit fade in the distance; he wouldn't be able to catch them now. Remaining on the ground, he looked at his wrist that he was sure would be bleeding from a cut he sustained from his fall. "Pas mal," he said, it wasn't as bad as he thought. He stood, walked back slowly to retrieve his police hat, then started to walk back from where he came.

"Déplacer!" The running man said, the woman not far behind. Williams didn't understand him at first, only turning to see where the command came from. "Déplacer!" The man said again, this time he was only a few meters away. Williams quickly moved to the side and stood as close as he could against the wall. There wasn't much room on Rue Clovis, an old street lined by stone walls and buildings. As they ran by, Williams realized the two were the cause for the whistle he heard moments earlier, that, for one reason or another abruptly stopped. The man made sure to look Williams in the eye as he sped past, the woman tried her hardest to look away.

"Merci," she said softly.

"Huh. Wonder what that was about?" Williams asked himself. He was walking again when he stopped and looked back, just seeing the two rounding the corner to the next street. He was sure he had seen that man before, wearing jeans, a sweater, and tennis shoes, someplace else. It was the sweater that kept coming to mind. The man was wearing a blue sweater, which Williams thought was odd since it was the middle of the summer. "Oh well."

Williams was due at the UPMC, Université Pierre et Marie Curie, around nine A.M., and he didn't want to be late. He looked at his phone, then quickly realized he was going to be early, too early, but didn't care. "My curiosity." It was his curiosity that was the reason Williams was now in Paris. An unexpected encounter with the head of the physics department at the university a month ago, and news of an exciting project that required his help. Williams couldn't pass it up, and François Legard knew it.

Legard showed up a few weeks ago, sat in on a few of Williams's classes, then dropped the news of a revolutionary new method of transportation he and his team were working on that promised to change the world as they knew it. But, that was all Legard said. He wasn't sharing anything else. No matter how many times Williams asked, it did no good. Instead, Legard simply gave him an envelope and told him he would see Williams in Paris in a few weeks. He knew curiosity would make that happen. The envelope, with travel arrangements, an ID badge, everything Williams needed, was at his side as he walked.

"To early," he said, checking his phone once again. He had about an hour to kill, so he stopped at a café, Le

Nouvel Institut, to have coffee. Williams took a seat in a corner outside the café in one of the wicker chairs. "I guess it's a Paris thing," he said quietly. The chairs were almost identical to those he had seen at a café near the Eiffel Tower two days prior, Café Alexandre. "Was that the name of that coffee shop?" he asked himself. "Damn. I'm getting too old. No matter."

"Bonjour Monsieur."

"Ah, bonjour. Un café noisette, s'il vous plait." Williams had had the drink before, a hazelnut coffee, and since he might not see the waiter again for a while decided to just go with it rather than check the menu and waste time. The sun wasn't near unbearable yet, so he sat outside, positioning his chair against the wall of the café so he could take in the morning commuters and patrons getting their day started. It was then that he noticed the woman sitting at the far end of the café.

He didn't recall seeing her when he first stepped up, but then again, he thought, there were other things on his mind. A wide brimmed sun hat covered most of her facial features, in fact he couldn't see her face at all but for a brief moment when she looked up for the waiter. She had a certain poise about her as she sat, refined even. "Gloves," he said, after noticing her cream-colored driving gloves. "I didn't think anyone wore those anymore."

"Café noisette," the waiter said as he delivered a coffee to the woman. For a moment, Williams contemplated walking over to her to start a conversation, but quickly decided against it. He was in Paris for a specific reason, but moreover, he didn't want to sound like an American idiot which would have been easy to do.

After a moment the waiter brought Williams his noisette, setting it on the table without stopping as he walked by. Williams settled back in to his people watching and took a sip of his hazelnut brew. Most of the people he saw walking by were young, almost all appeared to be college students. It made sense, he was meeting Legard at a university after all. And that started his mind racing again. *What could it be? Why would they need me?* There were too many unknowns, none yet answered by Legard. For each answer Williams dreamed up he would find himself asking two more questions. He was anxious, but he would see what it was all about in a short time.

Looking down the row of chairs against the café again, following the people walking by, he noticed the woman with the hat and gloves was getting up to leave. She said something to the waiter as if they knew each other, then turned and started to walk away. Williams wasn't the type to stare at anyone, and when he found himself doing so he felt terrible. But something about her was different, he was drawn into to her. It was the way she walked, always staying out of the sun, the way her hair bounced with each footstep against the stone walkway.

She stopped for a moment, turned, then looked over her shoulder at Williams. He wasn't expecting it, and caught off guard, tried to make it as if he was looking off into another direction. He spilled a few drops as he placed his coffee over half the saucer causing it to fall on the table.

"Damn," he muttered. It wasn't as bad as he thought, there wasn't much coffee left anyway. He looked up again, curious to see if she witnessed his clumsiness, but the woman was gone. "Today is a familiar one for sure. Maybe I'm just too excited." Williams dabbed off the few drops on the table with his napkin, then pulled out his phone to check the time. "For Pete's sake. Nice move Nick." The time had gotten away from him. He reached into his pocket, grabbed a few euro's, and placed them under the saucer of his cup. "Hope that covers it. Dammit, I'm going to be late."

Williams quickly realized, despite checking out where and when he was to meet Legard, he had no idea where he needed to go. The University, although built in the 1970's, was a modern piece of architecture by Parisian standards. As such, it all looked the same from the outside. He pulled out his phone to take a look at the picture he saved for himself the night before. Holding it up in front of him, it matched the façade, and the one to the left, and to the one down Rue des Fossés Saint-Bernard. The buildings, all perched atop thin steel pillars, looked similar at all angles.

"Way to go Nick. Way to go. Crap." He started to walk at a faster pace, looking for the first sign of an entrance he could find. "He said in the center, where the tall building is, in the center of the campus. I don't see it. Way to go." Williams stopped, for all he knew he was walking away from where he needed to be. He stepped aside taking a position near one of the trees that lined the street, then pulled up an aerial map of his location. "Bingo. There it is. Just around the corner." Williams stepped up the pace. He didn't want to run, he didn't want to appear out of breath and exhausted when he met with Legard. He also didn't want to be late.

"There you are." Williams could see his objective just off Rue Jussieu, shielded by some of the buildings lining the street. He stopped for a moment, checking the time on his phone. "Got a minute. Get yourself together." He was out of breath, but as far as he could tell, didn't look it. A minute or two would fix that, so he started to head in. He climbed the few cement stairs leading into the courtyard and headed toward the tall building. That's where Legard's instructions ended. He was simply supposed to wait outside of the entrance, that was all.

"Bonjour Monsieur Williams. I am glad you came," a familiar voice said, just as Williams made it to the entrance.

"Bonjour. And here I am. But you knew I would come, didn't you?"

"Oui. Your curiosity. Some things one can count on more than word. And you are here, so let's not waste any more of your time. I have something I want to show you."

"Good. I was hoping you were going to say that. Lead the way."

Legard walked in the building, a blue glass covered structure on the center of the courtyard. Williams followed. There was nothing special about the facility, at least from a perspective of a secret project, changing the world, that sort of thing. There was no security other than what looked like an electronic badge scanner in front of a small hall blocked by two pieces of glass. Williams thought for a second how it looked like one of those saloon doors from the wild west. Legard held his badge to the scanner, and with a beep, the two glass panes separated and allowed him to enter. Williams followed, but was shut out when the glass doors closed.

"Please," Legard said, motioning to the scanner. Williams would have to scan the badge Legard gave him to gain entry.

"Oh, yeah, I guess I should have gotten that out. Didn't know what I would need today, just brought everything." Williams rummaged through the envelope retrieving the badge. He placed it on the scanner and was admitted entrance. "What was that?"

"That?" Legard answered. "A mantrap. It only allows one person to enter at a time. The door will open, then immediately shut behind. Each person will have to scan their badge to get in. If you follow someone else close behind, security will have a fit."

"Gotcha." Williams hung the badge from his lanyard around his neck. "Where too?"

"This way. The offices above are merely administration, the lab Monsieur, is below." Legard made his way to an elevator, and for the first time, Williams could see some sort of security. It was an old man, most likely a retired policeman, sitting on a chair next to the elevator. He gave Williams a once over but didn't say a word. A few seconds later the man was back to reading his paper, *L'Équipe*. The elevator door opened, Legard entered, Williams followed.

"Security is pretty tight here then?" Williams asked. Legard just shrugged his shoulders.

That was odd. I would have thought there would be a little more security than this for something he explained would change the world. The elevator seemed to travel for a short distance before coming to a stop deep below the university. When the door opened Legard stepped out and began to make his way down the hall.

"You'll find security is.... Monsieur Williams? This way." Legard turned and looked back at Williams who had a blank look on his face, standing just outside of the elevator, the doors closing behind him. There were at least five security officers, all wearing full riot gear, standing just opposite of the elevator. Four of them where holding FN P90 machine guns, all at the ready. The fifth, holding a Benelli M3 shotgun, had it around his arm in a sling, and was wearing a belt of additional ammunition around his waist. But is wasn't the guns that caught Williams off guard, it was the dog. A small dog, a toy breed, handled by the man with a shotgun.

"What's with the dog?" Williams asked.

"You'll find security is very tight, as you say, Monsieur Williams. Le chien," Legard pointed to the small tan dog at the officer's feet, "he can smell explosives before anyone could even get off the elevator."

"Yeah, like I said, security *is* tight." Williams then slowly started to walk toward Legard, who by this time was past the officers and was heading into the next room. Beyond the doors the two men were met by a receptionist, sitting behind a desk and off to the corner of the small waiting room.

"Bonjour Adriane," Legard said. The receptionist gave him a cold look, then handed over a small sign in sheet. Legard glanced over to Williams, then started to fill it out. Adriane then walked over to a set of windowless double doors, entered a code on the keypad, then motioned for the two men to go in. Legard hurried past, Williams followed. The door shut behind them both.

"Friendly," Williams said.

"Cold. Monsieur. None colder than Adriane."

"So, what is the project? I can hardly wait any longer."

"We are headed to the lab now, you will see. I'll introduce you to the team, they will show you everything." Legard walked up to a solitary door, again with no windows, opened it and walked in. Williams was surprised what he could see. It appeared to be a very large open space, split into two rooms. Where he and Legard stepped in looked to be some sort of control room, with monitoring equipment, and what Williams could only guess where some sort of control terminals, or consoles.

"Morgen François. I did not expect to see you until this afternoon," an older man said. He was standing next to one of the terminals to the back of the control room.

"Ah, things change Gunter. May I introduce you to Doctor Nicholas Williams. Monsieur Williams, Doctor Gunter Vogel, one of the scientists on our project."

"The pleasure is mine Dr. Williams." Gunter reached out his hand.

246 | Corbin Deckard

"Please, call me Nick," Williams said in response.

"Hey Nick. Bob, Bob Engels. I'm from the states too," Engels said, as he made his way to the back of the control room to meet Williams.

"Hey Bob. Nice to meet you. Where about are you from?"

"Michigan. We'll have to catch up later, I need to talk to someone about American stuff for a while, it's been way to long. No one here knows what a pop is."

"Yeah, any time," Williams answered, welcoming the unexpected chance to work with someone from a familiar place.

"So, where can we find her? Do you not have a test scheduled for today?" Legard asked.

"She's in her office. She forgot to bring something we are going to use for today's test. She should be here in a-" Just then the door opened and a woman made her way into the lab.

Williams was caught off guard. The woman had very dark hair, almost black, and pale skin. She was about Williams's age, maybe younger as far as he could tell. He had seen her before, at the café this morning, while he was waiting for his time to meet with Legard. She was the woman who sat at the far end, the one in the hat and gloves who had looked back to see him spill his coffee.

"Ah, there you are, I was afraid you were not coming to the lab today."

"Bonjour François. Of course, it's the day we solve all our problems. I just left these in my office, we are going to use them today." The woman held up a small blue plastic bag with the name L'Épée de Bois printed on its side. In it were several red toy balls.

"May I introduce you to Doctor Nick Williams?" Legard motioned to Williams, who, still thinking about his seeing her at the café, didn't say a word.

"Ah, the American."

"The other American," Engels said.

"This is the new member of our team, oui?"

"Oui. Doctor Nick Williams, may I introduce you to Doctor Marie Lemaire, she is the leader of the team here at the university. You will be reporting directly to her," Legard said.

"Pleasure to meet you Doctor Williams. May I call you Nick, we are pretty informal here, right Bob?" Lemaire said, looking over her shoulder to Engels while she shook Williams's hand.

"Yep. That's true. Once you get past security upstairs, it's pretty relaxed here.

"Yes, yes, you can call me Nick, that's fine, Marie. It's nice to meet you."

"Good. Well, I'm looking forward to bringing you up to speed. We desperately need your insight on our project. As much as I think we are close, I don't think we are going to get it to work any time soon." Lemaire turned and started to walk to the console toward the end of the lab. That's when Williams noticed something.

"It?" Williams questioned, still not sure exactly what he was brought to Paris to work on, still not sure what 'it' was. Lemaire turned, and with a slight smile, motioned for Williams to come closer to get a better look.

"You'll want to get a good look at this," she said, still smiling, happy to show him around. He slowly made his way to the bottom of the control room, trying to get a hold of what he was seeing.

"Oh wow. Is that? Is that what I think it is?" Just beyond the control room was what seemed like kilometers of wires and cables heading from all directions into one large lab. He could see sensory equipment, monitors, and lights all focused on a void in the center of the room. It was surrounded by a structure that, from where Williams stood, was a most peculiar metal. "Is it for real?"

"Oui, Nick," Lemaire said walking closer to Williams and closer to the lab. "It is for real. We call it... Andromeda."

End.

The Andromeda Paradox.

The Andromeda Effect posed some challenges to write, as I suspected it would, simply because of the difficulty of paradoxes and how they can be explained, or not explained, within a story. I tried, successfully I hope, to illustrate why at times Nick and his team could see the world around them as different than what they remembered it to be. At other times, the world around them had changed drastically, but was completely accepted as what they thought to be true. The reason...well, the andromeda effect.

The more and more I wrote, the more complex this story about time travel became. Problems I encountered could be explained away but not without contradiction. Solving for those contradictions led to even more, which ultimately would manifest into something impossible to explain as part of an entertaining story. I later referred to that as the andromeda paradox, where the main points of the story become eclipsed by contradictory supporting elements. I realized, early on, that I needed the andromeda effect. Without it the story itself would have just been one long math problem so to speak, and I didn't want that.